TOUCAN KEEP A SECRET

This Large Print Book carries the
Seal of Approval of N.A.V.H.

A MEG LANGSLOW MYSTERY

TOUCAN KEEP A SECRET

DONNA ANDREWS

THORNDIKE PRESS
A part of Gale, a Cengage Company

Farmington Hills, Mich • San Francisco • New York • Waterville, Maine
Meriden, Conn • Mason, Ohio • Chicago

Copyright © 2018 by Donna Andrews.
Thorndike Press, a part of Gale, a Cengage Company.

ALL RIGHTS RESERVED

Thorndike Press® Large Print Mystery.
The text of this Large Print edition is unabridged.
Other aspects of the book may vary from the original edition.
Set in 16 pt. Plantin.

LIBRARY OF CONGRESS CIP DATA ON FILE.
CATALOGUING IN PUBLICATION FOR THIS BOOK
IS AVAILABLE FROM THE LIBRARY OF CONGRESS

ISBN-13: 978-1-4328-5575-8 (hardcover)

Published in 2018 by arrangement with Macmillan Publishing Group, LLC/St. Martin's Press

Printed in Mexico
1 2 3 4 5 6 7 22 21 20 19 18

ACKNOWLEDGMENTS

I continue to be grateful for all the great folks at St. Martins/Minotaur including (but not limited to) Joe Brosnan, Hector DeJean, Jennifer Donovan, Melissa Hastings, Paul Hoch, Andrew Martin, Sarah Melnyk, and especially my editor, Pete Wolverton. And thanks again to David Rotstein and the art department for another beautiful cover.

More thanks to my agent, Ellen Geiger, and the staff at the Frances Goldin Literary Agency for handling the business side of writing so brilliantly and letting me concentrate on the fun part.

Many thanks to the friends — writers and readers alike — who brainstorm and critique with me, give me good ideas, or help keep me sane while I'm writing: Stuart, Aidan, and Liam Andrews, Chris Cowan, Ellen Crosby, Kathy Deligianis, Margery Flax, John Gilstrap, Barb Goffman, David Niemi, Alan Orloff, Art Taylor, Robin

5

Templeton, and Dina Willner. Thanks for all kinds of moral support and practical help to my blog sisters and brother at the Femmes Fatales: Alexia Gordon, Dean James, Toni L. P. Kelner, Catriona McPherson, Kris Neri, Hank Phillippi Ryan, Joanna Campbell Slan, Marcia Talley, and Elaine Viets. And thanks to all the TeaBuds for two decades of friendship.

Special thanks to Suzanne Frisbee, who first told me about the real-life events that inspired this book's plot. Suzanne and Joni Langevoort remain my stalwart experts in all things Episcopalian. Father Lyndon Shakespeare also provided useful insight, and graciously agreed to let me steal his very evocative name for one of the characters. Any mistakes in church doctrine or custom are obviously things I forgot to ask them about.

And above all, thanks to the readers who continue to enjoy Meg's adventures!

CHAPTER 1

"You're still at Trinity? What in the world are you doing there???"

The ding of an incoming text had raised my spirits temporarily — I'd assumed it would be Michael, texting me to say that Josh and Jamie were safely asleep, and maybe even including a photo or two from their bedtime story session.

But this text was from Robyn. She was the reason that, instead of being at home to help my husband put the twins to bed, I was here at the church at nearly eleven o'clock — turning off lights, making sure everyone was out of the building, and checking that all the doors and windows were locked. Things the Reverend Robyn Smith, as rector of Trinity, would normally be doing.

Not her fault, though. She would much rather have been here, instead of home on enforced bed rest for the last three months of her pregnancy.

I studied my phone's glowing screen for a few moments, pondering what to reply. Obviously "doing your job" wasn't an option, no matter how cranky I felt.

"The vestry meeting ran late" would be the most truthful answer, but probably not a reassuring one. Robyn would know all too well the issues her parish's elected lay officials might be discussing, and none of them were likely to contribute to the calm, peaceful state of mind her obstetrician wanted her to maintain. Especially if she suspected that she was yet again one of the prime subjects of discussion. I'd overheard enough to figure out the Muttering Misogynists, as Mother and I called two of her fellow vestry members, had once again spent much of the meeting sniping about the expense and inconvenience of having the parish priest out on maternity leave. Of course, what they really didn't like was having a woman priest in the first place. The misogynists were a minority, both in the congregation and on the vestry. But that didn't mean they couldn't make life thoroughly miserable for Robyn in her present situation.

And mentioning that I'd had to unstop one of the toilets in the women's bathroom again would probably set her off worrying about whether Trinity needed a lot of expensive plumbing work that we could ill afford.

"The twelve-step meeting ran over," I finally texted back. It wasn't a lie. I'd been filling in for Robyn on the evening shift several nights a week for almost a month now, and I had yet to see a twelve-step meeting end on time.

"No idea why, of course," I added. Also true. I considered eavesdropping on the vestry one of the benefits of filling in for Robyn — in fact, almost a job responsibility. And difficult to avoid, given the amount of shouting that went on lately. But I tried very hard to give the twelve-step participants their space.

"Of course. But you're headed home now?"

"Yes," I texted back. "In your office now checking on the admiral."

"Give him a slice of orange for me."

"I will," I replied.

"And don't forget to talk to him."

"Roger. Later."

I shoved the phone into my pocket and studied the covered cage containing Admiral Nimitz, a three-year-old toco toucan that Robyn was looking after while his owner

9

was on active duty aboard the USS *Harry S. Truman.*

"Let's get you out of here," I said to the presumably slumbering bird. I felt slightly guilty, taking the bird away without telling Robyn. Toucans were gregarious, and she'd promised the bird's absent owner that she'd keep him at the church, where interacting with the congregation would fulfill his social needs.

"It's for your own good," I informed Nimitz. With Robyn away, her office didn't get anywhere near the traffic it usually did. And going into the office for the sole purpose of amusing the toucan was yet another burden on the already overworked volunteers. Frankly, most of the volunteers either didn't bother with Nimitz or ran out of time. So even though Nimitz was not only noisy but incredibly messy, I was taking him home, where my noisy, messy family could see to his social needs. My cousin Rose Noire, with her passion for everything vegetarian and organic, would probably relish the complicated challenge of his fruit-and-nut-based diet. The boys would love talking to him. And perhaps I could even pawn him off on my grandfather, who was not only a biologist and a bird fancier but owned a private zoo. Surely the Caerphilly

Zoo's aviary staff members were the best qualified to take proper care of Nimitz. And then —

My visions of a toucan-free summer were rudely interrupted by a loud hammering noise.

"What now?" I raced out of Robyn's office and stood for a moment, trying to figure out where the sound was coming from. The back of the church, apparently. I strode into the sanctuary and down the center aisle toward the altar. I didn't turn on the lights — partly to keep from alerting whoever was doing the hammering that I was hunting them down, and partly because I didn't need to. The full moon shone through the soaring two-story stained glass windows along both sides of the sanctuary, casting great mosaics of multicolored light over the pews and the altar. I could see just fine.

The noise wasn't coming from the sanctuary. Possibly from downstairs. Or more likely from the churchyard. I reached the back wall and peered out of one of the relatively tiny non–stained glass windows.

The churchyard would have been the perfect setting for filming a scary movie. One of those over-the-top Hammer Films with Peter Cushing and Christopher Lee. The full moon cast spooky shadows from the gravestones and the weeping willows. And at the far end of the churchyard, another small multicolored splash of light spilled over the flagstone path that led to the crypt.

"Someone's in the crypt," I said aloud.

And then I immediately corrected myself. The columbarium. Both Robyn and Mother were adamant about using the proper term for a room whose walls were filled with niches to hold the ashes of parishioners who'd chosen cremation.

But to me it would always be the crypt. It was a surprisingly large underground room that had been hollowed out of the side of the steep hill at the far end of the church-yard. In the middle of its gray stone front wall, a large medieval-style oak door with impressive wrought-iron hinges guarded the entrance to the crypt. As if deciding belatedly that the door made the place look too forbidding, the architect had added long, narrow stained glass panels on either side of the entrance.

Stained glass panels that were now lit from within — a dead giveaway that someone was inside.

My first impulse was to race out and accost the intruder. But I'd recently had a discussion with my dad, an avid reader of mystery books, about the Too Stupid to Live Syndrome.

"It's one thing to be a strong, independent heroine," he'd said. "And quite another to go racing unarmed into danger instead of sensibly calling 911. People just don't do that in real life. I know why authors do it, of course, because if the heroine just sat by and let the police handle everything, there wouldn't be a book. But still — they should at least make an effort to have their heroines behave intelligently."

"And why are you picking on heroines?" I'd replied. "Aren't there male protagonists who race into danger? And yet I bet you'd call them brave for doing exactly the same thing that gets women labeled Too Stupid to Live."

"An excellent point!" Dad had exclaimed, and we'd gone on to have a lively discussion about sexism in literature and film.

But I remembered the Too Stupid to Live Syndrome. So instead of racing out to confront whoever was in the crypt, I pulled out my cell phone and dialed 911 as I set out to investigate the source of the noise.

"There seems to be an intruder here at Trinity Episcopal," I told Debbie Ann, the dispatcher, as I strode back through the sanctuary. "Out in the columbarium."

"The what?"

"The crypt," I said.

"Oh right. Back of the graveyard, in the side of the hill."

"That's it. There's light coming from it, and there shouldn't be. There wasn't half an hour ago when I started making my rounds. And we normally keep it locked, although it wouldn't be hard for someone to get in — everyone at Trinity knows Robyn keeps a copy of the key on a hook in her office, so anyone who wants to visit a loved one who's buried there can borrow it."

In fact, Robyn usually kept two copies of the key on that hook. Only one there now, I noted, as I grabbed it.

"And there's a hammering noise coming from out there," I added. I stopped to lock up Robyn's office before I crossed the vestibule, on my way to the parish hall wing. Downstairs in that wing, at the end of a long hallway flanked by classrooms and storage rooms, was a door that would take me out of the building as close as possible to the crypt. "At least there was — I don't hear it anymore," I added as I dashed down the stairs.

"I'm sending a unit," Debbie Ann said. "In fact, you'll probably be seeing several.

14

Horace is only a few minutes away, and it's been such a slow night that everyone else is excited at the idea of backing him up."

"I look forward to seeing them." I had reached the end of the hallway and was unlocking the door, which led outside to a stairwell that climbed up to ground level. A wave of warm, lilac-scented air greeted me, replacing my vision of a creepy, haunted Transylvanian setting with the reassuring familiarity of a Virginia spring. Still, I stopped long enough to lock the door again behind me. Then I crept swiftly but silently up the concrete stairs and peered across the graveyard toward the crypt. I was reassured to hear the sound of a siren not too far away.

"Uh-oh," I said into my cell phone. "I think the intruder might have figured out we're onto him. The crypt door was closed when I looked before. Now it's wide open."

"Proves there was someone there," Debbie Ann said. "And if they did any damage, Horace is the one to figure out who they were." In addition to being an officer on the town and county police force, Horace was a trained crime scene specialist.

"Probably just kids," I said as I picked my way across the moonlit graveyard. "Pulling a prank. Or looking for a little bit of privacy."

And maybe kids who thought with Robyn out of circulation there'd be no one here to spot them at this late hour. Even if there wasn't any damage, I'd be in favor of having Horace track them down so we could make an example of them. And maybe it was time to rekey the crypt door and come up with better security for the new key. My heart, which had been beating a little faster than usual, was back to normal.

"Creepy place for a rendezvous," Debbie Ann said.

"I suppose I should be glad they were stupid enough to leave the door open."

"Teenagers." I didn't have to see her to know she was shaking her head.

"Don't blame their age," I replied. "Offhand, I don't recall doing anything like this when I was in high school, but I'm sure if I had, I'd have had the brains to leave everything as much as possible as I'd found it."

"I'm sure you were an exceptionally logical and sensible teenager."

The intruder or intruders hadn't just left the door open — they'd also left a light on. A dim light rather than the moderately bright illumination that had attracted my attention, but still. No common sense.

I'd reached the door. I stopped to the right of the doorway and waited for a few moments to see if I heard any noises inside. Nothing.

The siren was closer. I knew I ought to wait for Horace.

I'd have to reopen that discussion with Dad. Ask him if the heroines he was complaining about were really too stupid to live or maybe just too curious for caution.

I stepped into the doorway and peered inside.

The dim light was coming from a flashlight that lay abandoned on the crypt's stone floor. The flashlight's beam illuminated the body sprawled nearby. Both the flashlight and the ambient moonlight washed out color, but I was still pretty sure that the puddle around the body's head was blood.

"Tell Horace to hurry up," I said over the phone. "My prowler report just turned into a possible murder."

CHAPTER 2

"Murder?" Debbie Ann echoed. "Are you sure? Are you in any danger? Maybe you should go back inside the church."

"Could be just attempted murder. I'm going to see if the guy's still alive. Can you send an ambulance? And should you maybe notify my dad?"

"That's a yes to both," she said. "The ambulance should be there a few minutes behind Horace, and one way or another, we can use Dr. Langslow." Dad was both a semi-retired physician and the local medical examiner. "Stay on the line until Horace gets there."

I took another quick glance around to make sure no one was lurking in the nearby shrubbery or behind one of the weathered tombstones. Then I stepped inside. I started to grope for the light switch that, because of the stained glass panels flanking the door, was inconveniently located a couple of feet to right of the entrance. Then I stopped myself. The intruder could have left finger-prints. I turned my phone so I could use its edge to flip the light switch. Nothing happened. I flicked the switch up and down a few more times, even though I knew it was useless. Annoying that all the bulbs in both fixtures were burned out. I made a mental note to have a few sharp words with the church custodian. Then I opened my phone's flashlight app and used its tiny beam to scan my surroundings.

The crypt was ten feet wide and burrowed twenty feet into the side of the hill, so even adding my phone's illumination to the shaft of light coming from the fallen flashlight didn't do much to improve visibility, although the foot-square polished granite panels covering the walls did reflect the light a little. Still, I could barely see the doorway in the back wall — actually a fake doorway, intended to be replaced with a real door, if and when Trinity decided to expand the crypt.

But the victim wasn't that far back. He lay facedown on the flagstone floor about a third of the way along the room's length. His head, with its pool of what was certainly blood, was closest to me. One arm curled slightly above it in what seemed like a protective gesture, while the other lay at his side. From the way his legs were sprawled, I deduced that he'd been knocked down while making a break for the door.

I knelt at his side, trying to avoid the blood, and reached for his wrist.

"No pulse," I said over the phone. I turned its little beam onto the victim's head and quickly flicked it away again. "And he's got a nasty head wound, and there's a fair amount of blood here, but the wound's not bleeding much at the moment, which I'm pretty sure is a bad sign."

I took several deep breaths and looked away. Yes, I was the daughter of a doctor — a doctor who was also a lifelong crime fiction reader and, for the last several years, the local medical examiner. Thanks to Dad's peculiar ideas of suitable dinner table conversation, it would take something pretty awful to shake me. This was pretty awful. In my effort to focus, just for a few moments, on anything other than the head wound, I noticed that apparently the floor sloped toward the back of the crypt. The blood from the victim's head had run down the lines of grout between the paving stones and was pooling at the base of the fake door. I wasn't sure staring at the pool of blood was any better than looking at the victim.

The victim. I was trying not to call him "the dead guy," even though I was pretty sure it was accurate. Or would be long before the ambulance got here. It would be nice to know his name. And having something to do always calmed my nerves.

So even though I realized that every footprint I made potentially complicated Horace's job when he switched roles from deputy on patrol to Caerphilly's one-man forensic department, I took a couple of cautious steps to where I could peer down and see the victim's face.

"It's Mr. Hagley," I said to Debbie Ann. "The victim, I mean."

"Junius Hagley?"

"That's right." Junius Hagley, who up until forty-five minutes ago had been one of the loud voices coming from the vestry meeting. One of the Muttering Misogynists. I hoped Mother and all her fellow vestry members were alibied. They were sure to be high on the chief's list of suspects. Although if the list included everyone who wasn't fond of Mr. Hagley, it would be a long one.

"Look, whoever did it is gone," I said. "Not long gone, though, so maybe you could tell some of those officers heading this way to keep their eyes open for suspicious characters."

21

"Already done," she said. "Although I'm not sure what to tell them to look for."

"Yeah." I glanced around to make sure no one was nearby. " 'Be on the lookout for someone heading away from Trinity Episcopal' isn't terribly useful, is it?"

"And that's assuming he's headed away," Debbie Ann said. "And not circling back to get rid of a potential witness. Stay on the line until Horace gets there."

"Will do. Although if whoever did this has any brains, they'll know I'm useless as a witness and they're better off not returning to the scene of the crime." I said that last bit rather loudly, in case the intruder was still lurking outside in the bushes.

"Criminals aren't noted for their brainpower," Debbie Ann said. "Just stay on the line. The chief's headed your way, too."

"I'll be glad to see him." Since Chief Burke was also a retired Baltimore homicide detective, he usually took charge of major crime investigations himself.

From my new vantage point, I noticed something else. Around Mr. Hagley's head, a scattering of dirt and rocks littered the normally smooth, clean stone floor

No, not dirt and rocks. Human ashes — cremains, as Maudie Morton at the funeral home would say — and broken bits of at least one of the polished granite panels that normally covered the niches. Farther off I saw shards of china. Fragments of glass. A bronze urn with a big dent in its base. Another urn lying on its side. A granite panel broken into three or four pieces. A rectangular bronze plaque that had fallen off the panel — with a little more light I could have read the occupant's name and dates. Another largely intact panel with the bronze plaque still attached.

I flicked my phone's light up and ran it along the closest wall. Here and there gaping holes interrupted the wall's otherwise regular expanse of granite squares, with or without bronze plaques. I counted . . . three . . . no, four niches that had been opened up by prying off the front panels. One still held a bronze urn that had been tipped over on its side. The others were empty. An inspection of the opposite wall revealed two more vandalized niches.

And at the foot of the second wall I spotted something else that didn't belong — a crowbar. The light was too dim to see if it was bloodstained, but Horace would be testing that. And I didn't have to look back at Mr. Hagley's head to tell —

"Meg?"

I jumped. Even though I'd been absently

tracking the gradual approach of the sirens, Horace's arrival caught me by surprise.

"Sorry," he said. "Didn't mean to startle you."

"Murder victim," I said, pointing my phone's light at Mr. Hagley. I shifted it over to the crowbar. "Possible murder weapon. You'll find my sneaker tracks beside him, where I stooped to take his pulse, and here. You going to kick me out now?" I was actually itching to call Michael, to let him know what was happening before he heard about it from someone else.

"Maybe you should stay with me until some of the other officers have checked the premises, in case whoever did this is still lurking around," Horace said. "Stand in the doorway and let me know if you see anything suspicious."

"Can do."

"And can you turn on the lights?" he asked. "Unless there's a particular reason you were creeping around in the dark."

"The bulbs are burned out," I said.

Horace took the flashlight from his belt, turned it on, and trained it on first one overhead fixture, then the other.

"The bulbs are broken," he said. "Be interesting to know if the killer did this or if they were already out."

24

"If the killer did it, won't you find glass?"

"We'd also find glass if the bulb had been broken days ago."

"But it wasn't," I said. "With Robyn out, Mother gives the church a white-glove inspection almost every day. I'm pretty sure she did it earlier this evening, before the vestry meeting. If she'd found broken glass in here, she'd have told me."

"Could be."

He sounded dubious. Did he doubt Mother's attention to detail?

"And then there's the fact that there was light coming from here earlier," I added. "A lot brighter than that thing." I gestured to the fallen flashlight. "So unless the killer had an awesomely high-powered flashlight . . ."

"He broke the bulbs, then. Wonder why."

"The switch can be hard to find if you don't already know where it is."

He nodded, obviously filing away the information. He turned his flashlight on the body and whistled when he saw the head wound.

While Horace studied the crime scene with his trained forensic eyes, I tapped out a message to Michael. It took me a couple of tries to come up with wording that wouldn't bring him racing to make sure I was okay.

"Don't wait up," my final draft began. "I'm fine, but I found a body. Junius Hagley. Horace is here with me. Dad and the chief are on their way. They'll probably want to pick my brains before I leave."

Michael's answer came back so quickly that I suspected he'd started to worry and was watching his phone.

"You're sure you're fine? Rose Noire and Rob are here, so I could head over there."

"I'm fine, and with any luck I'll be on my way before you could even get here."

I wasn't actually that optimistic about an early departure, but I didn't want to worry him. And I didn't want him losing sleep over this. He had a busy day of classes and rehearsals tomorrow.

"OK," he texted back. "What happened to Hagley — heart attack? Stroke?"

"Crowbar," I texted back. "Homicide."

He didn't text back right away. I was about to put the phone away when his reply flashed onto my screen.

"Why do our local murderers always manage to commit their crimes when you're around?"

"Dunno," I tapped back. "Maybe the International Brotherhood of Thugs and Assassins insists."

"LOL. Could be, if your dad got to them. Well, at least he'll be happy." True enough — few things excited Dad as much as an opportunity to be involved in a real-life murder investigation. "Stay safe. Love you!" I replied in kind and then tucked my phone in my pocket.

"There's no place like home," I said under my breath. Then I turned back to see what Horace was up to.

CHAPTER 3

Horace, flashlight in hand, was now peering intently at the wound in Mr. Hagley's head. He seemed fascinated, but the better lighting wasn't an improvement from my point of view.

I focused on the other details of the crime scene. Horace's bright LED flashlight made for much greater visibility. I could see now that the china fragments were blue and white, and had probably once been a Chinese-style ginger jar. Most of the glass fragments were a soft green color, though I could also spot thinner fragments that doubtless had come from the light bulbs. The green glass looked familiar. I had a small vase that color at home, a souvenir of the Jamestown glasshouse. I could see a ginger jar as a container for ashes — in fact, a very similar jar containing a great-aunt of mine graced the mantel of Mother and Dad's farmhouse. But a glass vase?

28

"That's going to be a mess to sort out," Horace remarked.

Considering where his flashlight was aimed, I assumed he meant the ashes that had spilled out of the two broken containers, creating two wide swathes that merged about a foot and a half from the top of Mr. Hagley's head.

I didn't realize what he meant for a second — I had been thinking how lucky it was that all the blood had run downhill, away from the ashes, without contaminating them. Then it hit me. The two sets of ashes were all mixed up now.

"A total mess," I agreed. "And with our luck, the families of Green Glass and Blue-and-White China will turn out to be Caerphilly's equivalent of the Montagues and the Capulets. And they will both try to sue the diocese for allowing their loved ones' ashes to be sullied by contact with the other."

"Not sure what grounds they'd have for blaming the diocese," Horace said.

"That won't stop them from trying. Can we figure out whose niches have been vandalized?"

"Next up on my list."

"Excellent idea," came a voice from just behind me.

I started again, and then felt guilty. Horace had asked me to keep watch, and I'd been so busy gawking at the inside that I hadn't even noticed someone coming up behind me. Fortunately it was Chief Burke, not a grave-robbing murderer returning to up his body count.

"Provided we can do it without contaminating the crime scene before Horace works it," the chief added. I had a feeling that was intended for me.

"Staying put," I said.

Horace trained his flashlight on one of the fallen urns.

"P. Jefferson Blair," he read. "January 14, 1965 to November 13, 2000."

The chief pulled out his notebook and began scribbling. I just kept my ears open.

The other urn — the dented one — belonged to a J. A. Washington, who'd died in 2007. I wasn't surprised when the plaque still loosely attached to a cracked polished granite panel revealed that the blue-and-white ginger jar had probably contained Dolores Kelly Hagley.

"The victim's wife, I assume?" The chief glanced at me.

"Yes." I hadn't recognized Blair or Washington — Blair had died before I'd even heard of Caerphilly, and Washington before

30

I'd become as involved as I now was in Trinity — but I remembered Mrs. Hagley. "A very nice lady. And according to Mother, a sorely missed good influence on Mr. Hagley. She only died about a year and a half ago."

"Hang on." Horace focused his flashlight on a fallen bronze urn. "According to the engraving, that's Mrs. Hagley — I guess she rolled away. The broken china must belong to someone else."

"What a mess," the chief murmured.

Horace had turned his flashlight toward the wall and was peering at a fallen bronze plaque.

"Lacey Shiffley." He sounded surprised.

"Here in Trinity?" The chief's surprise echoed Horace's. And I understood. We all three knew — the way one does in a small town — that nearly every member of the sprawling Shiffley clan who attended church went to First Presbyterian. The only exceptions I knew of were one or two who'd married staunch Catholics and moved over to St. Byblig's, and a talented baritone who'd defected to the New Life Baptist Church to become a soloist in its nationally famous gospel choir.

"She died in 2006," Horace said. "Before my time."

31

"I was here then, but I hadn't yet gotten to know many Shiffleys," I said.

"I was here then, too," the chief said. "And I remember Lacey. But I didn't know she was buried here. We can check with her family to see how that happened."

The panel, belonging to the niche that still contained its urn revealed another surprise.

" 'Known only to God,' " Horace read. "That's weird."

"It's the customary inscription used for a poor soul who's unidentified," the chief said.

"But what's a John Doe doing buried here in the Trinity crypt?" Horace asked. "Not to sound crass, but I was under the impression that those little niches go for a pretty penny."

"A very good question," the chief said. "Let me have his date of death. I'm sure there will be something in our files back at the station."

"Depends on how far back the files go," I said. "January 12, 1995."

"A mere quarter of a century? No problem," Horace said. "I bet we've still got the wanted posters for the Lindbergh kidnapping around somewhere."

"I wouldn't be surprised to find a wanted poster for Benedict Arnold," the chief said. "Though thank goodness we've archived all

those really old files in the courthouse basement."

The owner of the sixth vandalized niche
was the third surprise — at least for the
chief.

"Beatrice Helen Falkenhausen van der
Lynden," Horace read. "The inscription's a
little smaller than some of the others — had
to be to fit her whole name in — but I think
the death date is 1993. I think the broken
china must be hers."

"Mrs. Van der Lynden," the chief exclaimed.

"Someone who died under suspicious
circumstances?" I asked.

"No," the chief said. "But she is connected
with one of the more interesting outstanding cases I inherited from my predecessor."

"What case is that?" I asked.

"Horace, why don't you get your forensic
kit and make a start." Evidently the chief
was not in the mood to discuss cold cases.

"Roger," Horace said. "And then —"

"What's that?" the chief said, pointing to
the far wall of the crypt.

"What's what?" Horace asked.

"I saw it too," I said. "When you turned,
something reflected your flashlight beam,
just for a second."

"Could be a piece of red glass," the chief said.

"Red glass?" I looked over at the two stained glass panels, hoping neither was broken. Horace was running his flashlight along the far wall. I was about to ask him to point it on the stained glass windows when —

"That's it," the chief said.

"Holy cow," Horace said softly.

Lying on the floor near the other wall was a ring with a red stone. A stone so large that common sense said it had to be a fake. Red glass.

No. Red glass might sparkle in the light. It wouldn't give off such a pure, intense, and ever-so-slightly sinister glow.

"Could that thing possibly be real?" I asked aloud.

CHAPTER 4

"I also see the ring," the chief said. "But I suspect that's not what you mean. I'm sure in due time Horace can figure out if it's a ruby or a garnet or just a piece of glass. For now, let him get on with processing the crime scene. I want to hear from you exactly what happened here tonight."

The chief and I left the crypt and sat just outside on a weathered concrete bench. Horace bustled past us, heading for the parking lot. The chief fished out his notebook, flipped it open, and attached a little clip-on book light to it. He paused to pull out his cell phone and call Debbie Ann.

"I want the files on a cold case," he said. "The Van der Lynden robbery case . . . late eighties, I think. Thanks."

I didn't exclaim "aha!" or anything — just sat quietly, trying to look like the sort of trustworthy and discreet person you'd want to discuss your cold cases with.

"Take it from the top." His pen was poised over the notebook.

Maybe later.

"Okay," I said aloud. "So this was one of my nights to fill in for Robyn until all this evening's scheduled events were over and I could lock up. I got here at seven P.M."

Horace hurried back with his forensic kit in hand and disappeared inside. While he was doing his examination of the crime scene, I filled the chief in on my evening. I'd texted Michael frequently while at the church with the sort of snarky comments that helped make my job bearable. The time stamps on my texts let me reconstruct a rough sequence of events. A text at 8:46 confirmed that by that time the Office Committee had finished folding, stuffing, and sealing the latest newsletter and the members had gone home, while the Altar Guild was long gone. The choir director had finished a powwow with the organist and a soloist at nine sharp, and the Food Ministry Committee had wrapped up at 9:14. The vestry didn't adjourn its latest stormy meeting until 10:15, and the twelve-step group members didn't leave until 10:25.

"Lord, what a hotbed of activity," the chief said. "Of course, it's much the same at New Life Baptist, I suppose, but I mostly hear about the choir." Not surprising, since his wife, Minerva Burke, was the choir's director.

"So from 10:25 until five or ten minutes before I called 911 I was going through the whole building," I continued. "Locking doors. Turning off lights. Testing window latches. Checking that all the faucets were off. Doing a few bits of housekeeping that couldn't wait, like unstopping a toilet in the downstairs women's bathroom and wiping up spilled sugar in the kitchen. Making sure no one was lingering anywhere."

"Was the parking lot empty?"

"Except for the church minivan, which usually lives here," I said.

"And your car."

"No, Mother gave me a ride in," I said. "I was going to drive the van home so I could take it in for service in the morning. So far Osgood Shiffley has been able to keep the old wreck running."

"Interesting." The chief scribbled.

"You mean because anyone familiar with how things work here at Trinity would assume everyone had gone home?"

"Unless you had a lot of lights on."

"It's my job to turn lights off, not go around leaving them on. The church wasn't completely dark, but there would only have been a couple of lights on. Mainly Robyn's office and wherever I was in my rounds. I spent rather a long time downstairs unstopping that toilet and then cleaning up after myself."

"How long?"

I pondered. The chief waited patiently with his pencil poised over his notebook.

"At least half an hour," I said. "The plunger didn't work, so I had to use the snake, and of course there was the cleanup. And there's no window in the bathroom, so I bet the church looked deserted."

The chief nodded and scribbled some more.

"There's also the question of how Mr. Hagley got here, if his car wasn't in the parking lot," the chief said.

"That's right," I said. "He usually drove himself. He has a dark blue sedan."

"We've already put out a BOLO on it. Go on — you were checking the whole church."

"Anyway I had just gotten back to Robyn's office to collect Nimitz when I heard a pounding noise."

"Nimitz?" the chief looked puzzled.

"Larry Baker's toucan," I explained. "Robyn is watching the bird while Larry's deployed overseas. At least she was until they put her on bed rest. I was going to take the wretched bird home where he'd be easier to manage. But when I heard the noise I went to look out a back window."

"And determined that the noise was coming from the crypt," the chief said.

"Columbarium, technically," I said. "Not that most of us at Trinity don't call it the crypt, but we try not to in front of Robyn or Mother or the half-dozen sticklers who get touchy about it."

"Looks like a crypt to me — but thanks for the warning." The chief stood and walked over to peer through the doorway. "Did you check the other room?" he asked.

"Other room?"

"Behind the door in the far wall."

"It's a fake," I said — and inside I could hear Horace saying the same thing.

"They were thinking long-range when they built it," I added. "Actually, Gothic George wanted the crypt to be three or four times as big, but a fiscally prudent vestry overruled him."

"Gothic George?"

"The Reverend George Burwell Nelson Page," I said. "Rector of Trinity at the time the crypt was built. Known as Gothic George for his taste in architecture — never met a gargoyle he didn't like. Or so the story goes — it was all before my time."

"And mine as well. How long ago was the cr— the columbarium built?"

"In the late forties," I said. "Space in the graveyard was getting tight, and Gothic George thought cremation was going to be the answer. Turns out he wasn't wrong — just a few decades ahead of his time. It's still only about two-thirds full, although I suspect most of the vacant niches have been sold. And you can blame him for its crypt-like appearance. He really wanted to put it underneath the church — beneath the existing basement — but when the vestry saw the cost estimates they put their collective feet down."

Just then my phone rang. I glanced at it and grimaced.

"It's Robyn," I said. "I don't know whether she's heard the news already or whether she's just worried because I haven't texted her to let her know I've gotten home safely. I should answer it."

The chief nodded, and I pressed the button to answer.

"Hey, Robyn," I said. "Can you hang on a sec?" I pressed the mute button and looked back at the chief. "I think we should tell her," I said. "You know how gossip gets around in Caerphilly, and I think it's better if she hears the news from me. Or you, if

40

you prefer."

He thought for a moment, then nodded.

"Tell her," he said. "We'll need her help unraveling this. Though I can probably wait until morning to talk to her at any length."

I unmuted my phone and put it on speaker.

"Meg? Is something wrong?"

"You're still lying down, right?"

"Of course I'm lying down. Don't nag me; it's not good for my blood pressure. What's happening down there?"

"It's Mr. Hagley."

"Oh, dear. What's he up to now?"

"He's not up to anything," I said. "He's dead."

A pause

"Oh, dear," Robyn said. "I feel so guilty."

"Guilty?" I echoed.

"I have had a great many uncharitable thoughts about him lately," she said. "If only I'd known he was not long for this world."

"The fact that he's dead doesn't mean he hasn't been a complete jerk lately," I said.

"Still, I hope he didn't suffer too much," Robyn said. "How did he die? Was it his heart?"

"He was murdered," I said. "I found his body in the columbarium. Someone hit him over the head with a crowbar."

"A crowbar?" Her normally low, calm voice rose to a squeak.

"Calm down," I said. "Is there someone there with you?"

"Yes, Matt's here. Oh, Meg — a crowbar?"

"Yes." I decided if her husband was there, maybe it was the best time to break the rest of the bad news. "A crowbar with which someone also pried the front of Mrs. Hagley's niche, and knocked her urn over."

"That wretched man! He couldn't be bothered to wait for the paperwork!"

"Paperwork?" I was relieved that annoyance at Mr. Hagley seemed to be displacing some of her distress.

The chief looked surprised.

"Mr. Hagley has been badgering me for weeks now about taking his wife's ashes home. I've lost count of how many times I've explained the proper procedure to him. It's not as if I can just walk out to the crypt, pop the niche open, and hand him her urn. The last time he called me, he lost his temper and said if I didn't give him his wife back he'd go out and fetch her himself. But I never thought he was serious. And why am I getting so worked up about that when the poor man's dead now?"

"Calm down," I said. "Talk it over with Matt, and tell him to bring you some of that herbal tea Rose Noire recommends."

"I'll be fine," she said. "I'm just sad that the poor misguided man has come to such a sorry end. I assume someone attacked him while he was trying to reclaim poor Dolores. You've called the police, I hope."

"Chief Burke is sitting with me now."

The chief pointed at the phone and held out his hand.

"And I think he'd like to talk to you."

CHAPTER 5

I was just as happy to let the chief tell Robyn about the other vandalized niches. I drifted closer to the door so I could watch Horace at work. I never ceased to marvel at the transformation Horace had undergone since discovering his calling as a criminalist. Growing up, he'd been painfully shy and awkward. In fact, he still was shy sometimes in social situations. But give him a complicated crime scene — even one involving a fairly gory body — put a crime scene camera or a jar of fingerprint powder in his hand, and the eager, capable, professional Horace emerged like a butterfly from a cocoon.

I watched him busily photographing and peering at things on the periphery of the crime scene — doubtless he was waiting to begin bagging things and hauling them away until Dad could examine the body undisturbed. A thought struck me.

"Whoever did this managed to cause an awful lot of damage in a really short time," I said. "The hammering sound didn't go on for more than a minute or so. Could he possibly have pried open all six niches that quickly?"

"I suspect what you heard wasn't the sound of him prying open the niches," Horace said. "He could do that fairly discreetly. A faint pop. I think what you heard was him trying to crack open the bronze urns. That would be pretty noisy. See, that one's kind of dented."

He fixed his flashlight on one of the fallen urns. Yes, something had made some ugly marks on it — probably the crowbar — though the vandal hadn't even come close to breaking it open.

"But why?" I asked.

"Dunno," Horace said. "Maybe they found the ring in the glass jar or the china urn. Maybe they were looking for more."

"They thought maybe it was customary for Episcopalians to take the contents of their jewelry boxes with them when they go?"

"Maybe they confused us with Egyptians," Horace said.

The chief, who had been pacing up and down while talking to Robyn, appeared at

45

my side.

"Robyn has something she wants you to do." He handed me the phone, and I could see that the mute button was on. "Actually, it's something she wanted to dash down here and do herself, but I convinced her that was a bad idea."

I took the phone and unmuted it.

"What's up?" I asked.

"The chief needs to know as much as possible about those poor souls whose remains were disturbed," Robyn said. "I'm not quite sure why — surely he can't possibly think any of their families had anything to do with this?"

"I'm sure he has to cover all the angles," I said. "And he probably does have to notify their families about the vandalism."

"That's true," Robyn said. "He does. But we need to follow up very quickly with a reassurance that Trinity will do everything we can to rectify this situation!"

"That's nice," I said. "But just what *can* we do to rectify the situation?"

"Well, that's what I need you to find out," Robyn said. "What they want us to do. The easiest thing would just be to tuck their loved ones back in their niches — once the columbarium is no longer a crime scene, of course. But it's possible that they might want us to have a little ceremony."

"Or maybe even a full-fledged second funeral." I could think of a number of people — including several I'd inherited DNA from — who would jump at the chance for a do-over on something as dramatic as a family burial.

"Also possible," Robyn said. "And there's always the chance that some of them may be so upset that they could decide to take their loved one's ashes back and reinter them elsewhere. Which would be terrible, but if that's what they want to do, we should be as helpful as possible. The crucial thing is that someone has to approach them very tactfully and sensitively. Soothe their ruffled feathers. And find out what they want us to do."

I had had a feeling why she was telling me this, and I didn't like it.

"Meg," she went on. "I'm counting on you. You're the only one I trust to do it!"

Which meant that if I refused, she'd probably start threatening to climb out of bed and overexert herself again.

"I'll do what I can," I said.

"There are some files you can use to figure out who the next of kin are," Robyn said. "In the overflow room. You can look under —"

"I'll find the files," I said. "And I'll talk to the next of kin as soon as the chief lets me — he will probably want me to wait until after he's notified them. But right now, it's past midnight. I'm hanging up so you can go back to sleep now."

I suited the action to the words. And stared at the phone for a while, daring Robyn to call back.

"I assume the files you're talking about are the ones that will help me figure out who to notify about the vandalism," the chief said. "I'd appreciate it if you could give me whatever information you can before you go home."

"Information coming up." I headed back to the church proper, and the chief followed me.

"If these were recent burials, I'd probably know just who to call," he said as we crossed the graveyard. "But only two of them happened since I came here. And the rest are nearly a quarter of a century old."

He watched in silence as I unlocked the back door and nodded approvingly when I locked it up again behind us. After all, there might be plenty of police on the premises, but they were focused on the crime scene, not the main building. I led the way up to the main floor, crossed the foyer to the of-

48

fice wing, and unlocked the overflow room.

It was a long, narrow room a few doors down from Robyn's study that had gained its name under Robyn's predecessor, Dr. Womble, who was a bit of a pack rat. While he was rector, this room, like half of the basement and all of the attic, had been packed with a century's worth of accumulation. Mother and Robyn had changed all that. The Ladies of St. Clotilda, Trinity's chief organization for good works, had held several huge rummage sales, and I'd lost track of how many times we'd filled the Dumpster with stubby candle ends, tattered vintage Christmas pageant costumes, mildewed pages from disintegrating hymnals, fading mimeographed copies of church bulletins from the 1960s, empty communion wine bottles, broken office furniture, and every other kind of ecclesiastical clutter.

Now the room held a long row of neatly labeled, securely locked file cabinets and a lot of empty space that came in very handy for temporary storage. Right now, for example, Trinity was running a drive to replenish the county food bank. A neat stack of a half-dozen boxes occupied one corner, waiting for the regular Monday morning delivery to the food bank.

I could see the chief glancing around with

curiosity — at the décor, no doubt. Mother and Robyn had been of one mind that a file room didn't have to be bland. The lime-green file cabinets looked quite striking against the bright teal walls. I'd have suggested putting Nimitz in here — he'd have fit in beautifully — but there was no way we wanted his messy self near the food or the files.

"Do you know where to find the records we need?" the chief asked.

"Not precisely," I said. "But I should have no trouble figuring it out. Mother and I helped Robyn organize them, once we all figured out that Dr. Womble's notion of filing was to shove all the loose papers on his desk into cardboard copier-paper boxes at random intervals. Finding anything was rather like conducting an archaeological dig."

I tried looking under *C* — for *columbarium* — with no luck. But then *B* for *burials* produced results. I pulled out a folder whose neatly organized contents proved to be exactly what I thought I'd remembered seeing: A neat map of the graveyard with all the plots numbered. A precise diagram of the columbarium, showing the numbers of the niches. For both graveyard and columbarium, a typed list of who owned each spot and whether or not they'd already taken up residence.

And behind that very useful folder lay a series of folders whose numbers corresponded to the graves and niches.

"Let's start with the file on the Hagleys' niche," the chief said. "Because notifying Mr. Hagley's next of kin is going to be one of my first priorities, and if Robyn's files contain that, it would save some time."

I consulted the list, found the proper numbered file, and handed it to the chief. I looked over his shoulder as he leafed through it.

"Deed of sale for the niche — steep price for a few square feet of rock and air," he said. "And the records from Mrs. Hagley's burial a year and a half ago. And yes, instructions on what Mr. Hagley wants for his own funeral. Seems there's a son down in Richmond. Charles Hagley."

The chief copied down the son's contact information, and then handed me back the file.

"I assume you could arrange for me to have a copy of the complete contents of the relevant files," he said. "There could be other information that would come in handy."

"I could make a copy now," I offered.

51

"Tomorrow will be fine," he said. "And by tomorrow, I'll have a better idea if there's anything else I need a copy of."

I nodded, and put the file on top of the cabinet — why refile it and have to hunt it down all over again in the morning? I was already looking up the next file.

"James Asmundsen Washington," I said, handing the chief the relevant file. "Buried eleven years ago."

"Mr. Washington I remember," the chief said. "Retired gentleman. Active in the Lions if memory serves. I think his widow still lives in town."

At least at the time of her husband's death she had, in a part of town where most of the houses were modest bungalows on small but tree-shaded lots.

"Do you know her?" the chief asked.

A reasonable question — after all, if Mr. Washington was buried here, the odds were that his widow was at least nominally a member of the congregation.

"Doesn't ring a bell," I said. "But she could be one of the people who only come occasionally. Or one of the shut-ins. Robyn would know better."

"One of the shut-ins is definitely a possibility," the chief said. "Her husband was seventy-nine when he died. Unless she was considerably younger than him, she's probably rather elderly. We'll find her, but I'd rather not bother Robyn about it just yet."

"Good point." I stacked the Washington file on top of the Hagley one. "I bet Mother will know. Who's next?"

"Since we seem to be moving in reverse chronological order, let's have Lacey Shiffley."

Lacey's file wasn't as informative as the other two. A copy of the purchase document for the niche, and a few documents related to the burial. Burial only — no funeral service; and the space to list the next of kin said, rather pointedly, *NA.*

"Downright peculiar." The chief frowned and shook his head slightly. "Hundreds of Shiffleys in this county, and not one of them she wants to claim as family?"

"Ask Randall," I said. Our friend Randall Shiffley was currently the de facto head of the sprawling Shiffley clan. Under other circumstances, that might have made him reluctant to share family secrets with outsiders — but since he was also Caerphilly's mayor and county manager the prospect of helping the chief solve a murder in his jurisdiction would probably outweigh any inclination he might have had to keep the family skeletons hidden.

"And no burial service," the chief went on. "That can't have pleased Dr. Womble. The man did a lovely funeral, you have to admit."

I nodded. The chief placed Lacey's file with the other two. I was already looking up P. Jefferson Blair.

"Not much here, either." I handed Blair's file to the chief. "Next of kin a Mrs. Parker Blair in Middleburg, Virginia."

"His mother," the chief said, scanning the file's contents.

"Who's probably getting along by now," I pointed out. "Blair was thirty-five when he died — he'd be close to retirement age by now, and his mother would have to be in her eighties."

"If she's still with us." The chief sighed and shook his head. "Still, Middleburg's a small, close-knit community. Shouldn't be too hard to track down the family, assuming there's anyone left."

He added the file to the stack on top of the file cabinet and looked at me expectantly.

"I'm looking for the John Doe," I said. "Who is not under the *D* for *Doe*. I may have to go through from A to Z. Wait a sec. . . . aha!"

CHAPTER 6

"Under *J* for *John,* I presume?" the chief asked.

"No, *K,*" I said. "For *Known Only to God.* Assuming this is the right file."

I glanced inside.

"The dates are right," I said, handing it to the chief. "It looks as if Dr. Womble donated the niche."

"But why?" The chief's face bore a puzzled frown. "I mean, why here at Trinity? I could understand his making a donation to cover the funeral and burial expenses of a John Doe. Exactly the sort of thing Dr. Womble has done, more than once, without any fanfare. But to bury him in the church? How would he even know for sure the poor soul was Christian, much less Episcopalian?"

"Found wearing a cross, maybe?" I suggested. "Or better yet, with a well-thumbed copy of the Book of Common Prayer in his pocket."

"Maybe," the chief said. "Still seems very odd."

"Dr. Womble's still around — you could ask him."

"I suppose I'll have to." The chief didn't look overjoyed at the prospect. Not, I was sure, because he had any dislike for the former rector of Trinity. More likely he had a good idea how time consuming and ultimately futile it would be, trying to get Dr. Womble to answer his questions sensibly and succinctly. I'd spent an entire afternoon at the Wombles' retirement cottage not long ago, trying to interview Dr. Womble for an article in the Trinity newsletter. I'd learned much about the Act of Uniformity of 1662, the cultivation of scented geraniums, and the most congenial pubs to relax in after a day of booking in the Welsh village of Hay-on-Wye, but had ended up crafting my article about Dr. Womble's early days at Trinity by spending the following morning in the archives of the *Caerphilly Clarion.*

"Since we're in the midst of the church files, can you look up when Dr. Womble came to Trinity?" the chief asked.

"Actually, I don't need to look it up," I said. "I profiled him for the church newsletter recently. May 1990."

"Then he'd have been the pastor here for all but the last of these six deaths," he said. "So I suppose I'll have to see what he has to say." The chief was visibly bracing himself at the thought.

"As will I," I said. "Assuming you're okay with me doing what Robyn asked — following along behind you and helping the bereaved families decide what they want done with their loved ones' ashes."

"Provided you leave the crime solving to me." He looked over his glasses at me. Then, as if suddenly remembering who he was talking to, he sighed and rubbed his forehead as if anticipating a headache. "Why do I even bother saying that? At least, please remember to report anything you learn during your interviews that could have a bearing on the murder."

"Absolutely. And particularly with Dr. Womble, getting any information out of him could be a time-consuming process."

The chief winced, and nodded slightly, which I decided to take as permission to interrogate Dr. Womble as freely as my time and patience permitted. I breathed a small sigh of relief. He could be prickly about civilians interfering in police business. But he'd learned over the years that I was scrupulous about bringing him any information I happened to run across — or found out by being nosy. And now that I was officially a Caerphilly employee, as special assistant to the mayor, and could be considered to have at least a tenuous official standing with the police department, he'd mellowed considerably. Not that he didn't still occasionally warn me against interfering, but he didn't go ballistic if I strayed across the line. It also helped that Adam, youngest of the three orphaned grandsons he and his wife were raising, was inseparable from Josh and Jamie, and our families had become close.

"And here's the final folder — Mrs. Van der Lynden." I handed it to him, and then decided to prod a little. "Victim, I gather, of some kind of still-unsolved robbery?"

"A jewel robbery," the chief said.

"And they never caught the robbers?"

"Oh, they caught them all right, but they never recovered any of the jewels."

"And you think that ring we found on the floor could be Mrs. Van der Lynden's?"

"No idea." He shrugged. "The case was already stone cold by the time I came to town. I have no idea if a ruby ring was part of the loot. And we don't know if the ring is real. A stone that size — I'd be surprised if it is."

"But still," I said. "Finding a ring — real or fake — in the crypt where the victim of a notorious local jewel robbery is buried . . ."

"Gets my attention." The chief was studying the contents of the folder. "Next of kin is a Mr. Archibald Falkenhausen van der Lynden, but his address is in care of someone named Wellington Blodgett." He flipped a page. "Ah. Not a person, Wellington Blodgett. A law firm."

"That's odd," I said.

"Could be useful." The chief was scribbling in his notebook. "I haven't run across any Van der Lyndens in the time I've been here in Caerphilly. But law firms don't tend to vanish without a trace quite as often as individuals."

I made a mental note of the name. A great many of my relatives were lawyers, and it might be interesting or even useful to find out what kind of law Wellington Blodgett specialized in.

"Anything else?" I stood posed by the file cabinets, demonstrating my eagerness to forage through the files for him.

"Not at the moment," he said. "Though I'm sure there will be, and I'll let you know. Any chance you could give me the key to the crypt?"

"I can give you a key." I handed him the

one I'd been carrying around. "But I can't guarantee it's the only key. There should be another copy in the office, though I don't think it was hanging on the proper hook when I was in there — maybe someone left it on Robyn's desk. And who knows how many extras are floating around the parish."

"We'll probably end up putting our own lock on it as well," the chief said. "But let's check on whether there's one in the office, if it's not too much trouble."

"No trouble at all," I said. "I need to collect the toucan anyway."

He waited while I locked up first the files and then the overflow room, and followed me down the hall to Robyn's study. I could tell he approved of the softer blues and greens in which she'd decorated her office.

I could hear feathers rustling beneath the cover, and realized it might be a good idea to make sure the bird was still okay. As far as I knew, the intruder hadn't entered the church, but you never knew. I whisked the cover off, and Nimitz greeted us with a volley of the low-pitched croaking noises that were a toucan's stock-in-trade. Not for the first time, I found myself marveling at how improbable he looked. The glossy black body and white vest were showy enough, but when you added in the orange-and-blue patch around his eyes and the bright-yel-low–and–orange beak that was nearly as long as his body, he looked less like a real bird than the result of turning three-year-olds loose with crayons.

I noticed the chief was staring at him, too.

"That beak is unreal," he said. "I assume they can't actually fly with that thing."

"They fly just fine," I said. "The beak's mostly hollow. But don't ask me to prove the flying part — the last time he got loose it took us hours to catch him."

The chief continued to study Nimitz while I did a quick search of Robyn's desk.

"The other columbarium key is definitely missing." I pointed to the key board on the wall, where the hook labeled COLUMB was now bare. "I noticed it while I was on the call with Debbie Ann. I wouldn't be surprised if that's how Mr. Hagley got in," I added, as I picked up the cover to Nimitz's cage.

"I see." The chief was frowning at the key board.

Seeing me approach the cage, Nimitz rubbed his head against the bars in a flirtatious gesture and uttered the soft noise, a cross between clacking and trilling, that he'd found most effective for charming bits of fruit out of passersby.

"What was that?" The chief had swiveled around and was staring at the bird.

"Just Nimitz," I said.

"I know, but what is he imitating? It almost sounded like someone being choked. Although it could be something mechanical. Can you get him to do it again?"

"I couldn't stop him from doing it again if I tried, but he's not imitating anything. He's a toucan, not a parrot." How many times had I already explained this to people visiting the office?

"So that's just the noise toucans make?" He sounded disappointed.

"One of the noises," I said. "They make a lot of noises, most of them rather mechanical sounding. But if you're hoping Nimitz is going to imitate the killer's voice or repeat Mr. Hagley's last words — sorry. Not something toucans can do."

"A pity." He turned back to his contemplation of the keys. Nimitz tapped his beak gently against the mesh of his cage, to get my attention, and then tilted his head flirtatiously again.

"I know perfectly well you're stuffed to the gills," I said as I covered his cage. "Goodnight, birdbrain."

I glanced down at the area around the cage and shuddered at the mess he'd made in the last few hours. He ate the fruit we prepared for him with untidy gusto, so the floor around his cage was always covered with splashes of fruit juice and partially pulverized bits of fruit. And then there were the droppings. I grabbed the roll of paper towels we'd taken to keeping near the cage and tackled the worst of it.

"My goodness." The chief had noticed what I was doing. "You definitely need someone to clean up after him."

"I've been cleaning up after him," I said. "We all do, several times a day, but there's just no containing the mess — which is why he's going to stay in our barn for the time being."

"Good plan. So you always keep the keys out in the open like that?"

He pointed to the key board, where most of the hooks — BOILER ROOM, VAN, SUPPLY CLOSET, and so forth — were still populated.

"Yes," I said. "About the only keys we try to keep reasonably secure are the ones to Robyn's office and the file cabinets. And even so, I'd be astonished if there weren't at least a dozen keys to both floating around the parish. Most of the vestry have them. Including, incidentally, Mr. Hagley."

"So Mr. Hagley could have used his own

key to gain entry here, to Robyn's office, and then taken the columbarium key off the board."

"Yes." I nodded. "In fact — hang on a sec."

Tending Nimitz had reminded me of something. I pulled out my phone, opened up a picture I'd taken earlier in the evening of Nimitz in all his Technicolor glory. I glanced at it and then showed it to the chief.

"I took this around ten o'clock," I said. "To show Robyn he was still healthy and happy."

"A nice likeness." His voice suggested that he was wondering why I was bothering to show him the photo.

"Look at the upper left corner," I said. "You can see the key board. Both columbarium keys are still there."

I used my fingers to enlarge the picture and showed it to the chief again. This time he nodded.

"I see," he said. "The background's a bit fuzzy, but no question that there are two keys there."

"Which means sometime after ten o'clock, someone got in here and took one of the columbarium keys. My money's on Mr. Hagley. I left Robyn's office locked when I ran out to see what the hammering was, but the rest of the evening if I wasn't in it, I locked the door behind me."

"Wise," he said. "But still, not a very secure system."

"You know how it is in a church," I said. "The focus is more on bringing people in than keeping them out."

"It's that way at New Life Baptist," he said. "And most of the time that's just fine."

"But most of the time neither church is the scene of a murder," I said.

"Exactly." He glanced at his watch. "Your father should be here by now, and I'd like to hear his first impressions. If you could let me out by whatever door's closest to the cryp— the columbarium, I won't keep you any longer."

Which was probably his polite way of suggesting he'd like me out from underfoot.

"I'll say hi to Dad on my way to the parking lot," I said as I snagged the van key.

CHAPTER 7

When we returned to the crypt we could hear Horace and Dad having a lively discussion about the red ring we'd found.

"The easiest way to tell if it's a real ruby is to see if you can scratch it," Dad was saying. "The only thing harder than a ruby is a diamond, so if you can scratch it with one of your tools we'll know it's a fake."

"Yes, I know." Horace sounded slightly annoyed.

"Or if you don't have any suitable tools, we could just drag it across one of the marble panels," Dad went on. "If any of the color comes off we'll know the stone is a fake."

"Right now the marble panels are part of my crime scene," Horace said. "I want them left the way they are. And besides, before I start trying to figure out whether it's a real ruby or not, I need to check it for fingerprints and DNA."

The chief stepped to the columbarium door. I stood behind him and peered over his shoulder. Dad was crouched by Mr. Hagley's body. Horace appeared to be inspecting the soles of Mr. Hagley's shoes. Dad's eyes were fixed, magpie-like, on the ring.

"Dr. Langslow," the chief said. "Any preliminary observations?"

"I'd estimate death occurred no more than an hour ago," Dad said. "Blunt force wound to the right posterior portion of the skull, near the lambdoid suture — that's the line of demarcation between the parietal and occipital bones." Luckily for those of us who hadn't taken Anatomy 101, he was pointing to the equivalent spot on his own head — the upper back right side.

"Could it have been done by that crow-bar?" the chief asked.

"Definitely the right shape for it," Dad said.

"And there's blood and other biological material on the crowbar," Horace said. "So I'd say that's a yes. Another interesting note — it appears the killer struck Mr. Hagley before he began prying the front panels off the niches — there's also biological material on the edges of several of the niches or panels."

Biological material. If he was just talking about blood, he'd have said blood. I decided not to think too much about what else he might mean. I pulled out my notebook-that-tells-me-when-to-breathe and added an item to my to-do list — organizing a com-mittee of strong-stomached parishioners to give the crime scene a thorough cleaning once the chief took away the yellow tape. And then I remembered something else.

"Dad," I said. "I don't want to wake her now — but any chance you could ask Mother to make sure there's someone reli-able assigned to help Robyn in the morn-ing."

"Of course," Dad said. "Help her how?"

"By preventing her from dashing down here, getting in the chief's way and putting herself and the baby at risk," I said. "I'm not suggesting she needs a keeper —"

"But she probably does," the chief said. "Good idea."

"Will do," Dad said. "Getting back to my findings — he was probably struck from behind — and with considerable force."

I left them to it. I made my way to the parking lot, which was filling up with vehi-cles. Dad's car, an ambulance, and four police cars. Evidently the ambulance was just here to transport Mr. Hagley when Dad finished with him — the two EMTs were leaning against its side, and waved when they saw me. Horace and the chief had come in two of the police cars. I suspected the occupants of the other two accounted for the rustling or crashing noises coming from the woods around the church.

I unlocked the elderly church van, started it after three attempts, and paused long enough to add *ignition* to the already long list of items that needed servicing. I texted Michael, "On my way finally. Don't wait up." Then I headed for home.

Instead of parking in my usual spot, I took the driveway that led to the barn. The door was unlocked, of course. I'd given up expecting the boys, or even Michael, to remember that my valuable blacksmith's equipment lived in the barn. But all my gear was safe inside what the boys called "Mom's jail" — a section at one end of the barn enclosed in heavy steel bars. Out of force of habit, I tested to make sure the jail door was safely locked. And looked longingly at the anvil I hadn't touched since I'd begun filling in for Robyn.

Then I set Nimitz's cage down on top of a couple of hay bales just outside the jail. I heard his feathers rustle slightly, and then he presumably went back to sleep.

"I should go straight to bed," I said to myself. "It must be nearly one o'clock."

In fact, it was a quarter past one. But however tired I was, I was more curious. Curious and maybe a little spooked. Someone had crept into Robyn's office, taken the columbarium key, and gone out there either to murder or be murdered, all while I was downstairs struggling with the stopped-up toilet. What if the toilet had been easier to fix? Or what if I'd given up after a slight struggle and gone upstairs to collect Nimitz earlier?

I checked to make sure I'd locked the barn door behind myself, then strolled over to my office — the former tack room, at the other end of the barn from my blacksmithing setup — unlocked the door, and turned on my laptop.

I wanted to know more about the people whose ashes the murderer had disturbed. While my laptop booted, I took out my notebook and wrote down the names, and what I remembered of the birth and death dates. Then I opened a search engine and typed in *Van der Lynden jewel robbery.*

Up popped a four-month-old article from the *Caerphilly Clarion* — part of its recurring "This week in local history" series. "Thirtieth anniversary of infamous local jewel heist!" read the headline. According to the article, on December 31, 1987, Mrs. Beatrice van der Lynden, widow of the late Archibald van der Lynden Sr., had graciously agreed to host the Dames of Caerphilly's annual New Year's Eve masked ball.

"It would be the Dames." The Dames of Caerphilly, while ostensibly a local historical society, had actually been merely a snooty social club dominated by the Pruitts, the family who had run Caerphilly like a personal fiefdom from the late 1800s until a few years ago. I had no idea if the Dames had formally disbanded or if they'd merely lapsed into oblivion after the disgrace and departure of most of the Pruitts, but certainly no one had heard from them in years.

The article went on to report that shortly before midnight shots rang out in an upper floor of the palatial Van der Lynden mansion. Several of the guests attempted to apprehend the jewel thieves. One of the would-be rescuers was killed along with one of the three intruders. The other two robbers were apprehended two days later, but Mrs. Van der Lynden's jewelry collection, valued at an estimated ten million dollars, was never found.

"Mrs. Van der Lynden never recovered from the trauma of this terrifying night," I read aloud. "And died of a broken heart shortly thereafter."

From what I'd remembered reading on her plaque, she'd died sometime in 1993. I wasn't sure five or six years qualified as shortly thereafter. Or that you could blame the death on a broken heart after so long. And was a broken heart really the reaction someone had to losing ten million in jewelry? Fred Singer, the owner, editor, and chief bottle-washer of the *Clarion,* did tend to get slightly melodramatic in writing these little historical vignettes.

I opened my notebook-that-tells-me-when-to-breathe, as I called the small three-ring binder that held my to-do lists, and made a note to talk to Fred tomorrow. In addition to being melodramatic, Fred tended to leave out anything that reflected badly on Caerphilly or its inhabitants — anything that might inspire anyone to sue him. A New Year's ball that ends in a pitched gun battle between a gang of jewel thieves and some of the invited guests? Surely there was more to the story.

I scrolled down to look at the pictures that had accompanied the article. The first few I could easily have mistaken for '80s photos of the cast of *Dynasty* — the men looking elegant in black-and-white tuxedos while the women were resplendent in long gowns, big hair, and enough sequins, lamé, and real gems that the onlookers had probably needed sunglasses. I didn't recognize anyone, but I deduced there were a lot of Pruitts in the crowd, judging from the number of short, stocky revelers whose heads appeared stuck directly onto their bodies without benefit of an intervening neck. And they all had masks, trimmed with feathers and rhinestones and for the most part carried on sticks rather than worn. Easier to manage with all that hair. Evidently a masked ball was very different from a costume ball. A good thing no one had invited me — I'd probably have showed up in some version of my Xena costume, and Mrs. Van der Lynden didn't look like the kind of hostess who'd appreciate it the way Michael and the boys did.

A third photo showed a mansion — the stately mansion of the Van der Lyndens, according to the caption. It looked curiously familiar. I studied it for a few moments.

"Of course! It's Ragnarsheim!"

Ragnarsheim was the home of Ragnar Ragnarsen, a drummer who, after surviving two decades in a series of heavy metal bands, had settled down to semi-retirement in Caerphilly. He'd bought a huge house on a large estate and had been busy ever since turning the whole place into his vision of a Goth paradise. I was pretty familiar with the house because a large part of his vision involved miles of intricate ornamental ironwork wrought by me.

How strange to see Ragnarsheim without a single bit of wrought iron festooning it. No gargoyles on the roof. No statues of dragons flanking the front door. No flaming torches, or —

I suddenly found myself yawning massively.

I glanced down at my list. I could type in the next name. But I felt another huge yawn coming on.

"Enough." I printed the article and stuffed it in my tote. Then I turned off my laptop and closed the cover. "Seven A.M. will be here before you know it."

I turned off the lights and took the path from the barn to the back door.

The kitchen was spotless. A quick check in the refrigerator showed the boys' school lunches already packed. In the front hall, their school backpacks and their baseball bags were lined up in a neat row.

I wondered for a few moments if Matt, Robyn's husband, would turn out to be anywhere near as good a partner in parenting as Michael.

Then I tiptoed upstairs, where everyone was asleep. I delivered stealth goodnight kisses to the sleeping boys — who had recently decided they were too old for such nonsense — and to Michael. Then I crawled into bed and fell asleep almost immediately.

CHAPTER 8

"Mom? Are you awake?"

I opened my eyes to find both Josh and Jamie looming over me. Their ability to loom seemed to be increasing exponentially of late, and I wondered briefly how few years it would take for them to zoom past my five-foot-ten height and set their sights on the more ambitious six-foot-four target Michael provided.

"Mom? I said are you awake?" Josh.

"No." I pulled my pillow over my face by way of emphasis.

"You can't possibly answer no to that question," Jamie pointed out helpfully.

"In this case, no doesn't mean I'm not awake." I pulled the pillow off my face, the better to glare at them. "It means I don't want to be."

"Oh." Jamie looked slightly chastened. But only slightly.

"But it's only fifteen minutes before you

have to get up anyway," Josh said. "And Rose Noire has questions about what to feed the parrot."

"Parrot? What parrot? We don't have a parrot." Unless Grandfather had come across a surplus parrot at his zoo and decided to give it to the boys as a present. I'd had to squelch notions like that before.

"The parrot you put in the barn last night." Josh hadn't yet mastered the eye roll — after all, he wasn't yet a teen — but he had the accompanying tone down perfectly.

Enlightenment struck.

"That's not a parrot," I said. "*That* is a *toucan.* His name is Nimitz, and he's the one from church, the one Reverend Robyn was taking care of while his owner's off doing his military service. We're filling in for her, just for the time being," I added, to make sure they understood the temporary nature of the bird's residence here.

"Will he start talking when he settles in and gets used to his new environment?" Jamie asked. Clearly he'd been paying at least a little attention to the many nature lessons Grandfather inflicted on us all.

"If Nimitz does start talking, you should tell Great right away," I said, using the boys' new shortened nickname for my grandfather. "Because he'd be the first toucan ever known to talk, and Great would want to do a television special on him."

"Would we be in the special?" Jamie asked.

"Wait — you mean he's never going to talk?" Evidently Josh was paying closer attention this morning.

"Never."

"What, never?" Michael sang from the doorway. He was clearly having a flashback to his appearance in some bygone production of *H.M.S. Pinafore.*

"No, never!" I sang back. Two could play at this.

"What, never?"

"Hardly ever!"

"He's hardly ever sick at sea!" we finished in unison.

The boys didn't say a word, but I could read facial expressions. Theirs said, "At least they're not doing this in public."

"Rose Noire needs to know what to feed the . . . bird," Josh said. Clearly Nimitz had fallen from his peak of popularity.

"The dumb toucan," Jamie added.

"You're not supposed to call anyone dumb," Josh protested.

"This kind of dumb just means he can't talk," Jamie said.

"Mom! Dad!"

"Enough!" Michael said. "Give your

mother some peace and quiet — she was up late last night. Tell Rose Noire that the toucan eats fruit, and if she needs more detail, Grandpa or Great can fill her in."

The boys thundered downstairs.

"So before they get back, fill me in," Michael said. "What happened at Trinity last night?"

Ah, well. I was completely awake by this time anyway. And beginning to feel impatient to get things done. So while I dressed and reduced my hair to a more civilized tangle, I gave him a blow-by-blow account of my discovery of Mr. Hagley and the beginnings of the chief's investigation.

"Damn," Michael said. "Hagley wasn't a very likable man, and no one in town's going to be prostrate with grief, but it's hard to think of anyone who would actually want him dead."

"Exactly. I mean, it's easy to joke, and say that I hope Robyn's alibied, and the vestry — but as far as I could see everyone was just annoyed with him. No one hated him."

"And speaking of Robyn, you're going to have your hands full today, carrying out her orders," he said. "How about if you take the boys to school and I drop the church van off with Osgood Shiffley. Then you'll already be in town with your car instead of having to scrounge a ride back here to get it."

"Deal," I said. "So maybe it's a good thing the boys woke me, since they need to take off in — yikes, five minutes."

The ride into town wasn't exactly peaceful, but the boys were in a good mood, and their noisy energy was exactly what I needed to keep me from brooding over the events of the previous night.

And almost enough to keep me from hearing my phone ring.

"It's Grandma calling," Josh, whose turn it was to ride shotgun, peered over at where my phone lay on the console between the seats.

"Do you want to answer it and tell her I'll call her back after I drop you guys at school?" I said.

"Nah." Josh slouched in his seat.

"I'll do it." Jamie's hand appeared between my seat and Josh's and snagged the ringing phone. Josh made an unsuccessful attempt to grab it back, then leaned back with a look of utter unconcern on his face.

"Hi, Grandma," Jamie said. "Mom doesn't want to talk to you now."

"That is *not* what I said to tell Grandma," I said.

"Dude, really?" Josh muttered.

"Yes, because she's driving us to school,

and doesn't want to be distracted," Jamie went on. "But she can call you back after she takes us to school . . . Uh-huh . . . Uh-huh . . . okay. Bye."

He sat back in his seat and looked very pleased with himself.

"Did Grandma say what she wanted?" I asked, when it became clear that Jamie wasn't going to volunteer any information.

"For you to call her back. She said that she's over helping Reverend Robyn with something, and that you'd know why she was calling."

So after I dropped the boys off, making sure they had their lunches and book bags — but leaving their baseball bags in the Twinmobile, since I'd be the one taking them to the game — I pulled into a space at the far end of the Caerphilly Elementary parking lot and called Mother back.

"Are you still at Robyn's?"

"No, I just pulled into the church parking lot. Robyn wanted to make sure everything here was okay. So what really happened last night?"

I settled into a more comfortable position and told her. Mother was always a highly satisfactory audience, exclaiming "No!" "You're joking!" or "Oh, my goodness!" at all the right spots.

"So I assume the columbarium is a crime scene for the time being," I said in conclusion. "Robyn's tasked me with talking to the next of kin, and I guess we'll need a special election sometime soon to replace Mr. Hagley. Although I suppose it would be rude to have it too soon after his death."

"Poor man." I could almost see Mother shaking her head sadly.

"What happened to 'selfish, heartless brute with a spreadsheet for a soul'?" I asked. "Or was it some other member of the vestry flinging that particular insult at him during last night's meeting?"

"Meg, really." She was using what Rob referred to as her Mother Voice. Somehow it had less effect on me now that I was perfecting my own version of it for use on the twins. "I can't believe that you would stoop to eavesdropping."

"I don't think it counts as eavesdropping when someone shouts loud enough to be heard all the way from the parish hall to the overflow room," I said. "I realize we're all going to have to practice saying nice, polite things about Mr. Hagley for the immediate future, at least in public. But you and I can at least be honest with each other."

"Good point," Mother said, in a more normal tone. "Although I really do feel sorry for Junius. He was never precisely the soul of cordiality, but he didn't go completely off the rails until poor Dolores died. She was such a good influence on him."

More likely Dolores had catered to her husband's every whim, made him feel important, and cushioned him against the harsh realities of a world that found him abrasive and annoying. It might have been better for the rest of us if she hadn't done such a good job of it.

"Robyn says Mr. Hagley has been trying to reclaim his wife's ashes for a while," I said aloud. "Any idea why?"

"Well, I couldn't possibly say for certain," Mother said. "I'd only be speculating, of course, and I wouldn't want any unseemly rumors to get out."

Which meant she had a very good idea indeed, and only needed a little encouragement to share it.

"Even a speculation would be welcome," I said. "And I can't help squelch unseemly rumors if I don't know what they are."

"He needed the money," Mother said.

"What, was he going to try to sell her ashes someplace?"

"No, of course not. He could sell their niche."

Okay, that made more sense. I'd seen the

bills of sale in the church files. Niches weren't cheap. But still . . .

"He was that desperate? And how do you know?"

"A whole lot of little things. He didn't use to like coming to church social events, but lately he hadn't missed a one — at least as long as there was food. He was always cadging rides to meetings — probably trying to save on gas. They'd had Wilma Shiffley cleaning for them for years, every two weeks, and six months ago he fired her. And terminated his lawn service. A lot of little things that add up."

I nodded, even though Mother couldn't see me. Okay, now I also felt a little sorry for Mr. Hagley. Maybe in addition to being a good influence on him, Mrs. Hagley had also been the financially savvy one. And maybe her death had reduced their income — would Mr. Hagley get less Social Security? I had no idea how that worked.

"And then there's the fact that he's nine months behind on his pledges to the building fund," Mother was saying. "Whenever anyone confronted him about it, he'd always have some excuse. Last night it was that he wasn't going to give the church any more money if they were just going to fritter it away on extravagances like a brand-new luxury minivan."

"Are we going to fritter any money away on a new van?" I asked. "Because Michael just took the current one over to see if Osgood Shiffley can keep it running for another few months. The list of things that need fixing takes up a whole page in my notebook, and if you ask me, spending any more on repairing it is just throwing good money after bad."

"We were discussing that very idea last night," Mother said. "Mr. Hagley and Mr. Sedlak were dissenting rather strongly."

"The two Muttering Misogynists," I said. "I do hope Mr. Sedlak stays in good health, or the chief really will be suspicious of the rest of you on the vestry. Getting back to Mr. Hagley — so you think he was going to resell their niche?"

"I'm almost certain of it," she said. "Did I mention that I've seen some of Dolores's things in the local antique shops lately? That little Chippendale footstool with the crewelwork cover. And that nice blue Wedgwood tea set of hers, the one she always used when she had us over for meetings of the Altar Guild."

"A lot of blue Wedgwood in the world," I said. "How can you be sure it was hers?" Not that I doubted her word — I figured she'd know somehow — some distinctive chip or stain, probably.

"Because I asked," Mother said.

Okay, that also worked.

"And according to Lettice — it was Lettice Forsythe's shop I saw it in — that's not the only thing he's sold."

"Poor man."

We both remained silent for a few moments. Perhaps Mother was also savoring the strange new sensation of feeling sorry for Mr. Hagley.

"Well, I should get busy," she said. "Because even though we probably need to wait a few days to announce the special election, there's no reason we can't start the planning."

"As long as you're at the church, could you do something for the chief? I think he'd like a copy of the files about the niches that were disturbed. I left them on top of the file cabinet."

"Of course. I'll do that first thing. And when I drop them off, I can find out if he needs anything else."

And while she was at it, she could try her hand at finding out where the chief was in his investigation. Why should I have all the fun?

CHAPTER 9

We signed off, and I decided to drop by to see the chief myself. Not to be nosy, of course, but to find out if the coast was clear for me to carry out Robyn's orders.

I parked in the police station parking lot and headed for the door. But when I reached the sidewalk in front of it, I met the chief coming out.

"Can I help you?" he asked.

"Just wondering if there are any next of kin I can start contacting," I said.

"I'm on my way to interview Mrs. Washington," he said. "Who, wonder of wonders, is still at the address we found in the church files. If you like, I'll text you when I've finished with her."

"That would be great," I said. "I expect the others will be harder to track down."

"The Hagleys' son will be coming up from Richmond this afternoon," the chief said. "I assumed you would be okay with me giving him your contact information as the person representing Trinity on this issue."

I nodded.

"The best information I've been able to find about Archie van der Lynden's whereabouts is that he's reputed to be at a residential substance abuse treatment facility."

"There can't be that many of those around," I said.

"You'd be surprised," he said. "And also, under HIPAA regulations, no reputable facility would even be allowed to tell me whether or not Mr. Van der Lynden was a patient there," he said. "Finding Archie could take a while, and if he was locked up somewhere detoxing he's not going to be our prime suspect. I still haven't heard back from the Blair woman in Middleburg, or the Van der Lyndens' law firm. Vern Shiffley comes on duty at noon, and I'm going to task him with figuring out who we should talk to about Lacey Shiffley."

"And I expect there's nothing you can do about the John Doe," I said.

"Actually, there might be." The chief looked pleased — almost smug. "Horace dug into the archives and found the file on him — the file and the evidence. They actually took tissue samples, so Horace can get John Doe's DNA analyzed."

"They couldn't have done that in 1994?"

"In theory they could have, but it would have taken forever and cost the moon, and they wouldn't have had anything to compare his DNA with when they got it. CODIS was just getting started up around that time. They kept his body around for almost a year before they accepted Dr. Womble's offer to bury him at Trinity. But someone back then had his head on straight, so before they released the body, they took the kind of tissue samples they'd need to do a DNA analysis, in case it ever proved useful."

"And now it will!"

"It might." His face fell a little. "We could come up blank. After all, most of the DNA in CODIS has been collected since it was established. It's not like our John Doe was out there leaving his DNA at crime scenes for the last twenty-four years."

"But it's always possible," I said. "Or you could find a relative."

"A relative's more likely, so that's what we're hoping for," he said. "Well, I'd better be off. Mrs. Washington is expecting me. Oh, and since you'll have some time before you're able to talk to her, any chance you could arrange to get me the contents of those files we looked at last night?"

"Actually, Mother's already working on

that. She'll drop them off later, or more likely arrange to have someone do it."

"Thank you."

He headed for his car. I didn't figure there was much more to be learned at the police station, so I did the same.

I decided to drop by my office at the town hall. Luckily, things had been slow lately in my theoretically part-time job as special assistant to Mayor Randall Shiffley. I suspected Randall, knowing how worried we were about Robyn and how much work her absence was causing, had done his best to keep it that way. But still, there were a couple of things I needed to do. And if Randall was around, all the better. The chief might be relying on Deputy Vern Shiffley for information about Lacey Shiffley. No reason I couldn't pick Randall's brains.

I was in luck. He was in his office with his feet up on the venerable oak table that served as his desk, frowning over some sheets of paper that I recognized as budget reports.

"Just the person I wanted to see." He tossed the papers back into his in-box. "The chief gave me the bare bones of what happened at Trinity last night. I want details!"

I gave him chapter and verse of what I'd seen, telling it all in order with one exception — I held back the names of the people whose ashes had been disturbed. And I topped off my story with what I'd learned from Mother about Mr. Hagley's motivation for wanting to reclaim his wife's ashes.

"Poor old Junius," he said. "And yes, I expect he was hurting for money. The town treasurer gave me a list of the citizens who weren't current with their property taxes, and he was on it."

"I wish we'd known he was in such dire need," I said. "We could have done something to help." Although no sooner had the words left my mouth than I found myself wondering if perhaps Robyn had known. Had known and had tried to reach out to help Mr. Hagley. Would he react to an offer of help from her with gratitude? Or would he resent what he might see as interference, reject her help, and lash out at her in anger?

I could ask Robyn. Better yet, Mother.

"So as soon as the chief gives the go-ahead, I'm going to start contacting the next of kin of the people whose ashes have been disturbed," I said. "As soon as he figures out where to find them all."

"So who are we talking about, apart from Dolores Hagley — and does he need any help?" Which was exactly what I'd expected Randall to say.

91

"He might with one — Lacey Shiffley."

"Lacey Shiffley!" His eyebrows rose in surprise. "Now there's a name I haven't heard recently."

"Probably not since 2006, when she died and ended up buried at Trinity instead of in the First Presbyterian graveyard."

"Lacey was always a bit of a rebel," Randall said. "A black sheep, to hear some of the old-timers talk."

"Just for turning Episcopalian? Where's your spirit of ecumenism?"

"That was one of the saner things she did," Randall said. "No, the reason she was on the outs with most of the family was that she eloped with a guy from Clay County. A Whicker, of all people." The Whickers, along with the Dingles, the Plunkets, and the Peebleses, made up more than half of the names in the Clay County phone directory. There was no love lost between the residents of the two counties. "And while I'm willing to concede that through some fluke of genetics even the Whicker family tree produces a few bright, hardworking, honest, likable saplings from time to time, Anse Whicker doesn't seem to have been one of them."

"How bad was he?"

"All I know is the family gossip, and who

knows how much that could have gotten exaggerated over the years?" Randall said. "But you could ask Aunt Jane. She and Lacey were first cousins, and almost as close as sisters growing up. I'm pretty sure Lacey kept in touch with Aunt Jane long after she turned a cold shoulder on the rest of us."

"I'll do that." I liked Judge Jane Shiffley, and the idea of talking to her appealed to me. "Would she also be the one to ask who Lacey's next of kin would be?"

"Definitely," he said. "For all I know, she might *be* Lacey's next of kin. Lacey was an only, and her parents would be long gone. She eventually divorced that no-count husband of hers, and I never heard that they had any kids."

"Is Judge Jane due in court today?" I asked.

"Probably," he said. "But not till ten or eleven."

"And it's only nine." I found myself thinking, not for the first time, that the school system was not kind to night owl parents.

"Which means you have time to tell me what other next of kins you're looking for," Randall suggested.

"The chief's going over to talk to Mrs. Washington, widow of James Washington. Middle name something with an A."

"I knew Jim," Randall said. "My dad took him on as night watchman for the construction yard after the Van der Lyndens fired him. They were tight with the Pruitts, the Van der Lyndens, and did their best to make sure no one would hire Jim, so Dad took him on just to spite the lot of them."

"Maybe the killer's choice of niches wasn't entirely random," I said.

"Maybe not," Randall agreed. "Because Jim Washington lost his job over the Van der Lynden jewel robbery."

"Why?"

"The way he told it, he was a scapegoat. He was on security duty that night, which meant he sat in the gatehouse and checked to make sure the people who pulled up were on the guest list before he let them in. And there was never anything to suggest the robbers came in the front gate — not with a couple miles of perfectly ordinary farm fencing around most of the estate."

"Still — James Washington was the Van der Lyndens' security guard at the time of the robbery."

"Security guard? He was their handyman and gopher. Firing him was just pure meanness. Who else?"

"Mrs. Van der Lynden herself," I went on. "And I'm beginning to appreciate the irony of her ending up buried in the same crypt as her ex-handyman."

Randall snorted with laughter.

"P. Jefferson Blair, who died in 2000."

"Not from around here," Randall said. "And I don't mean that in any negative sense — only that I've never heard the name."

"And a John Doe from 1995," I said. "So also presumably not from around here, or somebody would have identified him."

"Can't help with him, either, then," Randall said. "But Aunt Jane will fill you in on Lacey. So at least I've been of some use."

"Definitely," I said. "So unless there's anything here for me to worry about, I'm going to go have a talk with Judge Jane's bailiff."

"I have a better idea," he said. "Let me talk to him. Cal's dating one of my cousins. I could drop by and make sure he knows about some upcoming family event and mention, casual-like, that you're probably going to need to talk to Aunt Jane about Lacey. Cal's such an efficient son of a gun — I bet he'll just arrange it at her earliest convenience. And if you get there before the chief has a chance to talk to her . . . well, not your fault if Her Honor summons you."

"I'm not actually trying to sneak around

behind the chief's back," I said.

"But the sooner you talk to the next of kins, the better for Robyn's stress level. Or should that be nexts of kin?"

"Relatives will do," I said. "And thanks. I'm going to drop by the *Clarion* and see what Fred Singer knows."

"Good plan," he said. "And that's only two blocks away, so you can dash back if Cal tells me Aunt Jane's available."

Randall and I rode down in the elevator to the ground floor. He ambled down the corridor that led to Judge Jane's courtroom. I strolled down the long marble front steps of the courthouse and made my way around the town square until I reached the well-preserved Victorian-era building that housed our local paper.

I paused for a moment outside the entrance. Would the chief consider this sticking my nose into his case?

Not if I made it clear to Fred that I was mainly looking for information that would help me locate the various relatives Robyn had asked me to contact. Or at least convinced him to say that if the chief ever asked.

CHAPTER 10

When I stepped through the front door of the *Clarion*'s office, an old-fashioned bell tinkled to announce my arrival. The front room was small and divided in two by a counter to separate the public from the newspaper staffers — a holdover, I suspected, from the old days when the locals dropped by regularly to place classifieds, hand over announcements, and complain in person about the editorials or the delivery boys. Now all that was usually done by email, making the counter a pleasant anachronism.

Fred Singer, the owner and editor, popped out of the door behind the counter.

"Meg! Just the person I wanted to see! I want an exclusive interview on what happened last night at Trinity!"

"We can make a deal, then," I said. "I want to pick your brains about the late Mrs. Van der Lynden."

"Come into my lair, then," Fred said.

He led me through the newsroom — a room about the size of my dining room, containing three desks with computers on them, and more paper than I'd have thought it was possible to fit into such a relatively small space. Books, magazines, old newspapers, file folders, and stacks and stacks of loose papers weighted down the desks, filled every corner, and left only narrow paths between them. As we made our way back to Fred's tiny office, I could hear the rustling of papers as I brushed by them. Fred's office was much the same. The main path through the paper led to his chair — an old-fashioned wooden banker's chair on rollers, though the walls of paper around it left no room for rolling — with a branch trail to an old-fashioned wooden straight chair for his guest.

He must have guessed the direction of my thoughts from the expression on my face.

"I'm still waiting for that paperless office everyone keeps talking about," he said. "Every time I think about getting rid of some of this junk, one of the computers dies, taking several million words with it, and suddenly I'm glad I printed out most of it. Which is why I'm going to take notes about what happened to you last night on this stylishly retro yellow legal pad."

I knew a cue when I heard one, so I gave him my account of last night — leaving out anything I wasn't keen on having appear in the *Clarion,* and again saving the names of the people who'd occupied the opened niches for last.

"So I gather that's why you're suddenly so interested in Mrs. Van der Lynden?"

"Because she was one of the people whose niche was pried open last night."

"By Junius Hagley?"

"Or by whoever killed him. You'd have to ask the chief — that part was still up in the air last I heard. Anyway, last night when I went home, I did a search on Mrs. Van der Lynden's name, and the first thing that came up was your article on the New Year's Eve jewel robbery at her house."

"People love those little bits of local history." He preened — no doubt at the thought that his article was the first one in my search.

"I figured you could give me the real scoop," I said. "All the dirt you left out so you didn't get sued."

"Ha!" He slapped his knee as if pleased that I'd caught him sanitizing the town history. "Yes, the Van der Lyndens were litigious in their time. Might still be if there are any of them left. I can understand why my predecessor didn't print quite all the details he knew. For that matter, I'll have to be pretty careful myself when I write about the Van der Lyndens' connection to Mr. Hagley's murder. There's a difference between knowing what happened and being able to prove it. Frankly, I'm hoping the chief can dig up a few more hard facts I can use. And if you come across anything I can use —"

"I'll keep the *Clarion* in mind. So spill."

He leaned back in his old-fashioned chair, batting absentmindedly at some of the sheets of paper that brushed his head, and folded his hands.

"The Van der Lyndens. They moved here in 1970 or so. Bought the old Wentworth place and doubled its size. Made a big splash in local society."

"Even though they weren't from around here?" I asked.

"Folks'll overlook that if you've got enough money. The husband — Archibald Senior — died in the mid-eighties and there was just Mrs. Van der Lynden and Archie Junior, who was drinking and partying his way through college."

"At Caerphilly?"

"After he got kicked out of UVA and

100

University of Richmond. And quite possibly other schools that we never heard about. The old lady gave Caerphilly a honking big donation, and maybe the college thought with her right in town to keep an eye on him he'd behave a little better."

"And did he?"

Fred shrugged.

"If he didn't, they kept it pretty quiet. Made it to his junior year without getting sent home in disgrace. So anyway, the Dames of Caerphilly were having their annual New Year's shindig. This was back when they were still big."

I nodded. I could tell from his expression that he hadn't been any fonder of the Dames than I'd been.

"Mrs. Van der Lynden agreed to host the party. But unbeknownst to the Dames, she also planned to host a jewel robbery."

"Wait — she was behind the jewel robbery?"

"I can't prove it, but that's always been the conventional wisdom. Her money was running out. Not sure if she mismanaged it or if Archie Senior hadn't been the financial wizard everyone thought he was, but she was up against it. Me, I'd have suggested she find a millionaire to buy the estate, move someplace that was merely huge, and she could probably have hung on to the baubles. But she didn't think that way. She wanted to have her jewels and her palace and the money, too. So — they never proved this, mind you; a lot of conflicting testimony, but here's what I think happened — she decided to pull an insurance fraud. Told Archie Junior to arrange a fake robbery. You ask me that was her first mistake — relying on him for anything."

"Why did she need to involve him?" I asked. "She could hide the jewels, break a window, and call the cops."

"I think she had a premonition that the insurance company would be suspicious," Fred said. "So her plan was a little more convoluted. At the beginning of the party, she took a couple of the Dames upstairs with her — to help her pick out which jewels to wear."

"Thus establishing that the jewels were present and accounted for at the beginning of the party."

"Exactly. Then just before midnight, when everyone was gathering around the TV set to watch the ball descend in Times Square —"

"You'd think rich people could find some more exciting way to mark the occasion," I commented.

"Her plan called for a trio of supposed jewel thieves to come running down the main stairway, carrying the jewelry in the pink embroidered satin pillowcases from her bed, and waving guns to make sure no one got the idea to play hero. Instead, five assorted thieves began sniping at each other in the upper hallway and then came downstairs to conduct a pitched gun battle in the main hall. Panic ensued."

"I'm not surprised," I said. "Where did the surplus thieves come from?"

"From what Archie Junior said, he'd made a few overtures to the only actual crook he knew — his drug dealer — and figured out that any professionals he hired would want a big chunk of the loot. So he decided it would be a lot easier to recruit a few of his fraternity brothers to play the role of the jewel thieves. He only managed to get two takers, but he figured that would be enough. Unfortunately, the drug dealer decided to field his own team in the race to snag the jewels, and the real bandits arrived on the scene just as the two college students — whom some of the contemporary accounts referred to as the "gentleman bandits" — had finished loading all the jewel boxes into the pillowcases. The real bandits snatched the pillowcases, the gentleman bandits tried to recover them, and gunfire broke out."

"Who won?"

"No one, from what I can tell. One of the gentleman bandits and one of the real bandits were killed. The remaining gentleman bandit surrendered at the scene and confessed to what they were up to. He claimed it was just supposed to be a joke on Mrs. Van der Lynden, and it's possible he actually believed it. The two surviving real bandits were captured a day or two later. They claimed that when they dumped out the contents of the pillowcases and pried open the jewelry boxes, they found nothing but cheap costume jewelry and gravel. They all went to prison — real bandits, gentleman bandit, and Archie. But the jewels never turned up."

"Not ever?"

"Nope." Fred shook his head. "Not until you and Horace found the One Ring down in Trinity's catacombs. As it happens, the chief dropped by this morning to see what we had on the robbery, and we were able to give him copies of the pictures we had in the morgue of some of the more fabulous pieces stolen, including the Van der Lynden Ruby, as the old lady was fond of calling it. Either the ring's the real thing, or a damn good copy."

"Did Mrs. Van der Lynden go to prison, too?" I asked.

Fred shook his head.

"Why not?" Although I had a good idea, if Mrs. Van der Lynden could afford the right attorneys. Still. "Conspiracy to defraud the insurance company, accessory before the fact to murder — I'm sure they could think of a few more charges if they tried."

"They did — but they couldn't get around the fact that Archie took the fall for his mother. His story wobbled back and forth between claiming he'd only meant to play a prank on her to confessing that he was up to his ears in debt and hoped to sell the jewels to get himself free. But he stoutly denied that his mother had had anything to do with it."

"Maybe he was telling the truth."

"Maybe." Fred steepled his fingers in front of his face. "But no one who ever met him thinks Archie had the brains to think up something like this or the gumption to try it. And the smart money said he was more scared of his mother than of the law. They finally gave up trying to break his story." He spread his fingers as if setting free some winged creature he'd been clutching.

"So Archie went to prison, and Mrs. Van der Lynden lived happily ever after with the insurance money."

"She didn't get the insurance money."

CHAPTER 11

"Wait — Mrs. Van der Lynden *didn't* get the insurance money?"

"Not a penny."

"Why not?"

"The insurance company shared the general belief that it was an inside job. They dragged their heels for a couple of years, then denied the claim on some technicality — possibly something about her failure to provide adequate security for the stolen property, but I'm only guessing on that. Mrs. Van der Lynden filed suit against them, and that dragged on for a couple of years. Then she died, and the suit fell by the wayside when everyone found out how broke she was. I expect the lawyers figured out Archie had no money to pay for the work they'd already done, and they'd have had little appetite for running up more costs that might never be paid — especially when the smart money said sooner or later proof that she'd been in on it would turn up somewhere or other."

"And did it?" I asked. "Turn up, that is."

"Not that I've ever heard. Up until yesterday, if you'd asked me what I thought happened to the jewels, I'd have bet Mrs. Van der Lynden hid them somewhere, didn't tell anyone where, and took the secret to her grave."

"And now?"

"Either someone found where she hid the loot, or someone else had it all along."

"Had it and hid it in one of the niches at Trinity?"

He nodded.

"But why? Why go to all the trouble of stealing the jewels just to bury them?"

"Beats me. Maybe they thought they should wait until the statute of limitations ran out."

"I don't think Virginia has a statute of limitations on murder."

"Good point," he said. "But maybe the crooks didn't know that."

"They've had thirty years to figure it out — why wait until now?"

"Okay, here's another possibility: to spite Mrs. Van der Lynden. If they sold the jewels, she could always buy them back, and selling them would prove to the insurance company that they were stolen, so she'd get the insurance money. So — hide them until after she dies."

"Great idea, except that she's been dead since 1993. Why would whoever hid them wait twenty-five years?"

"Maybe the person who hid them died before she did."

I flipped to the page in my notebook where I'd jotted down the names and death dates.

"Of the niches that were disturbed, hers was the oldest," I said. "Everyone else that we know to have been involved in the case was still alive in 1993."

"Not such a great theory, then. Maybe they were hidden until one of the crooks got out of prison."

"Better idea," I said. "Except that it would mean the next of kin of one of those six people was in cahoots with the robbers. Because you'd need the cooperation of a family member to hide the jewels in some-one's niche."

"It's possible," he said. "But yeah, not likely."

"Have any of the crooks recently gotten out of prison?"

"They hadn't when I wrote that piece," Fred said. "I was going to include a 'where are they now' section to the article, but I really couldn't get much data and what I got was too depressing. Two real robbers and two gentleman robbers went to prison. One of the real robbers died in 2002, the other one — the ringleader, a hard case named Bart Hempel — was still up in Coffeewood, serving thirty to life for the murder. Archie Junior and Blair got much shorter sentences, so they got out in the nineties. I think they'd have made their move by now if they'd arranged for someone to stash the loot in the crypt. Archie has been in and out of rehab for the last twenty-five years. According to the police report Paul Blair shot himself while cleaning his gun, but isn't that so often what they say when they don't want to embarrass the family of a suicide? I didn't want to depress my readers with all that."

"Wait — Paul Blair?"

"You're wondering if he's the same one as the P. Jefferson Blair whose niche was disturbed. I haven't yet tracked down proof, but I'd bet real money he is."

"That seems weird," I said. "He turns up back here under a slightly disguised name, and ends up getting buried across from Mrs. Van der Lynden."

"Weird?" Fred grinned. "I'd call it downright suspicious. If it is the same guy. I'll let you know what I find out."

"But even if it is the same guy, I'm not sure I see how they could manage to sneak the jewels into the niche without anyone seeing them."

"Stranger things have happened. I had an aunt who wanted to be buried with the ashes of her Yorkshire terrier. I had my suspicions that the funeral home might not be keen, so I ended up putting the damned dog in a candy box tied up with a red ribbon and tucking it in her coffin at the funeral. I told everyone it was her love letters from her late husband."

"That was nice of you," I said. "Carrying out her last wishes like that."

"I suppose," he said. "It's put me right off Whitman's Samplers, though. Can't even look at the box. My point is that if someone asks for a moment alone with their dear departed, wouldn't the people from the church or the funeral home slip tactfully away?"

"Probably," I said. "But wouldn't it occur to whoever hid the jewels that they couldn't just drop by, pop the niche open, and reclaim them? They fasten those polished granite front panels in place pretty securely."

"I don't know," Fred said. "Could be a

good thing from their point of view. You wouldn't want a hiding place that was too easy to open, now would you?"

"True. And if Mr. Hagley's anything to go by, maybe people don't realize quite how involved a process it is to open up one of the niches."

"Yes." Fred looked thoughtful. "Curious, isn't it, how he suddenly got so fired up about reclaiming his wife's ashes. Maybe I should do some digging into Mr. Hagley."

I considered telling him Mother's theory about Mr. Hagley's dire need of cash and decided against it. For one thing, it was only a theory — and a theory built on information that was both unflattering and not really in the public domain. And for another, I rather liked the idea of having an inquisitive and persistent reporter poking into Mr. Hagley's possible motivations. If what he learned confirmed Mother's theory, all the better, and if it didn't, no problem.

"I should leave you to your digging." I stood up and hefted my tote bag onto my shoulder. "I assume I can drop by if I uncover any new information — or new questions?"

"I would be delighted to see you in either case," Fred said. "So will I see you at tonight's game?"

"Are the Eagles playing the Flying Foxes tonight, then?" Fred's grandson was the same age as Josh and Jamie and equally passionate about baseball. And on a rival team — which was unfortunate, because he was one of the best catchers in the league.

"Yes, the grand rivalry continues tonight," he said. "Just smack me if you hear me reverting to the old name and shouting 'Go Flatworms.' "

"Yes — Flying Foxes is a much better name." Not only a much better name but less likely to remind us of the much-reviled former president of the local youth baseball league.

So after we thanked each other for sharing information, Fred returned to his warren of an office and I stepped out into the town square and pondered my next move.

A little past ten. I checked my phone. No word from the chief to indicate he'd finished with Mrs. Washington, so I couldn't tackle her. I headed back toward the town hall. I could always do a little more online research, and I'd be handy if Judge Jane decided to see me.

I was in luck. I strolled into the courtroom hallway, just to see what was happening. Court wasn't in session yet, but the high-ceilinged oak-paneled courtroom was open and filling up with lawyers, plaintiffs, defendants, witnesses, and the usual handful of nosy Parkers who just loved to watch any kind of legal proceeding, even the routine ones that made watching paint dry look exciting. When Cal, the bailiff, spotted me, he waved and motioned me closer.

"Her Honor wants to see you pronto!" he said.

Several people who were standing nearby looked at me sharply, no doubt wondering what I'd done to incur Judge Jane's well-known ire. Just for the fun of it, as I followed Cal to the door behind the bench that led into Judge Jane's chambers, I tried to assume the worried expression of someone about to be thrown in jail for contempt of court.

"Glad you dropped by," Cal said. "With any luck, talking to you will put her in a better mood. She's always grouchy on her town days, you know."

A few years ago, when Caerphilly's financial difficulties had led to the town's main creditor repossessing all the government buildings, including the town hall, Judge Jane had started presiding over court in her barn. Most people hadn't minded — in fact, at least half of the people I knew had considered the barn ambience a distinct improvement over the stuffy courthouse. So even though we'd long since gotten our courthouse back, Judge Jane had been splitting her time between her official courtroom and her barn. Only the occasional attorney from out of town ever seemed to find this strange or inconvenient.

While I would have enjoyed a trip out to Judge Jane's farm, I had to admit that, given everything I had to do today, it was convenient that this was one of her town days.

"Come in and sit down," she called out when Cal announced my arrival.

I paused to let the half-dozen brown-and black hound dogs sharing her chambers sniff me. Judge Jane called them her deputies, and I hoped we never had to find out what they'd do to anyone who threatened her. They recognized me almost immediately and lifted up their heads to have their ears scratched. Between exchanging greetings with the dogs and stepping over and around the dog beds, chew toys, rawhide knots, and water bowls that littered the floor, it took a couple of minutes to reach the guest chair.

But perhaps I should be grateful that she didn't bring her horses to work.

When I finally took my seat, Judge Jane looked up from a document she'd been reading and fixed me with a glance that had been known to inspire hardened repeat offenders to confess and throw themselves on the mercy of the court.

My conscience was clear — well, mostly — but it was still hard not to squirm.

CHAPTER 12

"You had quite a time last night over at Trinity." Judge Jane pushed the document aside and leaned forward on her elbows. "Henry Burke caught the doer yet?"

I shook my head.

"Well, it's early times. I hear they broke poor Lacey's biscuit jar."

"The green glass thing she was buried in? Unfortunately. Do you know the story behind that?"

"I know where it came from," the judge said. "It was just about the one thing Lacey wanted when our grandmother died and we all went over to share out her possessions. No idea why she liked it so much. And definitely no idea she was planning to be buried in it. Of course, that was a good fifty years ago. She could have come up with the burying idea much later. Lord knows where I'm going to find another one like it."

I was startled for a moment — why would

she want another one like it? Then I realized she was thinking about reburying Lacey's ashes in the same container. Well, presumably it was what Lacey would have wanted.

"Was the jar an antique?" I asked.

"Must have been," she said. "In my earliest memories of Gran's kitchen, that jar was always there, full of cookies. And I'm nearly an antique now, so the jar must have been. Depression glass, I think they call it. I have no idea if it's valuable — I've got enough old things around the house without buying more. But I guess I'll find out."

"Since it's an antique, I can sic Mother on it," I said. "I'm sure she'll have no problem finding one."

"Kind of you," she said. "And I won't say no to her expert help."

"It's only fair." I took out my notebook and jotted a note about the biscuit jar. "Robyn asked me to talk to the next of kin of all the people whose ashes were disturbed, to see what they want done about reburial."

"Ah, so that's your angle." She laughed and shook her head. "I just figured your curiosity was getting the better of you and you were butting into Henry Burke's case to see what you could find out."

"I won't pretend I'm going to ignore any

evidence that would help the chief if I came across it," I said.

"Or if you can hunt it down," Judge Jane added.

"But he was okay with my talking to the next of kin as soon as possible. Randall and I figured either you were Lacey's next of kin or you'd know who was."

"I reckon I am. I was her executor, at any rate. I was the one who had to talk Maudie Morton into putting her ashes in that green glass jar, and break the news to the family that there wasn't going to be any funeral or even graveside services. There was hard feeling over that, I can tell you. But she laid out what she wanted in her will — bossiest will I've ever seen, if you want to know. She made her wishes known, and I did my best to carry them out."

"I'm glad to know she didn't quarrel with her whole family."

"She came damned close," Judge Jane said. "She had such promise and she ended up leading such a sad, lonely . . . useless life. I know that sounds harsh, and maybe she was perfectly happy in her own way, but — just damn. Hearing someone had disturbed her grave just brought it all up again."

"What was her story, anyway?"

"She was pretty as a picture and whip-smart." Judge Jane settled back in her chair with faraway eyes and a half smile. "And an only child, which was a big part of the problem. A lot better for everyone if Aunt Ida'd had a dozen or so kids to spread out all her energy on, but there was just Lacey. Aunt Ida and Uncle Ferd wanted Lacey to go to college, which wasn't exactly usual for girls in our family back then. They pushed too hard and she was going through a rebellious phase. I always thought if they'd given her an ultimatum that she had to find a job or a husband, she'd have moved heaven and earth to get to college. But instead she took up with Anse Whicker. A handsome devil, but already a troublemaker. And an ex-con to boot. If you ask me, she looked around to see who she could drag home to her parents that would hurt them the most and settled on Anse. And again, if they'd gritted their teeth and said 'that's nice, dear,' she'd have gotten bored with him. Instead, they wept and wailed and threatened to turn her out of the house, and she and Anse eloped."

"Yikes." I found myself remembering a few of my own youthful rebellions, which my parents had handled with grace, aplomb, and stoic patience. I wasn't sure I'd have gone as far as Lacey, but still, maybe I'd had some narrow escapes.

"And if you ask me, Lacey figured out what a disaster the marriage was pretty quickly, but she wasn't ever one to admit her mistakes. She held her head up and stuck by Anse. I've always suspected it was a relief to her when they sent him off to prison. She stayed loyal and visited him every week for a couple of years, but finally she'd had enough. Divorced him and moved back to Caerphilly."

"And continued to annoy her family by defecting to the Episcopalian church," I put in.

"You could be right." She shook her head and chuckled. "I've always thought the family was a little too happy to say 'I told you so!' and 'thank goodness you've come to your senses!' If everyone could have just kept their traps shut and started including her in all the family doings, I think things would have been different. She dropped her unsuitable Clay County friends, but she didn't come back and reconcile with her old ones, either."

"Instead she made a third set."

"She may have, but I never met any of them. Didn't hear any complaints about the lack of a funeral from anyone but family. I think she just became a recluse. And I bet I

121

can think of a reason why whoever vandalized Trinity would pick on her resting place."

"Do tell."

"After she moved back here, she got a bee in her bonnet about the jewel robbery. Thought Mrs. Van der Lynden had buried the jewels somewhere on her property. She kept sneaking over there in the middle of the night with a metal detector, hunting for them. Which didn't set well with the new owner of the property. The crazy lady who eventually sold it to that Viking musician."

"Mrs. Winkleson," I said. "Who sold it to Ragnar Ragnarsen."

"That's the one. The Winkleson woman kept calling the sheriff on Lacey. I finally convinced Lacey to back away for a while. Let the old bat settle down."

"And did she? Lacey, I mean — did she back off?"

"She did. This would have been six, maybe eight months before she died. If you ask me, she'd have started up again before too long — she was getting restless. Kept dropping by and complaining to me about how unfair it was for Mrs. Winkleson to keep her from her treasure hunt. But she died before she had a chance to start looking again. And maybe someone didn't understand the reason she quit looking."

"You mean maybe someone thought she'd stopped because she found what she was looking for."

Judge Jane nodded.

"Any chance they're right?" I asked. "That she let you talk her into stopping because she'd already found the treasure."

"I like the way your mind works," she said. "Reminds me a lot of mine. Yes, that did occur to me. I also considered that maybe the reason she was so gung ho about the treasure being somewhere on the old Van der Lynden place was that she'd found something there — something she thought was a little part of the treasure. Crazy idea, maybe."

"Doesn't sound that crazy to me."

"As I said, I was her executor, so it was up to me to clear out the little bungalow where she lived. Did every bit of it myself, and I left no possible hiding place untouched. If she ever found any part of the Van der Lynden treasure, she must have sold it and kept no record of the sale."

"What prison was Lacey's husband in?" Not the sort of detail most people would remember after all this time, and about someone else's estranged husband to boot, but I was hoping Judge Jane would have taken a professional interest in that kind of thing.

"He started out in the James River Correctional Institution over in Goochland County," she said promptly. "But then they moved him up to Coffeewood up in Culpeper shortly after that opened. Both medium security institutions. Why?"

"Did you read that article in the *Clarion* six months ago about the thirtieth anniversary of the jewel robbery?"

"Bit of a puff piece, but yes."

"Fred didn't mention it in the article but he checked on the whereabouts of the surviving players. The ringleader of the robbers was at Coffeewood at the time. I have no idea whether his path could have crossed with Anse Whicker's."

"But that would be an interesting thing to find out. There were four of them who did time for the robbery, in fact; even better odds that Whicker could have been in touch with one of them."

"I'll mention it to the chief," I said. "I'm sure he can find that out."

"If you mention it, mention I'll be contacting the prison authorities to request full information on the prisoners involved," Judge Jane said. "They tend to jump higher and work faster when it's a judge doing the asking. And I can let him know what I learn. So, just so we can tell Henry we took care of what you came for, let's go over what I want done about Lacey's reburial."

"I'm all ears." I held my notebook up so she could see it, and kept my pen at the ready.

"If you could ask your mother to find a nice replacement for the biscuit jar, I'd appreciate it. She can drop it off with Maudie Morton at the funeral home. And I will be reimbursing her; I have a strict rule about not accepting gifts from anyone who could ever come up before me in court."

"Yes, ma'am."

"Once Lacey's ashes are no longer part of the crime scene, I'd appreciate it if you could arrange for Maudie to pick them up, put them in a suitable temporary container, and hang on to them until your mother finds us a new biscuit jar. Then once the case is solved, and the notoriety has died down, and Robyn is back on her feet, we'll pop Lacey back into her niche. I might invite a few people to help me see her on her way, and if Robyn wants to say a few suitable words, that's fine with me. Will that cover it?"

"Pretty much," I said. "I assume if the front panel of the niche is damaged or destroyed, we should just replace it with an exact duplicate."

"Make it so."

"I hope all the next of kin are this easy to please." I tucked my notebook in my tote bag and stood up. "And now I'm going to let you get on with your day. I expect you have cases to hear."

"Unfortunately, yes. Crime may not pay, but that doesn't keep the local idiots from trying. My best to your family. And on your way out, tell Cal it's time to get this show on the road."

I passed the word along to Cal, the bailiff. I looked around for a quiet corner in which to make my calls to Mother, and maybe the chief. But in this part of the building, every quiet corner was already filled. Defendants conferring with their lawyers. Prosecutors bargaining with defense attorneys. People calling their workplaces and families to complain that they'd be stuck here a while longer.

I headed upstairs for the quieter corridor in which I had my office.

Mother answered my call on the first ring.

"Meg, dear. I was just about to call you. Robyn would like to see you."

CHAPTER 13

"Did Robyn say why she wanted to see me?" It didn't have to be another problem at Trinity, I told myself. "About anything in particular?"

"About several dozen things in particular, none of them particularly urgent or important." Mother's voice held just a touch of asperity. I deduced that Robyn must not be in the room. "This nonsense in the columbarium has unsettled her. I think it would help if you could drop by, fill her in on just where we are, and reassure her that you're dealing with things."

"I'll talk to Robyn if you can take on a small project for Judge Jane. It's more up your alley than mine, anyway." I explained about the biscuit jar for Lacey. "I have no idea what she's talking about — I was going to ask Horace to show me the photos and then start rooting around on the Internet."

"I'm sure I know exactly what she means.

But I can double-check with Horace. Leave it to me." Mother almost purred at the thought of going antique shopping — and with someone else's money.

Just then a text came in from the chief, saying that he'd be finished interviewing Mrs. Washington soon. So I thanked Mother and told her I had to run.

But before heading out to Mrs. Washington's house, I pondered whether to call the chief and tell him what I'd learned from Judge Jane. I decided to email rather than call him. I could avoid interrupting him, and perhaps gloss over the fact that I'd jumped the gun and talked to Judge Jane before he did. I called up my email program and spent some time — probably much more time than it was worth — coming up with just the right wording.

"Judge Jane Shiffley says she's next of kin for Lacey," I wrote. "Whose husband may have done time with one or more of the jewel robbers. She's getting info on that and will let you know."

I reread the wording and decided it worked. Without being inaccurate, it left room for him to think Judge Jane had dashed off to investigate with no prompting from me. I hit SEND and looked at the time. Almost eleven. Time to tackle Mrs. Washington. Presumably the chief had just left her house. If I could catch her in and interview her before I went over to see Robyn, I could report that I'd touched base with a third of the next of kin. And there were advantages to dropping by to see Robyn at lunchtime. With Robyn on strict bed rest, every cook in the parish — in fact, in the whole town — had joined the effort to keep her properly fed. Her husband, Matt, was already starting to worry that he was gaining almost as much weight as she was. What they couldn't eat went to the women's shelter and the homeless shelter and the parish shut-ins, but they wouldn't mind sharing a bit with me.

I double-checked Mrs. Washington's address and headed out to visit her.

Mrs. Washington's house was a tiny bungalow on a postage-stamp lot in a block full of similar houses and lots. None of the houses looked run-down or neglected, but none of them looked glossy and shiny, either. No bright colors. No toys in any of the yards. The whole block had a faded, careful look about it.

Mrs. Washington's house looked better than most, I decided as I parked in front of it. Her white picket fence wasn't actually in dire need of paint. Her gate latch was tricky, but not actually broken. You had to watch your step a bit on the flagstone walk, but it wasn't so horribly uneven that you'd have to repair it immediately.

When the door opened, I could see that the interior matched the exterior, neat but faded. Mrs. Washington, though, did not. She was tiny but stood ramrod straight. She wore a simple navy-blue dress with white collar and cuffs that flattered her slender form, and her iron-gray hair was done up in a skillful French braid.

"Yes?" She stood in the doorway, not unfriendly but not exactly welcoming, either.

"Mrs. Washington? I'm Meg Langslow. Robyn Smith sent me —"

"Come in." She stepped aside and gestured for me to enter. I stepped past her into the tiny beige and blue living room. Tiny, but at least she hadn't made it look overcrowded by squeezing in too much furniture, too many bright colors, or any large items. The love seat where she gestured for me to sit and the small armchair on which she perched were perfect for the space. And the almost complete lack of extraneous objects also helped.

But however soothing her minimalist décor might be to the claustrophobic, it was also irritatingly devoid of any clues to her personality and history.

"I understand that Trinity will take care of reinterring my husband in the columbarium," she said.

"That's right," I said. "We just need to know your wishes."

"My wishes?" She uttered a short noise that could have been a mirthless chuckle or just a snort. "To have him back in his niche where he belongs, with a minimum of fuss."

"We can take care of that," I said. "Trinity will repair or replace the panel that covers his niche, and also the urn if that was damaged, and reinter him as soon as Chief Burke allows."

She nodded.

"If you should decide you want a small service when the reinterment takes place —" I began.

"I'm not an overly religious person," she said. "He's already had one funeral; I think that should be sufficient."

Well, that was that. I'd fulfilled Robyn's orders to find out what Mrs. Washington wanted. The fact that I hadn't learned anything to bring me any closer to knowing what had happened was, after all, my problem.

I was wondering if I should take my leave

when she spoke up again.

"What other niches were disturbed?" she asked.

"Dolores Hagley, P. Jefferson Blair, Lacey Shiffley, Mrs. Van der Lynden, and a John Doe who was buried at Trinity for reasons I haven't yet learned." I watched her face as I recited the list of names, but she didn't seem surprised by any of them.

"Then they'll be dragging up that wretched robbery again." Her face wore a look of . . . distaste? Nothing stronger, really.

"Seems likely," I said. "Though I have no idea why anyone would kill anyone over a thirty-year-old crime."

"Because they still haven't found the jewelry." Her voice was bitter, but it was an old, faded, well-used bitterness. "My husband was shunned and suspected for twenty years, thanks to her. Mrs. Van der Lynden, I mean. First she fired him. Then she tried to blame him for letting the robbers in. She even accused him of being in cahoots with them himself, when everyone knew it was her and that son of hers. The case may be thirty years old, but some of us are still living with the aftermath."

"I'm so sorry to hear it," I said.

"They say Henry Burke is a pretty good detective."

"He is," I said. "Though I'm not sure even he can solve a thirty-year-old cold case."

"Particularly one that was so badly bungled from the start," she said. "But he can try. Which is more than they did thirty years ago. Yes, I'm bitter," she added, with a wry smile. "Tell me, will there be any difficulty with burying me beside Jim when my time comes?"

"No — why should there be?" The question surprised me, and not just because of the sudden shift in subject. "The niches are designed for two urns, you know."

"I'm not technically Episcopalian," she said. "Left the Catholic Church to marry Jim and never regularized things with your lot."

"I'm not sure anyone would bother about that," I said. "After all, your husband was Episcopalian. I don't think anyone at Trinity would want to put you asunder."

She smiled slightly at that.

"If you don't mention it, I imagine everyone will just assume you *are* Episcopalian," I went on. "I certainly won't tell. If there's nothing in the records, everyone will blame Dr. Womble. And remember that Trinity took in the John Doe who was found in our graveyard. We have no idea if he's Episcopalian or not. For all we know, he could be an

133

atheist."

"I always wondered about that," she said. "Wondered if someone actually knew who he was and told your minister. If that's why he was taken in."

"Not that I know of," I said. "But it's an interesting idea. I'll ask Dr. Womble when I see him. Since he was the one who arranged to have the John Doe buried at Trinity, I'm considering him the next of kin, unless they manage to get a DNA match and figure out who he is."

"I remember when they found that body," she said. "Even after I heard no one recognized it, I kept hoping it would turn out to be young Archie — I think he was out by that time. Out after less than five years. I never thought that quite fair. Archie and his college friend get token sentences, and I bet the other two are still in prison."

"One died there," I said. "And the other was still there in December, when Fred Singer wrote his article about the thirtieth anniversary of the robbery."

"I thought as much."

"You said 'everyone knew it was her and that son of hers,' " I began.

"That would be Mrs. Van der Lynden and Archie," she said.

"So I assumed. But who do you mean by

everyone?"

"The rest of the staff. We kept in touch with some of them even after Jim was fired. They all knew the truth."

"That he was innocent?"

"And that she'd have thrown any one of them under the bus if Jim hadn't been around to blame it on."

"So who did the staff think was to blame?"

"They were all sure Mrs. Van der Lynden had set up the whole thing. Most of them were convinced she still had the jewelry. A few of them thought maybe Archie had screwed up — dropped the jewelry some-place, hidden it and forgot where, or maybe hidden it someplace so obvious that the real crooks found it. Want to know what Jim always said?"

I nodded.

"He said he bet Archie rowed out to the middle of the lake with the jewelry boxes and dropped them in. And then he cut a notch in the side of the boat so he'd remember where he dropped them."

I was so unprepared for her to say any-thing even slightly humorous that it took me a few moments to recognize the old joke.

"Almost had you there," she said, with a slight but genuine chuckle.

"Was there actually a lake?"

"And several boats, and Archie was almost that dim. But I think the insurance company had the lake dredged at some point."

"Darn," I said. "I guess I'll take back the scuba gear I rented."

Her mouth twitched in what I guessed was a fleeting smile.

"You work for Randall Shiffley, am I right?" she asked.

"That's right." Her sudden jumps from one topic to another were slightly disconcerting, but at least they kept me from being bored.

"Doing what?"

"Officially, special projects. Christmas in Caerphilly, the Un-Fair, things like that."

"And unofficially?"

"Anything he wants done that isn't getting done. Or isn't getting done the way he wants it when he wants it."

She smiled faintly.

"That's good," she said. "Randall's father took Jim on when no one else in town would hire him. And Randall kept him on long past the point he could do the job, to keep us going until Jim was eligible for Social Security. It may not look like much" — she waved her hand to show that she meant the house around us — "but I wouldn't have this much if not for them. They're good people, those two. You tell Randall hello when you see him."

"Will do."

"What's the procedure for going to visit Jim — once he's back in the vault? I went over there once or twice, and the door was always locked. Don't Episcopalians go in for visiting graves? Leaving wreaths?"

"Absolutely," I said. "Just ask in the church office to borrow the key. We lock it up to prevent problems — vandalism, kids trying to spook each other, teenagers looking for privacy even in the least appropriate places —"

"Grave robbers," she added.

"Especially them," I agreed. "But mourners are always welcome."

"That's good to know. I was a little resentful the first time I found myself locked out. Now, I realize perhaps you were trying to prevent exactly what occurred last night."

"I only wish we could have prevented that," I said.

"Thank you. I know it's distressing to everyone at Trinity."

"Though not nearly as distressing as to the families whose loved ones were disturbed. We'll be working with the chief to see if there's anything we can do to improve security — without making it even harder for families to visit, of course."

"Good."

"And I won't take up any more of your time," I said. "Just let me know if you have any questions about what's happening with Mr. Washington's ashes." I scribbled my cell phone number on a sheet of paper and handed it to her.

She took it, nodded, and set it in lone splendor on the otherwise empty coffee table. Then she saw me to the door and said good-bye with just a hint more warmth than she'd shown on my arrival.

Not exactly a people person, Mrs. Washington, I thought, as I returned to my car. And I still felt a certain nagging curiosity about her. Why? I paused for a moment to analyze the question. I didn't exactly see her as a prime candidate for coshing elderly but tallish men over the head and using a crowbar to pry open niches. Of course, I could think of nothing to prove she hadn't hidden the ring and the other jewels in her husband's niche in the first place. But if they'd had the jewels all those years, they wouldn't have needed the jobs that Randall and his father had provided. And she sounded genuinely grateful about that.

And I got the sense that if she knew who had the jewels, she'd almost certainly have told me — or the chief — in the hopes that it would provide posthumous vindication for her husband.

My nagging curiosity was probably just that. Curiosity. In fact, nosiness. I could think of no good reason to pry any further into poor Mrs. Washington's sad, lonely life.

Especially since Mother could probably tell me everything I could possibly want to know if I later decided my curiosity had any useful purpose.

My stomach growled as if to remind me that my next stop was Robyn's — where with any luck I could feast on the town's bounty while calming down Robyn.

I was more optimistic about the feasting than the calming.

CHAPTER 14

Robyn and her husband, Matt, didn't live that far from Mrs. Washington, but the neighborhood was entirely different. Large houses on large lots — at least by town standards. Robyn and Matt's two-story Victorian house was typical. Although not as inconveniently large as the house Michael and I had bought, Robyn and Matt's would have plenty of room for their new baby, and a few siblings — even a nanny or au pair if they decided to go that route. But they wouldn't have so much room that visiting family members felt free to drop by to stay for a few months — although so far we'd managed to keep the permanent residents down to my brother, Rob, and my cousin Rose Noire.

Robyn and Matt had even done a great job of preparing the yard for the baby's eventual enjoyment. Matt and Dad and several of the more practical members of the garden club had repaired the fence and then scoured the yard, digging up any plants that were poisonous or could cause contact dermatitis and transplanting them to the yards of people without small children.

Now if we could only convince Robyn that it was time to make a similar childproofing effort inside the house. I knew Mother was going to try. As I rang the doorbell, I found myself hoping that she'd tackled the idea today, perhaps as a way of distracting Robyn.

But my hopes were dashed when the door swung open, revealing Robyn and Matt's foyer in all its warm, welcoming, vibrant, artistic, cluttered glory.

"Good to see you." I realized Robyn's current doorkeeper was Viola Wilson, wife of Reverend Wilson of the New Life Baptist Church. I'd never figured out if Mrs. Wilson was significantly younger than her husband — who was in his eighties — or if she'd hit a genetic jackpot and just didn't look anywhere near her age. Her medium-brown skin was only lightly wrinkled, and she moved less like a senior citizen than someone in middle age. Vigorous middle age. Like maybe a dedicated marathoner.

"How is she?" I asked, as I stepped inside.

"Restless," Mrs. Wilson said. "Can't blame

her. All this foolishness happening over in her church, and her not able to do anything about it. Angus would be climbing the walls by now. And this on top of all the stress she had already. I'm hoping you can ease her mind a bit."

"I can always try," I said.

Mrs. Wilson led the way down the hall. As I followed her, I was mentally cataloging all the things Robyn and Matt seemed to love that would make childproofing their house so problematic. Their furniture, most of it Victorian, seemed chosen to maximize the number of sharp corners and protruding bits. At least half of the pieces were heavy enough that if they fell over they could easily flatten a small child, while the rest were so spindly and rickety that they quivered whenever anyone walked by. And every horizontal surface was covered with the pottery and glassware that Robyn collected — everything from delicate cut glass and fragile bits of porcelain to bold, modern abstract glass pieces and brightly painted dishes from all over the world — tiny Japanese tea cups, Moroccan tagines, New Mexican black vases, African tribal pots. And mixed in with the glass and pottery, of course, were a large number of crosses, inspirational and devotional plaques, and statues of saints — not more than you'd expect for the home of an Episcopal priest, but certainly a more diverse collection than any I would have imagined. Nearly all of these things were beautiful or interesting, and the few that didn't seem to fit into either category were probably beloved, heartwarming presents from friends or parishioners. Or perhaps souvenirs of Robyn's own enthusiastic dabbling in arts and crafts. I'd have been hard-pressed to pick out many items that struck me as hideous, out of place, or unworthy of their inclusion in her life. Still the overall effect wasn't beautiful but cluttered. Or was I only seeing it that way because I was imagining what would happen if you turned a crawling baby loose in it?

Matt's enthusiasms revealed themselves in the paintings, drawings, and prints — his own work and those of artists he knew or admired — that covered every available bit of wall space, from right above the chair rails to just below the crown moldings of the soaring twelve-foot ceilings. Intermingled of course, with the crosses, crucifixes, and plaques. Stacks of paintings also leaned against the wall here and there below the chair rail. I liked his paintings, especially when I saw them in a gallery or in someone else's home. Here the sheer number of them made me unable to enjoy any of them as much as they deserved.

Then there were the half-finished do-it-yourself projects — every room had its share. Patches of new plaster waiting to be painted. Areas where he was slowly replacing dry-rotted woodwork with new. Partially dismantled lamps. Bits of furniture in need of — or possibly in the middle of — regluing, reupholstering, re-just-about-anything. Though at least Matt got points for trying. When Michael and I had figured out how many little projects our house needed, we'd thrown up our hands and paid various Shiffleys to fix everything.

And everywhere there were books. Tall bookshelves on at least one wall of every room, along with stacks of books that wouldn't fit on the shelves. Paperbacks lying facedown on chairs or sofas, so that they'd forever after fall open at the point where the reader had been interrupted. Hardbound books sporting an unusually varied range of makeshift bookmarks — paint samples, feathers, programs from services, pledge cards, scraps of fabric, grocery store receipts — even a two-dollar bill. The range of their library was fascinating — books on theology and religious history rubbed shoulders with Ray Bradbury and Agatha Christie. Practical manuals on plumbing and woodworking shared shelf space with tomes about yoga and mind/body studies. C. S. Lewis held pride of place, but so did Elizabeth Peters and Sue Grafton. I'd been raised to believe that there was no such thing as having too many books, only having too few shelves. Robyn and Matt were so woefully short of shelves, considering the size of their book collection, that even my dad, when he saw it, might gently suggest that a little thinning of the herd was in order.

Mrs. Wilson noticed my expression and guessed exactly what I was thinking.

"Yes, a great deal to be done here," she said. "And it won't be a picnic doing it. Every stick of furniture has a story — though it's usually some variation on how they bought it for pennies in a flea market and lovingly restored it. And I think at least half the knickknacks were presents from relatives and parishioners who, Robyn is sure, will be devastated if they hear that their kind gifts were sold."

"Maybe we could talk her into having a yard sale for some good cause," I said. "Whatever's her current favorite. How could anyone be insulted if, after much soul-searching and prayer and in loving celebration of the new life to come, Robyn and Matt made the difficult and self-sacrificing decision to donate a nontrivial portion of their worldly goods to those less fortunate."

"You're good," Mrs. Wilson said. "Your mother and I can use you when we start working on Robyn again."

"As long as you wait till I've finished chasing down the relatives of all the people whose ashes were disturbed," I said.

"There's time. You do what you need to do. Sufficient unto the day is the evil thereof."

And with that cheery thought she swung open the door to the master bedroom.

"Meg's here!" she announced, in the upbeat tone one uses with a fractious child.

The room still showed signs of its hasty conversion from a shared home office. Books and papers were stacked waist high all around the perimeter. Along one wall, a vintage drop-front desk was piled with cosmetics and toiletries and stacks of Robyn's clothing. Along another wall, a rolltop desk held Matt's gear. The queen-sized bed in the middle of the room left very little floor space, and it was so covered with books, files, notebooks, magazines, newspapers, cards, letters, papers, knitting projects, dishes of food, board games, bed jackets, tubes of anti–stretch mark cream, and — well, everything else Robyn had been using all day — that you saw almost nothing of the pale green sheets beneath.

"This does not look like bed *rest,*" I said. "This looks like trying to work just as hard as ever with the added handicap of doing so in a makeshift work space."

From the doorway I could hear Mrs. Wilson's snort of laughter.

"I know, I know." Robyn cringed slightly, almost like a child being scolded for something she knew she shouldn't have been doing. "But I've been so worried! What's happening at the church? Has the chief found out who attacked poor Mr. Hagley? Is there much damage to the columbarium? Have you seen the families? How are they taking it? Can you —"

"Time out!" I said. "The answers are 'I don't know, no, I don't know, some of them, and pretty well so far.' If you calm down, I'll tell you the details."

I sat down in a rocking chair by the side of the bed and took a few slow, calming breaths. Not that I needed calming all that much, but I was hoping it would rub off on Robyn. And I started telling her about everything that had happened last night and this morning. I lingered over anything amusing or heartwarming. I didn't leave out the one really bad part — finding Mr. Hagley's body — but I kept my description of it as short and calm and non-sensational as possible.

Mrs. Wilson helped by delivering, first, cups of hot tea in handmade gray mugs with cobalt-blue stripes, and then matching plates loaded with small portions of a dozen or so of the different dishes people had dropped off. We nibbled country ham, roast chicken, string beans, butter beans, broccoli, tomato aspic, tossed salad, ham biscuits, apple pie, chocolate cake, and Beacon Hill cookies — one of Mother's specialties. Which didn't mean that she'd cooked them, of course, only that she'd found someone she trusted enough that she could rely on them to bake the gold standard of Hollingsworth family desserts for Robyn.

And to my relief, Robyn gradually calmed. When I'd first walked in, she'd been trembling like a Chihuahua in a snowstorm. Between the food and my resolutely upbeat account of recent events, she was starting to look less frazzled.

"So what are you doing next?" she asked, while nibbling a bit of pie crust.

"Next?" I pointed to a nearby clock. "Unless that thing is completely wrong, next I pick up Josh and Jamie at school, take them home for a quick dinner, and then watch their Summerball team play its game."

"But what about the rest of the next of kin? And we don't know what the chief has found out and —"

"Chief Burke's youngest grandson is on the same team as the boys," I reminded her. "So I will have a whole six innings to find a suitably low-key way to pick his brains."

"Good," she said. "Because we need to find out when we can get the columbarium back."

"Oh, do we have a burial coming up?"

"Well, Mr. Hagley, I assume. Unless all this upsets his son so badly that he decides to take his parents' ashes elsewhere."

"I doubt if the younger Hagley will blame us if the funeral has to be delayed until the chief releases the columbarium," I said. "After all, it's his father's murder the chief is investigating. And remember, Mother is also taking a keen interest in getting everything at Trinity back to normal."

"That's good."

I made a sudden snap decision. Now was the time.

"And then after the baseball game, Mother

and I are going to come over for a little while to help you with your next project."

"My next project?"

"Getting this house ready for the baby," I said. "Starting with this room."

"But the baby won't come for a few more months, and he or she won't start crawling right off, and —"

"Oh, and once the baby comes, you're going to have so much time — is that it?"

She opened her mouth to protest again and then laughed instead.

"And of course I know what you're much too polite to say," she said. "I'm the one who nagged the entire congregation into cleaning out Trinity from attic to basement. Why can't I do the same for my own house?"

"You had the necessary detachment for cleaning out Trinity," I said. "You don't here. But Mother and I do — so we'll come over and help. Starting tonight. With you in the room, approving every little thing we do. And Randall Shiffley's been asking what he could do to help you out, and we should take him up on it. He's got plenty of workmen — one of them can finish some of the repairs that Matt won't have time to get to. Send over a couple of strong backs to help us rearrange things so they're more convenient."

"Well . . ." Robin looked around and frowned as if suddenly seeing her study turned bedroom for the first time. "I hate to impose. But yes, the mess is driving me crazy. I would be eternally grateful."

"We're on, then." I stood up. "After the ball game. And only for an hour or two. And while we work I can fill you in on anything else I learn about what the chief is up to."

"It's a deal."

In the doorway, out of Robyn's line of sight, I saw Mrs. Wilson grinning and giving me a thumbs-up with both hands.

"Off to collect the boys, then." I stood up and turned to leave. And then paused while Robyn said a short prayer asking God for his blessing on my endeavors. I wondered if the Eagles upcoming game counted as one of my endeavors.

Out in the hallway, Mrs. Wilson pressed a large brown paper grocery bag into my hands.

"So you don't have to cook anything," she said. "Because Lord knows, you have enough on your plate. But bless you for talking her into letting us get this place in shape."

I was about to make the obligatory protest

151

that she shouldn't have gone to so much trouble and that there were others who needed the food more than we did, but then I thought better of it. If I was going to spend long hours here helping Robyn get the house shaped up . . .

"Thanks," I said. "Dare I hope you put in some of that country ham?"

CHAPTER 15

I got to the school a few minutes early and pulled into the pickup lane. Josh and Jamie could have ridden the bus, of course, but its roundabout route through our rural part of the county made for a long ride. So especially on baseball game or practice days, I liked to pick them up.

While I waited, I called Randall.

"I have a project for you," I said. "If you're willing to take it on."

"Fill me in."

"Have you seen Matt and Robyn's house?"

"I was there a week ago, taking over a casserole from my mom."

"Then you probably noticed the place isn't child-friendly."

"It's not even sane-adult-friendly. That man needs an intervention — makes no sense whatsoever to keep disassembling parts of your house if you haven't got the

153

time or the skills to reassemble them. And with all due deference to the fact that you ladies like your trinkets and knick-knacks, the reverend needs to corral hers with some shelves or cabinets or something. I think the damned things are breeding behind her back."

"You get the mind-reading award for the week," I said. "So can you spare a few workmen to finish the unfinished do-it-yourself projects? And maybe even to build those shelves or cabinets? Just let me know how much you think it will cost, and I'll get Mother to organize a collection."

"Heck, I'll donate the materials, and if you just feed my men when they're over there, with some of that food people keep dropping by, I'll throw in the labor to boot."

"Deal. Gotta run; school's out."

I could already see Josh and one of the boys' good friends, Mason, dashing down the sidewalk toward my car. Jamie and Adam Burke had made a beeline for Minerva Burke's car. Jan, Mason's mom, seeing where her son was headed, strolled over to join me.

All four boys were pleading for a sleepover together, pointing out that, after all, it was Friday! From their tone you'd have thought Friday was a rare and unpredictable occurrence whose mere existence required a celebration.

Fortunately Jan, Minerva, and I had already foreseen not only the arrival of Friday but also the probability that the Four Horsemen, as we called the boys, would want to celebrate it together. We confirmed that the boys were happy with the plans we'd already made — that after their baseball game, the herd would go home for a Friday night sleepover with Mason, and then sometime around noon-ish Saturday, Jan would deliver them to Michael and me for baseball coaching with my grandmother and a Saturday night sleepover.

With their weekend arranged to their liking, all four boys boarded the appropriate cars and began loudly pointing out to their wayward adults that we needed to take off now so they could eat and change for the game.

The next two hours passed in a blur. The enormous bag of food Mrs. Wilson had given me disappeared with unnerving speed. The boys went out to the barn with a handful of blueberries as an appetizer for Nimitz, while Rose Noire, before departing for the yoga class she was teaching, prepared a large bowl of organic fruit for his main meal. Despite their disappointment over his inability to talk, the boys had fun feeding the toucan.

Although apparently they still had hopes of turning Nimitz into the world's first talking toucan. I overheard them working on the project. Though they couldn't quite agree on what his first phrase should be. Jamie favored "Go Eagles!" while Josh was working hard on "Here, Spike!"

I gave up trying to convince them that their efforts were in vain. Teaching them to feed him properly was enough of a job.

"Josh, the fact that he throws the chickpeas across the room probably means that he doesn't like them," I explained. "Just tell Rose Noire not to include them next time."

"But I think he enjoys throwing them," Josh protested.

"And are you going to enjoy picking them up?"

"Wow, look!" Jamie said. "His poop is coming out blue!"

"That's because of all the blueberries you fed him."

"But that was only a couple of minutes ago. He can't possibly have digested them already." Both boys were peering at Nimitz with concern.

"It was fifteen or twenty minutes ago. Toucans have a very short digestive tract so they process whatever they eat pretty quickly." I said this with great authority, although I owed most of my newfound expertise in toucans to lectures from Dad and Grandfather.

"This could be really interesting on Fourth of July," Josh mused.

"Or Christmas," Jamie added.

I reminded myself that with any luck, the bird would be out of our barn before the boys could engineer seasonally themed toucan poop. And changed the subject.

We spent a little less time than usual turning the house upside down looking for their baseball garb, and thank goodness their equipment bags were already in the Twinmobile. I packed overnight backpacks for each of them. After making sure that my own bag contained chewing gum, bug spray, and sunscreen, I herded them into the Twinmobile and set off for the baseball field.

Michael, who was the Eagles' assistant coach, had come straight from class and was already there. So were all the rest of the team, meaning that once again, even though we lived only two miles from the field, the boys were the last ones to arrive.

I watched as the boys scampered out onto the field to join their teammates. Tory Davis, the head coach, waved Josh and Jamie over to where she was working with two of the team's pitchers — Manuel Espinoza and Danny Takahashi. Michael was taking the majority of the team through a fielding drill — yes, including Adam Burke. This early in the season, the boys' uniforms were still pristine, and the red shirts and white pants were vivid against the background of fresh spring grass.

I glanced around and saw the chief standing just outside the chain-link fence on the far side of the home dugout, watching as his grandson practiced. I strolled over to join him.

"Team's shaping up," I said.

"It is indeed. Frank would be so proud."

I nodded. Frank Robinson Burke had been an outstanding college baseball player. His untimely death a few years ago, in a car crash that had also killed his wife, had made the chief and his wife custodial grandparents of Frank Robinson Burke Jr., Calvin Ripken Burke, and Adam Jones Burke, my boys' buddy. The chief still tended to get a little choked up occasionally at how much Adam favored his father.

Probably a good thing if I distracted him.

"So tell me to get lost if you like," I said. "But do you have any more next of kin available for me to visit?"

158

"Unfortunately no," he said. "I confess that I have not had the opportunity to interview anyone other than Mrs. Washington. Other things have claimed the lion's share of my time."

"Other things?" I echoed. "You mean things unrelated to Mr. Hagley's murder?"

"Unrelated to anything a sane and reasonable person would — Sorry. I should have said that remains to be seen. Do you know Mr. Scott Sedlak?"

"Alas, yes." And now I understood his outburst — sane and reasonable were the last adjectives I'd have used to describe Mr. Sedlak. "Goes to Trinity. Currently serving on the vestry. The surviving half of the dynamic duo Mother and I refer to as the Muttering Misogynists. Why?" I suddenly wondered if anything had happened to Mr. Sedlak.

"Mr. Sedlak has been filling me in on his theory of the crime," the chief said.

"And probably doing so at great length, if he's in his usual form," I said.

"He seems to feel that Mr. Hagley was terminated — his word, not mine — because of his involvement in Trinity's vestry. And that he — Mr. Sedlak — is destined to be the killer's next victim."

"Who does he think is going to . . .

159

terminate him?"

"Radical elements who have seized power within the church," the chief said. "I never knew Trinity was such a hotbed of intrigue. Or could he be talking about the Episcopal Church at the national level?"

"He's probably referring to the vestry," I said. "He's not fond of the Council of Presiding Bishops, but I don't think he feels personally threatened by them. Trinity's vestry used to be all male until an embarrassingly recent date. Clearly Mr. Sedlak isn't happy with the change."

"Yes," the chief said. "He seems to find your mother particularly . . . intimidating."

"He does have some common sense, then," I said. "He should be intimidated by Mother. Of course, he's crazy if he thinks Mother would need to kill him — or Mr. Hagley — to free the vestry from their noxious influence. She already had everything in place for a peaceful change of regime."

"In what way?"

"She recruited several very nice people to run for the vestry," I explained. "Much nicer than either of the misogynists, though I suppose it's terrible of me to speak ill of the dead in Mr. Hagley's case."

"So they'd be running against Mr. Sedlak

and Mr. Hagley, if he had not been killed."

"You know, I don't know," I said. "Usually the problem is to get enough people to run for the seats in the first place. I can't recall a contested election since I've been there. I don't know if they would try to talk the misogynists out of running, or put them on the ballot and hope common sense prevails and they lose. Mother would know. Although wait a sec — come to think of it, once you serve your three-year term you have to be off for at least a year, so it's not a case of defeating them this time so much as making sure there's no chance of them sneaking back in a year or two from now."

"How did your misogynists get elected in the first place?"

"Mr. Hagley was elected right after his wife died," I said. "He was a lot . . . calmer then. And I suppose people thought, 'oh, good, serving on the vestry will help take his mind off his loss, poor thing.' Took him a few months to show his true colors. Mr. Sedlak, now . . ."

I thought about it for a bit.

"No clue, really," I said. "From what I hear, he's spent the last thirty years criticizing everything the previous vestries and pastors have done, even when it was entirely men doing the running. No idea why he decided to stand for election, but I guess people must have thought it would do him good to find out what it was like to be on the receiving end of the criticism for a change. Inside the tent peering out, as it were."

"And how has that gone?"

"Badly," I said. "Dad and I have to calm Mother down after every vestry meeting. Mr. Sedlak and Mr. Hagley are the only men on the vestry at the moment, so they think they should do most of the talking. A lot of mansplaining going on."

"I can imagine how your mother would react to that." The chief was repressing a smile.

"Yes — as I said, badly! But not homicidally. She says 'bless his heart,' a lot in that steely tone that makes it mean just the opposite. So if Mr. Sedlak has gotten the impression that the rest of the vestry members don't like him, he's absolutely right. But that doesn't mean any of them killed Mr. Hagley or want to kill him."

"His fears did seem a little overblown," the chief said.

"And even if Mother wanted to kill him or Mr. Hagley, do you really think she'd do it on the church grounds? Shedding blood on holy ground — sacrilege! And with a crowbar? A stiletto, maybe, or a tiny little vintage pearl-handled revolver, or an obscure untraceable poison that causes the victim no pain. But a crowbar?"

"Not quite in character, I admit." The chief had given up the battle to keep from chuckling.

"And the same goes for any of the other ladies of the vestry, for that matter. Even if they wanted to off somebody, they'd pick a secular scene of the crime. I'm sure some of them are already saying we should schedule doing the Restoring of Things Profaned. Which is kind of like an exorcism, only less drastic, and done for buildings and things instead of people."

"Sounds like a sensible thing to do," the chief remarked. "But you'll have to wait till the crypt's no longer a crime scene."

"We'll probably also have to wait until Robyn's on her feet," I said. "I suppose we could have the supply priest do it, but I don't think people would find it as comforting if it came from anyone but Robyn."

"Supply priest?" The chief looked puzzled.

"Ecclesiastical equivalent of a substitute teacher," I said. "Another bone of contention for the misogynists. We're a small parish, so we only have the one priest. Any time Robyn isn't available for services, we

163

either have to get the diocese to send a supply priest — which isn't free — or we can't have the whole enchilada with communion and all — just a morning prayer service led by one of the deacons. Mr. Hagley and Mr. Sedlak were mutinous about how much money the parish is having to spend on supply priests with Robyn out on enforced bed rest."

"Wouldn't that also be the case if a male priest were out on extended sick leave?" the chief asked. "I seem to remember Dr. Womble was on bed rest for several months after his heart surgery."

"Ah, but that's different," I said. "Don't ask me how, but it is, at least according to the misogynists. The real problem is that they disapprove of the church's decision to ordain women, and loathe the fact that Trinity now has a woman priest. But since their side already lost that battle, all they can really do is criticize everything we women accomplish."

"So in your opinion, while Mr. Sedlak is not well liked, it's unlikely that the vestry members have designs on his person, either individually or collectively."

"Highly unlikely."

"Was he speaking figuratively, do you think, when he asserted that some of the

164

women were practicing witchcraft against him?"

"Damn. I hope so," I said. "But he could be that paranoid. I haven't seen anyone sticking pins into voodoo dolls, if that's what you mean."

"The word 'paranoid' did spring to my mind unbidden several times during our discussions. And do you have any idea what the Philadelphia Eleven is? I gather it was some ghastly crime committed against the church. He referred to it several times as if he assumed I would be familiar with it but — Is that funny?"

I had burst out laughing.

CHAPTER 16

"I'm sorry," I said when I could speak again. "Are you sure he said the Philadelphia Eleven?"

"Yes." The chief was frowning. "I'd rather assumed it was something rather sinister, from his tone of voice."

That set me to giggling again.

"I'm sure Mr. Sedlak finds the Philadelphia Eleven sinister," I managed to get out. "Before the 1970s, the Episcopal Church didn't ordain women as priests. In 1974, a few renegade bishops ordained eleven women without going through all the usual procedures. Big scandal; everyone got very worked up, and the upshot was that the General Convention approved the ordination of women two years later. I have no idea if the Philadelphia Eleven helped bring it about or if it would have happened anyway. But of course Mr. Sedlak would loathe them, individually and collectively."

"Difficult to see how church politics nearly half a century gone by could have anything to do with a present-day murder," the chief said.

"Not so difficult," I said. "As long as people like Mr. Hagley and Mr. Sedlak are around, trying to turn back the clock. Did the Thirteenth Amendment put an end to racism?"

"Good point," he said. "Still, I don't think the ladies of the vestry are going to be high on my suspect list. How did Mr. Hagley and Mr. Sedlak get along?"

"I like the way you think." I thought about it for a few moments. "Mother might know better than I do," I said finally. "I doubt if they were buddies, but I also doubt if Mr. Sedlak would want to do away with Mr. Hagley. He'd have one less ally against the insidious creeping forces of modernism."

"Makes sense," the chief said. "I don't know whether to thank you for explaining all this to me, or be exasperated to find out that I've wasted nearly two hours of my day talking to a loon in the grip of a conspiracy theory."

"Oh, dear," I murmured.

"Although it wasn't completely useless," he said. "I did learn one interesting fact. Apparently Mr. Hagley was in the habit of giving Mr. Sedlak a ride home. Mr. Hagley begged off last night. Said he had to go somewhere else in a hurry."

"At ten fifteen at night?" I asked. "Because that's when the vestry meeting broke up."

"Mr. Sedlak also found this improbable, which I suppose was why he mentioned it. He ended up scrounging a ride from your mother."

"She and Mrs. Willis must have loved that. He lives all the way on the other side of town."

"On the plus side, it means your mother and Mrs. Willis are very well alibied for the time of the murder."

"And Mr. Sedlak, too, I assume."

"Not necessarily," the chief said. "By my calculations, Mr. Sedlak would have had just enough time after they dropped him off to drive back and attack Mr. Hagley. I don't think he did it, mind, but it's possible. Your mother and Mrs. Willis, though, alibi each other until shortly after you called 911."

"That's good," I said. "Not that I suspect Mother, but maybe if Mr. Sedlak knows she's alibied, he'll calm down a bit."

"I'm not optimistic," the chief said. "He even finds it suspicious that she gave him a ride without asking for gas money — apparently Mr. Hagley expected it. At any rate, if

168

Mr. Sedlak shows up in my office again, I will seriously consider charging him for obstructing justice."

I made a mental note to tell Mother. Even if the chief didn't do anything of the sort, the very idea would please her enormously.

"On a more practical note," he went on, "I'm meeting with Chuck Hagley, Mr. and Mrs. Hagley's son, tomorrow at eight. After I finish with him, he's all yours. He'll be staying at his parents' house. I can give you his cell phone number."

I pulled out my notebook and jotted down Chuck's contact info.

"I also heard from the Blair family," the chief said. "The mother's dead, but there's a sister who still lives in Middleburg."

"Is she coming down here?"

"No." He grimaced slightly. "She wants nothing to do with him. Says that his going to prison broke their mother's heart, and his suicide finished her."

"It was suicide, then?"

"Officially, accidental death," the chief said. "But nothing I saw in the files looked the least bit accidental. What a waste."

We both fell silent for a moment. I remembered the dates on Blair's plaque. Only thirty-four years old.

"The sister did give us the name of one of

Blair's friends and said he can make any decisions that need to be made. A professor James Donovan. Law school faculty." He handed me a slip of paper with Donovan's name, phone number, and office address. "Anyone you know?"

"Not that I know of." I shook my head. "Possibly someone I've met in passing at faculty events."

"I'm meeting him at nine tomorrow. You're welcome to contact him after I finish. And I'd appreciate it if you could fill me in after you talk to him."

"Fill you in on what? What he wants us to do with Blair's ashes?"

"And any other information or insights you might gain from the meeting," he said. "I didn't get the impression that he was particularly pleased at the notion of talking to the police about his old friend. I wouldn't exactly call his attitude truculent, or even unfriendly, just . . . rather cool. But maybe he'll warm up a little if you can convince him that I have no intention of raking up old scandals or blackening his friend's name all over again — that I'm just trying to solve a murder."

"Then again, he's not just a lawyer but a law professor," I said.

"Of criminal law, according to the faculty

170

directory," the chief said. "So it's entirely possible he might be more forthcoming with you than with someone official like me."

He might be right.

"So I play the faculty wife card and see if he unbends."

The chief nodded.

"On the positive side, so far I haven't had to deal with any distraught family members," I said. "Mrs. Washington just wants us to tuck her husband's ashes back where they belong."

"Not the hysterical type at all." The chief sounded as if he approved.

"Judge Jane might have a little send-off for Lacey, but both of them were pretty calm about the whole thing."

"Although Her Honor does seem fired up to get me the information I need to examine the possible ties between Lacey's ex-husband and the jewel thieves," the chief said, with a smile. "I'm not at all sure how relevant it will be. Yes, Lacey was obsessed with the idea that the jewelry allegedly stolen from Mrs. Van der Lynden was actually hidden somewhere on the estate. Kept going out there with her metal detector, trying to find it. By that time Mrs. Winkleson had bought the place, and she didn't take too kindly to trespassing treasure hunters, so we were constantly having to send officers out there to chase Lacey off. I went to talk to her a time or two myself. Impressive lady, really. Imagine Judge Jane, only six feet tall and thin as a rail. She'd be out there in a flowered dress, hiking boots, and a safari hat, methodically running her metal detector over the ground in the fields or the woods. Rain or shine, heat wave or blizzard. Made no difference to her. It got to the point that Mrs. Winkleson's butler would just call and say 'she's here again,' and we'd send a deputy out to chase her home."

"Hard to see what that could have to do with a murder over a decade later."

"Very hard. But at this point, anything related to the jewel robbery is potentially interesting and useful. Because with all due deference to Mr. Sedlak, I think this murder will turn out to have a lot more to do with the jewel robbery than with Episcopal Church politics."

I nodded.

"Any idea when you're going to see Dr. Womble?" I asked.

The chief sighed and closed his eyes briefly.

"Sorry," I said. "It's just that I'm impatient to get all my next-of-kin notifying done, and he's the closest thing we have to a next of kin on the John Doe."

"That could change," the chief said. "And possibly a great deal more quickly than I'd have anticipated. Apparently shortly before my predecessor retired, he started a campaign to solve all the department's cold cases. He sent off several tissue samples for DNA analysis — including samples from the John Doe. So instead of having to wait weeks or even months to get the DNA results back, all we have to do is submit the results that were already in the case file to CODIS, which Horace is going to do as soon as he gets back to the office tonight."

"That's great," I said. "But why wasn't it done a long time ago?"

"Probably because the first DNA report they got back and submitted to CODIS implicated Mayor Pruitt's brother-in-law in a 1991 murder case," the chief said. "Orders went down that the department had better things to do than waste their time on cold cases and they should get rid of all those useless DNA reports."

"That sounds like Pruitt-style justice," I said. "How did you figure it out?"

"Apparently the as-yet unidentified officer who was working the cold cases balked at destroying evidence. So he filed all of it in the John Doe case file — not just the John

Doe DNA report, but three other inconvenient DNA reports, and the memo from the mayor ordering him to get rid of the DNA reports."

"So we might find out who the John Doe really is," I said.

"We might indeed," the chief said. "Of course, now there are several other cases I need to examine, to see if the suppression of evidence resulted in any more guilty Pruitts getting away scot-free with crimes."

"Or any innocent people being sent to prison in their place," I added.

"Precisely." The chief looked grim. "So, as you can see, today was perhaps the worst possible day to have to waste time on Mr. Sedlak's blitherings."

"I can understand that," I said. "I'll try not to nag you about the next of kin. And while we're on the subject, I realize that right now the crypt is a crime scene and you don't have a crystal ball to tell me when you're going to release it, and it's not as if we have anything scheduled there — at least not until we get to the point of interring Mr. Hagley. But just to make my next conversation with Robyn easier, let's pretend I asked you how soon we get our crypt back."

"Okay," he said. "And you can also pretend that I said I'm doing my best to finish with it. I'd be tempted to say sometime tomorrow, but I'd hate to get her hopes up and then disappoint her. Looks as if your grandmother has been coaching the boys in their batting again."

I could take a hint. Time to drop the subject — not that I minded his choice of a new subject. My grandmother Cordelia had played a few seasons with the All-American Girls Professional Baseball League in her youth, and she was the Eagles' not-so-secret weapon in their quest to win the league championship again.

"She's down this weekend especially for the baseball," I said. "Minerva and I have already arranged for the Four Horsemen to have a sleepover Saturday night so Cordelia can work with them."

"Good. Ah, there's your father."

Dad, who had been setting up comfortable canvas chairs for Mother and my grandmother Cordelia, beamed and waved when he saw us.

"I expect he'll be over here in a minute to tell me about the autopsy," the chief remarked.

"You don't sound very excited."

"If your dad had found anything exciting, he'd have called me earlier. Quite possibly

175

before he'd completely finished the autopsy, in case I wanted to see his interesting findings for myself. No, I'm not expecting anything but a confirmation that Mr. Hagley's death resulted from being hit over the head with that crowbar."

I could see his point.

"Chief!" Dad exclaimed as he bounced over to us. "You'll have my report by morning, but I can give you the highlights now. I found Mr. Hagley to be in perfect health —"

"With the tiny exception of that whole being dead thing," I said.

"Precisely." Dad nodded. "I've ordered the routine toxicology tests, but I doubt if they'll show anything odd."

"So he died from being hit over the head with the crowbar by person or persons unknown," the chief said, to head off any possibility that Dad would explain Mr. Hagley's demise in dense, polysyllabic medical terms. "And if not for our killer, he might have been with us for a good long while to come. Which makes no difference in the eyes of the law, of course, but it still feels more heinous. Excuse me, but I should take this."

He pulled his cell phone, which had indeed buzzed discreetly while he was speaking, and stepped few paces away.

I resisted the urge to sidle a little closer, and wondered how hard it was to learn lip reading. It would be such a useful skill sometimes.

CHAPTER 17

To my surprise, Dad wasn't trying to eavesdrop on the chief's phone call. He stood quietly, his fingers twined in the chain-link fence, his eyes following Josh and Jamie as they practiced. But I could tell his mind was elsewhere.

"Poor Junius," Dad said. Then he frowned. "Did people really call him Junius?"

"I didn't," I said. "I called him Mr. Hagley."

"But what did his friends call him?"

"I think most people called him Mr. Hagley."

"What would the nickname for Junius be? June? Junie? Juno?"

I refrained from saying that none of them sounded very likely. Dad's expression showed that he'd already figured that out.

"What did your mother call him?" Dad asked finally.

"I don't think she considered herself his friend."

"But surely she must have . . ."

"Pretended to be his friend? Mother?"

"Good point."

"I think she called him Mr. Hagley, too," I said, after pondering for a few moments. "Sometimes 'my dear man,' when she was really annoyed with him."

Dad sighed and seemed to abandon his quest to humanize Mr. Hagley.

"Well, that's beside the point," he said. "I need you to go out with me to the Van der Lynden's mansion."

"It isn't the Van der Lyndens' mansion anymore," I pointed out. "It belongs to Ragnar now."

"And you and he are such good friends." Dad beamed at me. "You can help me talk him into it."

"Talk him into what?" Ragnar was a friend, yes. And increasingly becoming a good friend, which was strange, since about the only thing we had in common was a love of wrought iron. But it was hard not to like Ragnar.

"A reenactment of the crime!" Dad exclaimed.

"You mean the jewel robbery? But that was thirty years ago!"

"Yes, that's going to make it a challenge," Dad said. "But I think it will be worth it if we can shed some light on the location of the jewels."

"Everything will have changed," I said. "And what's the point? What could you possibly accomplish by doing that?"

"Everything hasn't changed," Dad protested. "Not the floor plan, for example."

"We don't know that." I noticed he was ignoring my question about the point of the reenactment. "I don't think Ragnar has made any sweeping architectural changes, but who knows what Mrs. Winkleson did to the place while she owned it."

"We can at least try," Dad said. "Fred Singer is searching through his archives for any photos that might help us out — he's already given me a guest list; here, I made you a copy. I need your help figuring out how to cast all the participants."

He handed me a sheet of paper that contained a long list of names. The cream of Caerphilly society circa 1987, presumably. Almost no one I knew, though a few of the last names were familiar.

"And I have a copy of the floor plan that appeared in the paper," Dad was saying. "Ms. Ellie at the library is ferreting around in her historical files. So all we have to do is talk Ragnar into letting us do it."

Knowing Ragnar, I didn't think much persuasion would be needed. In fact, the reenactment sounded like the sort of lunatic project he'd enjoy just as much as Dad would.

"You never answered my other question — what do you hope to accomplish with your reenactment?"

"We might be able to find out what really happened thirty years ago," he said. "And locate the rest of the jewels. We have a real unsolved mystery right here on our doorstep — we have to do something."

I was working on finding a tactful yet firm way to convey how silly I thought this idea was when it occurred to me that if Dad was busy reenacting the thirty-year-old jewel robbery he'd be much less likely to interfere with the chief's present-day murder investigation. Maybe the reenactment would serve some useful purpose after all, even if not the one Dad intended.

"So you want me to go out there with you to talk Ragnar into doing this?" I asked.

"And then we can start planning all of it!" Dad threw his arms out in an expansive gesture. "We could go right now."

"And miss your grandsons' game?"

"After the game, then. Ragnar's a night

181

owl — he won't mind."

"After the game, I'm going over to help Mother with a project for Robyn, and by the time we finish with that it could be bedtime," I said.

"But —"

"I'll check with Ragnar tonight," I said. "And see what time will work for him."

"Let's try for tomorrow morning."

"Late morning, maybe. He's a night owl, remember? And besides, it will take Fred and Ms. Ellie a little time to dig up those photos. If Ragnar's at all reluctant, I bet the photos will convince him. And you might want to check the county archives. If Mrs. Winkleson or Ragnar were doing any remodeling, they'd have to file building permits, wouldn't they? With architectural drawings. That could be useful."

"An excellent idea!" Dad beamed at me. "See, I knew you were the right person to ask about this. So sometime tomorrow — for sure?"

"If it's okay with Ragnar. I'll talk to him. And we might need to postpone if I haven't finished all the other things Mother has me doing for Robyn."

Actually, Mother hadn't delegated anything to me lately, but I was sure she'd be happy to if I decided I wanted a good excuse to weasel out of helping Dad with his reenactment project. But Dad looked so disappointed that I relented a little.

"I'll go and see if I can clear it with Mother — the fact that I might need to postpone a few of her projects," I said.

"Excellent!" His face brightened.

"You stay here and watch the practice," I said. Dad nodded and stayed intertwined with the fence. I strolled over to where Mother and Cordelia were sitting.

"Good news," Mother said as soon as I was in earshot. "I have a very nice green glass biscuit jar on its way. Horace was so helpful about getting me close-ups of the glass bits without anything . . . unsuitable in the frame."

I made a mental note to apologize to Horace for any stress I'd caused him by sending Mother his way.

"I found it online, at an antique store's website — in mint condition," she continued. "I'm having it shipped directly to dear Maudie at the funeral home."

I wondered if the "dear Maudie" bit meant the funeral home owner had done Mother some service lately, or only that Mother was planning to ask her for a favor and was mentally buttering her up beforehand.

"Awesome," I said. "Any chance you could do a couple more things?"

Mother cocked her head like a bird, to indicate that she was listening with eager anticipation.

"First, can you come over with me to Robyn's for a couple of hours after the game?" I asked. "I talked her into starting to declutter her house. I figure I can do the hands-on sorting and organizing while you keep her spirits up and reassure her that it's already looking better."

"Of course, dear. Long overdue."

"I can help for a few hours if you like," my grandmother Cordelia said. "I'm no slouch at organizing."

"Excellent." I felt relieved. With Mother and Cordelia involved — two of the most organized people I knew — Robyn's clutter didn't stand a chance. "Second, can you convince Dad that I'm doing several million things for you, and can't quite spend the whole day on his latest pet project?" I explained about Dad's reenactment plan.

"Life's never dull with James around," Cordelia said.

"Of course, dear," Mother said.

"Third and last request — can you help me find a Dame?" Seeing that Mother looked puzzled, I handed her the list and elaborated. "Fred Singer gave Dad the guest list from Mrs. Van der Lynden's party — which was actually organized by the Dames of Caerphilly. My social circles don't usually intersect with the Dames. Can you help me figure out which of the guests are still alive? And also, since my impression is that the Dames membership list consisted mainly of Pruitts and their toadies, whether any of the surviving guests might be willing to talk to someone who's a member of the new regime?"

"Of course, dear," Mother purred. She took out her elegant reading glasses to study the list.

"And this is going to help you with your mission of contacting the next of kin . . . how?" Cordelia had a twinkle in her eye. "Because of course I know you wouldn't be trying to horn in on Chief Burke's investigation."

"It won't help a bit with contacting the next of kin," I said. "But it will help me keep Dad from driving the chief crazy. If I give him a real, live party guest to play with, I bet he can spend hours interrogating him or her about things like what was on the menu and what the weather was like. Keep him out of the chief's hair."

"Yes, your father can be very . . . enthusiastic when he's interested in something, can't he?"

Cordelia merely rolled her eyes.

Mother sighed and held up the copy of the party guest list. "Time has not been kind to Mrs. Van der Lynden's friends."

"You don't recognize any of the names?"

"I recognize all the names, dear," Mother said. "From my work on the town history project. But only two of them are still alive, and I'm not very optimistic about getting either of them to talk to your father. One is Mrs. Belinda Pruitt — and you know how the Pruitts feel about anyone who's friendly with the Shiffley clan."

"She's a dead end, then," I said. "And the other?"

"Poor dear Mr. Jackson at the nursing home."

"The one who's still fighting the Civil War?"

"Actually, these days he's under the illusion that he was wounded at the Battle of Chancellorsville and is recuperating in a Confederate field hospital," Mother said. "I rather doubt he'd be interested in returning to the 1980s."

"Let's not tell Dad yet," I said. "He'll be happier if he thinks we're still combing the town for party guests."

"Of course." Mother tucked the list back in her purse. "By the way, dear, I was thinking of something. In dear Dr. Womble's day, we had people called Key Holders. It was an official volunteer post. Perhaps it's time to bring that back."

"What did they do?" I asked.

"More or less what you and the other volunteers have been doing since Robyn's been out," Mother said. "Making sure everything is shipshape and locked up at the end of the day. Because while Dr. Womble is a lovely person, very erudite and wonderfully spiritual, the mundane, practical aspects of running a church were simply beyond him."

"I can see that." Dr. Womble was famous throughout the diocese for having broken both legs by falling down the stairs while walking around with his nose in a book. Nobody in the parish was surprised, actually, but the bishop, hearing about it, had noticed that Dr. Womble was overdue for retirement. Probably a good thing the bishop had made himself scarce in Caerphilly for the next year or so, until the Trinity congregation had figured out that Robyn was a wholly worthy successor, and that Dr. Womble was, to his surprise, enjoying retirement.

"And the duties of the Key Holders were rather more onerous in those days, because one of the main responsibilities was to make sure Dr. Womble hadn't wandered off to some out-of-the-way part of the building and picked up a book," Mother went on. "Because, of course, given his wonderful powers of concentration, once he'd lost himself in a book you couldn't expect him to answer you."

Actually, once he'd lost himself in a book, Dr. Womble probably wouldn't have paid much attention to a five-alarm fire or a major earthquake. So while I wasn't sure "wonderful powers of concentration" was the term I'd use, I had to agree that being a Key Holder was apt to have been even harder in his day.

"Sounds like a useful system," I said. "Why did we do away with it?"

"Perhaps Robyn thought it was something we'd implemented as a way of coping with Dr. Womble's charming eccentricities," Mother said. "Something that shouldn't be necessary with an energetic young rector at the helm."

More likely Robyn, faced with a congregation who were not entirely thrilled at having her replace their beloved rector, had set out to prove to the doubters what a dynamo she

188

was. As someone who had trouble learning to delegate, I could totally understand her motivation. But . . .

"Maybe it's time to reintroduce the Key Holder system, then," I said. "Because even if we were okay with Robyn continuing to run herself ragged, she has other responsibilities now, ones that are just as important as the parish."

"Precisely," Mother said. "And everyone I've talked to is in favor of the idea, so if you like you can start calling yourself a Key Holder. I've put it on the agenda for the next vestry meeting. Along with the special election to replace poor dear Mr. Hagley."

I found myself wondering if hearing Mother refer to him as "poor dear Mr. Hagley" could possibly cause Hagley to roll over in — well, not his grave, since he was still down at the funeral home. To roll over in whatever Morton's kept their clients in until the police gave the go-ahead for the cremation and funeral.

I could always ask Maudie.

But later. The Eagles took the field, the first Flying Fox batter stepped up to the plate, and we all put aside other worries to enjoy the game.

At least most of us did. During the bottom of the fifth inning, the chief stepped away from the bleachers to take another phone call, and then after a quick word with his wife, strode rapidly over to his car and drove away.

I probably wasn't the only grown-up who had trouble concentrating after that. Was there a break in the case? Or some new and possibly unrelated crime?

CHAPTER 18

I shoved my worries aside and cheered the Eagles on to a 7–5 victory.

After the game, Michael and I saw the boys safely off in Mason's mother's car. Then he headed back to the college for a rehearsal — he had a large role in a student-directed production of Thomas Kyd's *The Spanish Tragedy,* a particularly gory and melodramatic Elizabethan play. I headed over to Robyn's house. Mother followed, carrying Cordelia. I'd have given my grandmother a ride, but when she saw the mess the boys had created when they'd thrown their baseball gear into the Twinmobile, she opted for the more civilized transportation experience available in Mother's impeccably maintained sedan.

And for the next several hours we worked on clearing out Robyn and Matt's office-turned-bedroom. What amazed me most was how much of the clutter wasn't even

191

really theirs. We found boxes of papers from various long-past church projects and committees that people had dropped off because they no longer wanted to give the stuff houseroom. Books lent to Robyn by people under the misguided impression that she'd have plenty of time to read them, since obviously the clergy had a flurry of activity on Sunday and spent the rest of the week loitering about having virtuous thoughts. Boxes of things belonging to several of Matt's artist friends who were either currently between lodgings or had been at some point in the last few years. We even collected an entire box of things Dr. Womble had left behind at Trinity that Robyn had been meaning to return to him when she had the time.

"I'll take charge of that box," I said.

"You don't have to," Robyn said. "It will be nice to have an excuse to visit him when I'm up on my feet again."

"I'm sure you can find some other excuse," I said. "Always plenty of church topics you could ask his advice on. But I need an excuse to visit him now."

"Be my guest, then," Robyn said.

Although I wasn't going to give Dr. Womble the box until I had a chance to inspect its contents, because I'd already

noticed an exceedingly interesting item —
an unopened letter addressed to Dr. Womble
at the church's address. In the top left
corner of the envelope were the initials *AvdL*,
along with an address in someplace called
Barking Tree, Virginia.

A few minutes later I made a trip to the
bathroom so I could look up Barking Tree
on a state map without having to make long
explanations. It was in Lee County, the
westernmost county in Virginia — in fact,
most if not all of Lee County was farther
west than the entire state of West Virginia,
and it had a population of less than 25,000
— would that mean Archie would be easy
to find? Or would Barking Tree turn out to
be one of those places that closed ranks
against outsiders? Of course, if that was the
case, Archie would also be an outsider, even
if he'd moved there several decades ago
after getting out of prison.

I noted with interest that the county
contained a high-security federal prison.
Could that account for Archie's presence
there? No — the address I remembered
from the envelope seemed to correspond
with something called The Inchness Center
— whose website revealed that it provided
caring, individualized treatment in a peaceful rural setting for individuals with sub-

stance abuse issues.

"Aha!" I exclaimed — but quietly.

"Meg, dear," Mother called. "Are you all right?"

I flushed the toilet and returned to the decluttering.

A little while later my phone rang. I glanced down at it. A local number, though not a familiar one. But I could think of any number of people who might be trying to reach me for reasons related to recent events at Trinity, so I answered it anyway.

"Meg?" A familiar voice. "It's Maudie Morton down at the funeral home. Are you still looking to talk to Chuck Hagley? That's Junius and Dorothy Hagley's son."

"Definitely."

"Then you might want to come down here quick. The chief's interviewing him right now over in my arrangements room."

"Right now? I could have sworn the chief told me he was interviewing Mr. Hagley tomorrow."

"I gather that was the plan," Maudie said. "Originally Mr. Hagley was going to stay over at his parents' house and talk to the chief in the morning, but I gather now he's planning to drive back to Richmond tonight."

"Bet the chief was annoyed."

"Yes. So if you hurry you might be able to catch Mr. Hagley before he goes."

"I'll be over as soon as I can, then. Thanks."

"Something important?" Mother was looking expectantly at me. For that matter, so were Robyn and Cordelia.

"I should have put the phone on speaker to save time." I explained the reason for Maudie's call.

"You go on, dear," Mother said. "It's past ten o'clock — probably time we let Robyn get some rest, and even if it wasn't, I think it's time your grandmother and I called it a day. But we made a good start, didn't we?"

She beamed at the room. Which did, indeed, look much better, although it was still far from tidy or organized by any reasonable standards — much less those Mother, Cordelia, and I shared.

"It wasn't nearly as awful as I expected it to be," Robyn said. "That is — I mean —" She threw up her hands. "Just thank you, okay?"

"And come again?" Cordelia prompted.

"Absolutely." Robyn looked around and sighed, but it was a sigh of contentment. "This place already looks several hundred percent better."

Cordelia followed me to the front door.

"Any chance you could fit a couple of boxes in your car?" she asked. "All those boxes of stuff she agreed to sell or donate or return to the owners — we should get as much as we can out of the house in case she starts having second thoughts."

"I've got the Twinmobile," I said. "So plenty of room for boxes."

"And there are a few boxes your mother wants to take charge of," Cordelia added. "Nice if you could load those in her car before you go."

While we were loading the Twinmobile, I decided it was a good thing Robyn couldn't see its interior, or she'd lose all confidence in my organizing and decluttering abilities. The bats, helmets, gloves, batting gloves, athletic cups, baseball socks, cleats, baseball hats, water bottles, and who knew what else — all the items that should have been in the boys' baseball bags — were strewn throughout the car. Just for a moment, I contemplated how satisfying it would be to clean it all up. And then a wave of tiredness washed over me. I'd save the satisfaction for the morning. Better yet, I'd look forward to the even greater satisfaction of supervising while the boys did it.

I called Michael to tell him I'd be home a little late, and why.

"Quiet night," he said. "Not only are the boys out, Rob and Rose Noire are, too. So when I got back from rehearsal I went out and read my lines to the toucan."

"Sorry!" I replied. By which I meant, sorry to have left him alone. I couldn't say I was sorry to miss the line-reading portion of the evening's entertainment. *The Spanish Tragedy* might be an important historical document and a milestone in the development of western drama, but it didn't exactly amount to an enthralling evening for a modern playgoer. Even when it was Michael doing the orating, a little bit of Kyd went a long way. "I'll run lines with you when I get home. Or better yet, tomorrow."

"No problem," he said. "There's plenty of time. And the bird's a great listener. Hangs on every word I say."

I made a vow to be less critical of the play the next time I helped Michael run lines.

"He's probably hoping you'll feed him when you finish," I said. "When he cocks his head on the side as if he finds what you're saying fascinating, he wants a grape. And he won't repeat your lines back to you, you know. No matter how much you read to him."

"And that's a blessing," Michael replied. "If I thought he could learn the lines, I'd be reading to him from a much better play."

We said goodnight, and I reached to start the car. Then I remembered the letter from Archie in the box of Dr. Womble's stuff. The box was on the seat beside me, so I reached over, rummaged around in it, and pulled out the envelope.

CHAPTER 19

I turned on one of the map lights and used my phone to take a picture of the front of the envelope. The whole front, showing not just the return address, but also the fact that it had been sent to Dr. Womble at Trinity, and was postmarked six months ago. Dr. Womble had retired several years ago — had Archie not heard about that?

Of course, it was always possible that Dr. Womble wasn't too keen on giving his home address to a convicted felon.

Chief Burke would figure it out. I emailed the picture to him. I didn't wait for a reply — after all, he was presumably still talking to Chuck Hagley — and I needed to get over to the funeral home before he finished.

On the way to Morton's Funeral Home, it occurred to me to wonder what went on in an arrangements room. Doing flower arrangements, perhaps? Surely most of that would happen at the florist. I hoped it had nothing to do with arranging the dear departed for the viewing. I'd learned to cope with Dad's passion for sharing what he considered interesting medical details about his patients — or, worse, his autopsies. But behind-the-scenes mortuary knowledge was something I could live very happily without.

Even without the prospect of finding out just what went on in an arrangement room, I had to admit that I wasn't looking forward to visiting the funeral home. If you walked into one of the rooms there without knowing it was a funeral home, you'd look around and find the surroundings pleasant and peaceful, if a little on the conservative side. Rather like a hotel that wasn't trying to be trendy. I liked Maudie Morton herself, especially when I ran into her outside the funeral home — doing her shopping, or attending her grandson's baseball games. And the several times I'd been there to help friends or relatives with funeral plans, Maudie had always been brisk, no nonsense, and reassuringly calm.

But still. Funeral home. Not a place where I wanted to be in any capacity.

I was relieved to find Morton's parking lot almost empty. I'd had a brief vision of arriving to find myself in the middle of a visitation for someone I knew whose death I hadn't heard about. Or worse, in the middle of the funeral of someone I knew — someone who, not being a churchgoer, had opted for whatever kind of nondenominational or secular services they would hold at the funeral home. Of course, there was still the chance Maudie might want to show off one of her success stories — someone on whom they'd had to do a lot of work to get the body suitable for an open casket — for example, Mr. Hagley. She'd definitely done that a time or two with Dad — who didn't seem to mind. In fact, he probably found it fascinating, and having autopsied the people in question, he was in a better position than anyone to marvel at the transformation. Sometimes people assumed that being Dad's daughter I shared his interests and his imperturbability in the face of medical trauma. I only hoped Maudie's people skills were sufficiently well-developed that she'd figured out there was a reason I'd gone into blacksmithing rather than medicine.

When I walked through the door I found her sitting behind the reception desk.

"Meg, dear." She rose and gave me a quick hug and a kiss on the cheek. "You're in plenty of time. The chief is still visiting with Mr. Hagley."

I was startled for a moment until I realized that by Mr. Hagley she meant the son.

"Would you like some tea or coffee? It's late, I know, but we have decaf."

"Tea would be nice," I said. "With or without caffeine, whichever's easiest. After all, I need to stay awake to talk to Mr. Hagley and then drive home."

I took a seat on a prim-looking but surprisingly comfortable sofa in front of the fireplace, in which a gas fire was doing a reasonable job of pretending to be real logs. Maudie went over to a sideboard that held two gleaming coffee carafes and two teapots under quilted cozies. She poured two cups from one of the teapots and brought them over on a silver tray with a full complement of the usual supplies — napkin, teaspoon, cream, sugar, non-dairy cream substitute, and three kinds of artificial sweetener. I began to feel soothed and pampered. I could well imagine how comforting the bereaved found these little luxuries. My own shoulders began to release the tension of the day.

"Thanks." I took my cup and inhaled the steam while Maudie stirred a tiny amount of sugar into hers. "How long have they been talking?"

"Nearly an hour now." She glanced at a

Dresden china clock on the mantel. "I called the chief as soon as Mr. Hagley arrived, and by the time he came, Mr. Hagley and I had mostly finished discussing the cremation and burial arrangements."

"Oh — so that's what the arrangements room is for," I said. "I was thinking flowers. Look, if you talked to him about arrangements for his father, you probably have a good idea what he wants done with his mother as well. That's really all I need to talk to him about — well, that and expressing Trinity's official regrets over what happened."

"He wants a small, intimate funeral," Maudie said. "Followed by interring his father — and reinterring his mother — in the columbarium at Trinity."

"Interesting," I said.

Maudie cocked her head as if to ask why.

"Mr. Hagley had been badgering Robyn to get his wife's ashes back," I explained. "Didn't seem to grasp that there was a process, or was too impatient to follow through with the process. We were under the impression that the reason he was out there with a crowbar was to take them back himself."

"But why?" Maudie looked puzzled, and perhaps a little shocked. "Did he have some quarrel with the church?"

"He was always quarreling with the church and everyone in it," I said. "So maybe that was it. But informed sources say he needed money and was planning to sell their niche."

"Ah." She frowned slightly. "Perhaps it's a good thing that the funeral and burial can't go forward immediately. That will give young Mr. Hagley time to assess his father's situation."

"You mean, figure out if he can afford to bury his parents in their niche or if he needs to sell it to help settle their debts."

"Precisely." She sighed. "And if there really is financial need, I could arrange to offer a discount."

"That would be nice," I said. Nice, and very typical.

"It's only fair," she said. "After all —"

Just then the door of the arrangements room opened. Chief Burke appeared, nodded to me and Maudie, then turned back to the man who had followed him to the doorway.

"I appreciate your time," he said. "If you think of anything else that might be relevant, don't hesitate to give me a call. You've got my card."

"Yeah, right." Chuck Hagley's tone suggested that he didn't much expect to need the card. He took the chief's extended hand and shook it with the sort of facial expression that suggested he was graciously overlooking some shortcoming in the way he'd been treated.

I studied him with interest. I didn't see much of either parent in him. Dolores Hagley had been a short, plump, motherly, self-effacing woman. Junius Hagley had been bony and angular and gave such an impression of disjointed height that I was always vaguely surprised to stand next to him and find that we were eye to eye at five ten. Chuck Hagley was at least two inches over six feet and rather beefy. He didn't appear particularly sad or stricken — more like someone who'd really rather be almost anywhere else.

The chief had pulled out his phone and was studying it. He glanced up at me and held up the phone.

"Where'd this come from?" I assumed he had just found the picture I'd sent him.

"A box of Dr. Womble's stuff that Robyn asked me to take over to him."

"Ah." He nodded. "Thank you."

"So is there anything else?" Chuck Hagley's gaze drifted from the chief, over to me, and on to Maudie.

"Mr. Hagley, this is Meg Langslow,"

Maudie said. "She's with Trinity."

"Not in the mood to be prayed over," Hagley said. "Thanks all the same."

"I'll be running along." The chief looked as if he was dashing away to avoid bursting out laughing.

"Praying's not really my line," I said.

"Aren't you the minister?" Hagley looked confused.

"Robyn Smith's the minister, and she's out on maternity leave," I said. "I'm just filling in for her on a few practical things."

"Practical things?" Hagley allowed Maudie to herd him back into the arrangements room and ease him into a chair. She set the tea tray down on the mahogany conference table that filled most of it and refilled Hagley's coffee cup. I trailed after them with my teacup.

"Well, I was supposed to find out how you wanted Trinity to handle arrangements for your mother as well as your father," I said. "Though I gather Maudie's already taken care of that."

Maudie nodded and beamed at me as she slipped out of the room, closing the door behind her, leaving me face-to-face with yet another next of kin.

CHAPTER 20

"You just need to know what to do about Mom?" Hagley asked. "That's easy. Whatever the old man wanted is fine with me."

"I'm also supposed to convey Trinity's regret about what happened, and our condolences to you," I went on.

"Consider them conveyed." He took an impatient gulp of coffee.

"Because you have a long drive ahead of you and you're wondering how soon you can get rid of me and hit the road," I said. "No problem; I'll skip the rest of the conveying."

"Ha!" He looked surprised and genuinely amused. "Yeah, that's pretty much the size of it. And I know your chief of police is just trying to catch whoever killed Dad, but I don't know any other way to explain that I have no idea who could have done it. He should be asking people here in town. I mean, yeah, Dad drove everyone crazy, and

I'm sure a lot of people had to fight the urge to smack him occasionally, but you don't murder someone just because he's an old fussbudget."

"Then you see the chief's problem," I said. "Because so far no one in town can figure out why anyone would have done this. I just wanted to say that if you have questions of your own about what happened to your father, I was the one who found him. So if there's anything you want to know about that, just ask. Not necessarily tonight — I'm sure you want to get home. But whenever. Here's my number."

I handed him one of my business cards — one of the blacksmithing cards, not the much more bureaucratic-looking ones I had for my job as Randall's assistant. He barely glanced at it — but he was staring at me.

"You found him," he echoed. "Do you have any idea what he was doing out there?"

"Not really," I said. "One theory is that he wanted to reclaim your mother's ashes."

"With a crowbar?" He looked incredulous. "I mean, isn't there a process for that?"

"A process that Reverend Robyn explained to him more than once."

"But of course he couldn't be bothered." Hagley closed his eyes and shook his head. "He just barks and expects everyone to carry out his orders. And why would he want to move Mom's ashes, for goodness' sake? He's always been so . . . involved with the church. Pretty damned close to obsessed, if you ask me."

"It's also possible that he went out there for the same reason I was out there when I found him," I said. "He could have seen a light, gone out to investigate, and surprised a vandal. He'd been there earlier at a vestry meeting, and I thought he'd gone home like everybody else, but maybe he stayed behind to police the grounds or something." I didn't actually think this was too likely, but I suspected Hagley might find it more comforting to think of his father as the self-appointed guardian of the church instead of a grave robber.

And I was right. His face lit up at the thought.

"That would be just like him," he exclaimed. "He could be such an old busybody, and it would never occur to him that he was putting himself in danger. No common sense."

But the tone of his voice was a little warmer — almost affectionate.

"Look — I may take you up on your offer to talk," he went on. "Some other time. Right now I still haven't taken it all in, and

I have no idea what to ask. I don't know when I'll be back here — my aunt's going to help me plan the funeral and all, but we can't schedule it until the police release the body and the crypt, and your chief would like me to leave the house as is till he has time to search it for any possible clues — no idea what he's hoping to find, but he's welcome to try. Nothing for me to do here except hang around feeling useless, so I might as well go back home. But call me if there's anything you need to know."

He handed me his business card. Charles H. Hagley, Esquire, and an office on Broad Street in Richmond.

"You're a lawyer," I said.

"Don't tell me you're one of those people who hates lawyers." His voice was more than a little defensive.

"I'm fine with lawyers," I said. "I have several dozen in my family. And I find them very useful indeed. What kind of law do you practice?"

"Mostly personal injury," he said. "If you lived in Richmond and watched a lot of late-night television, you'd recognize my face from the annoying commercials. 'Injured? Don't haggle over the settlement! Let Chuck Hagley do it for you!' " He delivered his lines in the stagy, overdramatic manner of an anxious amateur — something I had indeed seen on far too many late-night commercials.

A thought hit me — he was a lawyer from Richmond.

"Ever heard of a Richmond firm called Wellington Blodgett?" I asked.

"Out of my league."

"What's their specialty?"

"Rich people," he said. "Wills, trusts, estate planning."

"Do they do any criminal work?"

"Not on your life." Hagley seemed to find that amusing. "Although if any of their exalted clients were so unfortunate as to be mistaken for a common criminal, I'm sure they'd know how to arrange for a suitably high-powered defense attorney. Why do you ask?"

"I heard their name somewhere and it sounded vaguely familiar," I said. "I figured if you were from Richmond you might know. But that's not a firm I'd ever have dealt with, so I must be confusing them with someone else."

"They all sound alike, the snooty-sounding names of the really elite firms," he said. "Well, I'm going to hit the road."

We shook hands, and I followed him out into the reception area. He thanked Maudie

211

and took off.

"He seems in a much better humor than when he arrived," Maudie said, as we watched Mr. Hagley stride across the parking lot. "Good work."

"I think he was just tired of being asked if he knew anyone who'd want to knock off his dad," I said. "Time for me to hit the road myself."

Although after I got into the Twinmobile I sat for a few minutes, pondering. If Wellington Blodgett was a snooty firm catering to the wealthy and influential, how did they end up as the point of contact for Archie van der Lynden — an ex-felon whose family had supposedly lost all its money?

I made a mental note to ask one of those many family lawyers when I got a chance. Then I started the car and headed for home.

Out of habit, I took the route that went past Trinity. Which was, fortunately, not my responsibility tonight. Someone else was the Key Holder and had probably already locked up and gone home. So I was just going to drive past — no stopping to make sure everything was locked up properly — even though some of my fellow Key Holders were careless. Not my problem. I had a rendezvous with my pillow.

But when the church came into sight, I

couldn't help glancing over at it.

Why was there still a light on in the building? A light that flickered, darker then brighter, and moved from one window to another.

Someone was moving through the church with a flashlight. Unless Trinity was experiencing a power outage, why would anyone be walking around inside with a flashlight? I could think of no reason.

No legitimate reason, anyway.

I pulled into the parking lot. No cars — not even the van, which was still in the shop. Even more suspicious. Anyone with a good reason to be there would just park near the front door.

I came to a stop in the middle of the parking lot, with my car parallel to the building in a place where I could keep my eye on both the front door and the side exit. Then I pulled out my cell phone and dialed 911.

"Meg, what's wrong now?" Debbie Ann asked.

"I think there's an intruder at Trinity." I leaned to the right a bit to get a better view. "Someone's moving around inside with a flashlight, and —"

Two popping noises startled me, and the window to my left exploded into several million tiny little beads of safety glass. I threw

myself sideways and ducked under the dash-
board.

"Meg! What was that?"

"Someone's shooting at me."

CHAPTER 21

Normally Debbie Ann might have muted her phone for a few seconds while she put out the radio call. This time she didn't. An oversight, or did she guess how reassuring I'd find it, hearing her ordering all units to the Trinity parking lot?

"I feel like a sitting duck here." I was sprawled awkwardly over the Twinmobile's center console, covered with tiny little glass beads, with my nose buried in someone's clay-covered baseball socks.

"Keep your head down!" she ordered.

"And let the shooter sneak up to my car and finish me? I'm going to start the car and put some distance between me and whoever's out there."

"Maybe I should ask the chief what he wants you to do," Debbie Ann said. "Sammy's only a minute or two away."

But my gut told me that safety lay in flight. I listened to my gut. The first thing it told me was to get a weapon, and for a second or two I groped on the floor. Then I reminded myself that the only weapon I was likely to find was Josh's bright orange metal bat, which wouldn't be all that useful against a shooter. Okay, if I couldn't arm myself I needed to get out of there. I counted to three before pulling myself upright again and gripping the steering wheel. I looked wildly around as I started the car. No one in sight. I put the car in gear and took off. Since the church was on my left, it was a pretty good bet that the bullets had come from that direction, so I floored the pedal and steered toward the parking lot's exit, sending gravel flying behind me.

I hesitated when I reached the road. Homeward? Or back toward town? Town, definitely. I didn't much like the idea of running into the shooter on the long, lonely country road between here and home. In town there were more likely to be lights and witnesses. Besides, the sirens were coming from that direction.

I could hear faint noises coming from the floor on the passenger side of the car, where I'd dropped my phone. I decided to put a little more distance between me and the church before I stopped to pick it up.

I was relieved when, a few blocks later, I spotted a patrol car heading rapidly toward me. I slowed down as it approached, and then, when it zoomed past me toward the church, I stopped by the side of the road and snatched up the phone.

"Meg? Meg? What's happening? Meg, are you okay?"

"I'm fine," I said to Debbie Ann. "I drove out of the parking lot with no problems, and I just passed a patrol car heading that way. I'm going to turn around and head back to Trinity. I expect by the time I get there every deputy in the department will have arrived, so it should be the safest place in town."

"Don't get in their way," Debbie Ann warned. "And remember, there's still an active shooter out there."

I made a cautious U-turn and headed slowly back the way I'd come. Three police cars were already parked in the middle of the lot, lights flashing, and I could see figures bearing flashlights striding around the grounds.

I spotted the chief's blue sedan near the cluster of police cruisers and drove over to park near it. The driver's-side door was open and the chief was standing between the door and the body of the car, talking on his radio while his eyes followed the officers.

"She's here," he said into the radio. "Meg — you're okay?"

"I'm fine," I said. "The Twinmobile, not so much. It's going to need a new driver's-side window. When it's light, I guess I'll figure out if there are exit wounds on the passenger side or if there are still two bullets rattling around in here."

"Actually, we can figure that out for you. Although if there are any bullets, they'll probably be embedded in something, not rattling around." He picked up the radio handset. "Horace, soon as you get a chance, grab your forensic gear and meet me at Meg's vehicle. It's parked right beside mine."

I heard Horace's static-ridden "Yes, sir."

The chief returned the handset to its holder and turned back to me.

"I know you weren't on duty here at Trinity tonight," he said. "Since you were at the ballgame and then at Morton's. What brought you back here?"

"Inability to delegate," I said. "I should have headed straight home, but since I was passing by anyway, I couldn't help glancing over, and I spotted someone with a flashlight inside the building. So I pulled into the parking lot to take a closer look and called Debbie Ann to report it, and while I was talking to her, someone fired two shots at me."

"Speaking of inside — do you have your key to the building with you?"

I nodded and fished in my purse for the separate key ring on which I kept my Trinity keys. My friend Aida Butler, one of the chief's deputies, was just pulling up, and at the chief's request I handed her the key ring and showed her which key opened the front door. The chief diverted Vern Shiffley, another deputy, from searching the graveyard and assigned him to go with Aida to clear the inside of the church.

It was slightly disconcerting to see how, after Aida had unlocked the bright red double doors, she and Vern had taken up tactical positions on either side of the gray stone doorway. And then to watch them slam open the doors and step in, guns at the ready, Aida facing right and Vern left, in what looked to my admittedly amateur eyes like a precision tactical maneuver.

Just like on television, I couldn't help thinking. Which would actually have been rather cool to observe in real life if it had been happening anywhere other than the quiet small-town church where my family and I spent so many peaceful hours.

"Chief?"

Horace had arrived. I turned over my car to him and looked around for a place to sit. The chief waved me toward the front passenger seat of his sedan.

I slumped gratefully into the seat. It had been a long day. But I left the car door open, the better to follow what was going on outside. And I pulled out my phone to update Michael.

"I was just about to call you," he said. "I was getting a little worried — I thought you'd be home by now."

"So did I," I said. "Do you think you could pick me up at Trinity?"

"Actually, Rob and I are already on our way," he said. "The fire department just sent out a call to all volunteers. Is something on fire? And what are you doing there? And is something wrong with the Twinmobile?"

"No fire that I can see," I said. "I'm fine. So is the Twinmobile, except that someone shot out the driver's-side window. When Horace finishes processing it for evidence, I'm going to ask the chief if he can have someone drop it off at Osgood Shiffley's repair shop. I'd rather not have to explain the missing window to the boys, much less any bullet holes Horace may find in the interior."

"Agreed — but for heaven's sake, fill me in."

So while Rob and Michael raced toward Trinity, I gave him the rundown on my evening. As we talked, I kept an eye on what was happening around me. Flashlight beams revealed where some of the deputies were combing through the woods. The lights inside Trinity let me follow the progress of the inside search. I overheard a deputy reporting to the chief that the lock they'd put on the crypt was still intact. Eventually the chief grew tired of questioning me and asked if I could put him in touch with whoever was supposed to have been serving as Key Holder this evening. Luckily I had the duty roster, complete with the volunteers' contact information, in my cell phone. The chief strode a few paces away — was he seeking a better view of the church or just getting far enough away from me that I couldn't eavesdrop while he called the duty Key Holder? I didn't really care which. I sat back and watched the action.

After a couple of minutes, a fire engine pulled into the parking lot. The skeleton crew manning it began unloading some kind of equipment. I reported this to Michael.

"But there's still no sign of a fire," I

added. "So I have no idea why they've called you out. Surely they're not going to send unarmed firemen out to search the woods for an active shooter."

"I suspect they're going to have us set up the big lights to help with their search," Michael said.

"That makes sense." And also gave me a sense of relief that the chief wasn't sending Michael into danger. "So maybe once you get here, I could take Rob's car home. Assuming you two can probably get a ride home from one of the other firemen."

"Absolutely. Just sit tight for a few more minutes — your transportation is on its way. I should hang up now and get the rest of my gear on."

After we ended the call, I got out of the car and strolled over to where the chief was talking to Vern Shiffley, who had just emerged from the church.

"Anyway, someone was obviously looking pretty hard for something," Vern was saying. "Every door's been unlocked — a few forced open. Even closets. But not a lot of ransacking — no drawers turned out or anything like that."

"So whatever they were looking for isn't small," the chief said. "Can you tell if anything was taken?"

"Hard to tell," Vern said. "Like I said, nothing's messed up. Pretty darn clean and tidy everywhere. I expect we're going to have to get some people from the church to look things over to be sure."

I sighed and closed my eyes. Given how much time I'd been spending at Trinity, I was sure I'd be one of the people asked to help look things over. I hoped tomorrow would do.

"And a lot of easy pickings just left there," Vern went on. "Stuff that you'd expect any petty thief would snatch right up. Computers, a nice camera. Bottles of communion wine. None of that touched."

"So our intruder was looking for something in particular," the chief said.

"But about the only thing missing is the parrot," Vern said.

"Parrot?" the chief echoed.

"The one the minister had in her office," Vern explained.

"He's a toucan," I said. "And he's not missing. He's just not here."

"He's completely missing, cage and all," Vern said.

"Because I took him home last night, after the murder," I said. "I figured we had enough to worry about here without him underfoot."

"I remember you said you were doing that," the chief said. "So let's not worry about the toucan," he added, turning back to Vern.

"Uh, yeah. Hang on a sec." Vern looked embarrassed. He pulled out his radio. "Debbie Ann? Can you cancel the BOLO on the parrot?"

Chapter 22

"You put out a BOLO on the bird?" I asked. From the expression on the chief's face, I could tell he'd been about to ask the same question, although perhaps not in the same mild tone I'd used.

"I figured the bird was here during the murder," Vern explained. "Maybe the killer realized he'd left a witness behind and came back to silence the parrot."

"And it would have been an ingenious theory, if the bird actually was a parrot," the chief said, in a much more gracious tone than I'd have expected.

A thought hit me.

"Chief — actually it is a pretty ingenious theory. Vern thought the bird was a parrot — so do more than half the people who've seen him in Robyn's office. What if the killer thought so, too? Because if he thought Nimitz was a parrot, maybe he's worried that Nimitz could repeat something that would identify him."

The chief frowned, as if considering the idea and not altogether liking it. Vern had perked up at my suggestion and was watching the chief's face.

"It's possible, I suppose," the chief said. "Where is the bird now?"

"At the moment, he's in our barn," I said. "But should you feel the need to inspect him, you'll probably need to go out to the Caerphilly Zoo. Because that's where I'm taking him first thing tomorrow morning. Or should I say later this morning?"

"No, tomorrow's good," Vern said. "Still five minutes of twelve."

"First thing tomorrow morning, then," I said. "And I'm going to tell as many people as possible that the miserable bird is out at the zoo. Because whoever was searching the church fired two shots at me, and if the bird really was what the shooter was looking for, I do not want him showing up at our house."

"I don't suppose you want him showing up at your grandfather's zoo, either," the chief pointed out.

"Not really," I said. "But unlike our house, the zoo has a state-of-the-art security system."

The chief nodded.

A brilliant light suddenly flooded the

parking lot — evidently the fire department had gotten the first of its floodlights working.

"Go show them which way to aim the lights," the chief told Vern.

Another fire engine was entering the parking lot, with several other cars behind it — including Rob's sleek little blue convertible. I waved at the new arrivals.

Rob parked his car at the far end of the parking lot, the better to prevent his fellow first responders from sideswiping it in the excitement of their arrival. He might actually appreciate my taking the convertible out of harm's way. Michael got out, already dressed in his bulky gear, and loped over to us. Behind him, I could see more firemen arriving, and a flatbed truck from the Shiffley Construction Company, loaded with more portable lights, was turning into the parking lot.

"Your chariot awaits, milady." Michael handed me Rob's keys, gave me a quick kiss, and hurried over to where the other firemen were setting up another light.

"I'm finished with the van," Horace said. "You could actually take that if you want."

I explained my plan of dropping off the Twinmobile for repair, and the chief promised to arrange it. Horace helped me gather all the baseball gear, shake out the million little cubes of glass, pack everything in the baseball bags, and stow those in Rob's car — in the passenger seat, since the convertible's trunk space was so minuscule as to be nonexistent for all practical purposes. The donation and recycling boxes would have to wait.

"Oh, we're going to have to keep your clock for the time being," Horace said.

"My clock?"

"The one that was in this box." Horace was pointed to the box of stuff I'd be taking to Dr. Womble. "One of the bullets ended up embedded in it. We'll give it back when we're finished with it."

"Actually, it's Dr. Womble's clock," I said. "And since he left it behind when he retired and has been doing without it for at least five years, I don't think he'll mind if you keep it as long as you need to."

"That's good," Horace said. " 'Cause it's pretty much toast, that clock."

"Do you think you can fit that box in as well?" I asked. "I want to take it to Dr. Womble tomorrow."

"Sure." Horace hefted the box and managed to wedge it in the convertible's passenger seat along with the baseball bags.

As he was doing so, a sudden blinding

light flooded the entire parking lot. A helicopter hovered overhead, shining its spotlights down on the crime scene. Strange that I hadn't noticed the noise of its arrival. Then again, the firemen and the construction workers were making such a racket that the helicopter hadn't stood out all that much. And the increased light revealed that not all the police vehicles in the parking lot were from Caerphilly. Evidently the chief had called for reinforcements from nearby jurisdictions.

Several Shiffleys who trained tracking dogs had arrived and were unloading their charges — a mixed crew of Labradors and bloodhounds. I wasn't sure I understood just how the dogs were supposed to figure out which of the many human scents that might be found in the church was the intruder. I had visions of the dogs leading their handlers unerringly to the homes of the various vestry members. Perhaps I should warn Mother.

The chief and Randall Shiffley were standing by the chief's car, looking up at the helicopter, their hands shading their eyes against the light. It looked like an outtake from *Close Encounters of the Third Kind*.

"FBI, you think?" Randall asked.

"More likely the State Police," the chief replied.

I decided to assume the arrival of the helicopter would turn out to be the high point of the evening. I climbed into Rob's convertible, shoved one of the baseball bags aside so I could reach the gearshift, and headed for home.

I had to admit I was a little anxious about parking Rob's car in the shed he'd fixed up to keep it in. By way of distraction, I contemplated what an eyesore it was. All the other sheds that had littered our yard when we first bought the house had either been fixed up, torn down, or hauled away. Granted the shed was in as unobtrusive a spot as possible, but still — an eyesore. Rob's idea was that no one would look for an expensive convertible in such a run-down building. Tonight, it occurred to me that if anyone were looking for a good place to hide from the police — or to lurk while keeping an eye on our house for someone to return — the shed would seem perfect. Maybe I could get Rob to allow a little cleanup by pointing that out.

Tomorrow. Tonight I had to brave the shed to park the convertible.

But not alone. Before driving out there, I stopped at the back door to let the dogs out.

Tinkerbell, Rob's Irish wolfhound, bounded joyfully over and gave me several sloppy doggy kisses before scampering off to a discreet corner to pee. Spike trotted out and stared accusingly at me for a few moments as if to ask what I'd done with the boys — Josh and Jamie were the twin lights of his life, and he only tolerated Michael and me because he'd learned from experience that biting us upset the boys. Then he sat down on the porch and stared up at the sky as if hoping the boys would return by helicopter.

"I was hoping for a little canine protection service," I muttered as I got back in the convertible and drove it to the shed. But I reminded myself that if there had been anyone in there — or anywhere else in the yard — the dogs would be all over him. On at least one occasion, Tinkerbell's strenuous efforts to make a new friend had so terrified a would-be burglar that he'd panicked and fled, leaving behind a full kit of lockpicks, glass cutters, and other housebreaking tools that Dad had found fascinating to play with. And Spike had a long history of chasing away intruders, although his zeal was made less helpful by the fact that his definition of intruders included quite a few people we actually wanted to visit us for the purpose of delivering things, fixing things, or just having dinner with us.

The dogs followed me back inside and accepted treats in return for their bodyguard duties. Then they disappeared. I could hear Tinkerbell's toenails clacking down the hall to the living room, where she liked to sleep in front of the fireplace, even in the hottest days of August when it contained nothing but a large arrangement of dried flowers. Spike headed upstairs to wait in Jamie's room. He normally started the night sleeping with Jamie, who tended to fade much earlier in the evening than his brother. At some point in the wee small hours, Spike would trot across the hall to finish the night with Josh, who liked to sleep until noon on days when he didn't have to get up for school.

Alas, Spike would be waiting in vain tonight.

The house was very quiet. Rose Noire was on a camping trip with several like-minded herb fanciers who wanted to gather something or other under a full moon. And for once we had no other visiting relatives staying with us. Not only had the shooter tried to kill me, he'd also ruined one of the few chances Michael and I had had lately for a quiet romantic evening together.

Although I couldn't manage to stay awake long enough to work up a good head of resentment over that.

I woke briefly when Michael returned home at around 3:00 A.M. I wanted to ask him if they'd caught the shooter, but by the time I was awake enough to string a coherent sentence together, he was fast asleep.

So I lapsed back into slumber myself.

CHAPTER 23

Saturday morning dawned bright and sunny.

Or so I deduced when I woke up, at eight thirty, grateful that we'd installed blackout shades in the master bedroom. I'd have joined Michael in sleeping even later but, although my notebook was tucked away out of sight in my purse, my to-do list kept nudging me awake.

I dressed quietly and slipped out into the hallway.

"Grrrrrr."

Spike was waiting for me. He didn't actually snap at my ankle — clearly he was mellowing a bit, or maybe just slowing down. But he did fix me with a baleful stare, and I realized he was missing the twins.

"Sorry," I said. "They're having a sleepover. They'll be back in a few hours."

My words didn't seem to mollify him, but he followed at my heels down to the kitchen, allowed me to let him out into the yard, and then deigned to accept a bowl of dog food. Tinkerbell was visibly more grateful for her visit outdoors and her food.

Since Rose Noire wasn't back, I let the chickens out into the yard and scattered some feed for them. Although the llamas watched me with the intense interest they always showed in human activity, I decided they could wait for their grain until Michael was up. Though they did like apples and carrots as treats, so I sliced up a few for them while I was preparing the toucan's meal.

The toucan.

As I watched him eat his fruit — from a safe distance, so he wouldn't splatter me with juice in his enthusiasm — I considered my options. I could just show up at Grandfather's zoo with the toucan and pretend I thought people dropped off random birds at their aviary all the time. Probably not a great idea. Then again, if I asked Grandfather to take the bird in, there was a chance he'd say no, since toucans were neither endangered nor particularly fierce, two qualities that tended to endear creatures to him.

Still, if I played my cards right, I could get him to cooperate. Perhaps I should just pretend we'd already discussed the toucan and he'd already agreed to foster it. Yes, that was the ticket.

So I pulled out my phone and called him. "What now?" he said when he picked up. Was I the latest in a string of annoying callers, or was he under the erroneous impression that this was the new phone etiquette?

"And good morning to you, too," I said. "Are you at the zoo? I need to bring you the toucan. If you're not there, I can just drop it off with Manoj — he's still the head aviary keeper, right?"

"Yes — fine young man. I plan to promote him when something opens up. But what's this about a toucan? We already have a pair — we don't need any more toucans."

"That's a relief," I said. "Because you don't get to keep this one, remember? He's the one that belongs to Robyn's parishioner, who's going to want his bird back when the *Harry S. Truman* returns from wherever it's currently traveling. But with Robyn down for the count, the toucan's in danger of being neglected. He needs expert care — and where better than at a zoo! Didn't we already discuss this?"

"We're not an avian boarding facility," Grandfather protested. "We can't just take in every stray pigeon that some do-gooder wants us to take care of. Clarence boards animals at his veterinary clinic — why not ask him to take the bird?"

"Well, that was my first idea," I improvised. "But Mother said she knew you would be willing to take the bird in, seeing how everyone else in town was doing their bit to help Robyn." Grandfather wasn't afraid of anything on two or four legs, but he did try to avoid crossing Mother. "And Cordelia said if you wouldn't do it, she'd pick up the tab for boarding at Clarence's," I added, hoping to make productive use of the perennial sniping between Grandfather and Cordelia.

"Nonsense," Grandfather said. "There's no need for her to pay for anything. Stupid idea."

I made a mental note to tell Mother and Cordelia what they were supposed to have said, just in case it ever came up.

"When shall I tell Manoj to expect you?" Grandfather asked.

"I can head over with the bird now."

"I'll be in the small mammal house," he said. "Awaiting the birth. Got to run."

"Birth of what?" But he'd already hung up.

Well, I'd find out when I got there.

Assuming I ever got there. With the Twin-mobile in having its window replaced, I was left with my ancient blue Honda, which still ran reasonably well, in spite of being nearly old enough to vote, thanks to Osgood Shiffley's expert (though not inexpensive) care. But the Honda's interior space was limited, and there was no way I could fit the toucan's capacious cage in it.

So I transferred the toucan to the dog carrier we kept for Spike's visits to Clarence. Fortunately for the toucan, the carrier was much larger than you'd normally use for an eight-and-a-half-pound fur ball, because we'd found the larger the carrier, the fewer times we got bitten during the process of stuffing Spike into it.

The toucan clearly wasn't crazy about leaving his usual home, and I was wary of that huge, powerful bill, but unlike Spike, he confined his protests to squawking and pooping copiously.

"It's only for the ride," I told him, as I stuffed a few orange slices into the carrier to placate him. "And you'll love what's waiting for you at the other end." At least I hoped he would. I made another mental note to warn Grandfather and Manoj that like many caged birds the toucan might not have had much experience with his own species.

Then I turned to look at the empty cage.

What if whoever had ransacked Trinity figured out that the toucan had moved here? And didn't get word that he'd moved on to the zoo? I didn't much like the notion of Mr. Hagley's killer rummaging through our barn, and maybe even invading the house.

So with the toucan carrier in tow, I went into my office, turned on my laptop, and typed out a notice in very large, bold letters: DO NOT CALL THE POLICE TO REPORT THE TOUCAN MISSING! HE IS NOW HOUSED AT THE CAERPHILLY ZOO!

I printed out two copies. I taped one over the toucan's cage and the other on the main barn door. Then I laid down a tarp in the back of my car, in case Nimitz still had a reserve supply of poop, loaded the carrier in, tucked the box of stuff for Dr. Womble in the trunk, and headed for the zoo.

Evidently Grandfather's initial reluctance to take in the toucan had turned into enthusiasm. When I arrived at the zoo, I found two uniformed keepers waiting for me just inside the entrance. I recognized the slight but energetic one as Manoj. Both keepers came scurrying out to the car.

"Welcome, Meg!" Manoj said. "Axel, get the . . . dog carrier?"

"The toucan's cage wouldn't fit in the

car," I said. "And I figured he wouldn't need it here anyway."

"No, we have a splendid habitat waiting for him."

Axel, who was burly and blond and almost a head taller than Manoj, picked up Nimitz's carrier as if it was a matchbox and headed into the zoo with it. Manoj and I fell into step behind him.

"By the way," I said. "I have no idea if he's ever encountered another toucan in his life. I assume you're not just going to turn him out in the habitat with the other toucans —"

"Of course not!" Manoj looked slightly shocked. "We will keep him in quarantine until Clarence has given him a clean bill of health. And then we will introduce him gradually to the other toucans, under careful observation. Don't worry — we have lots of experience with integrating new individuals into existing flocks. Even individuals who haven't been properly socialized with their own species."

"Good," I said. "Not that I ever doubted you, but keep in mind that for the last couple of days I've been dealing with people who don't even know that toucans can't talk."

"Seriously?" Manoj looked even more

shocked at that notion.

"Yes, which brings me to something that I probably should mention — at least one of the clueless people who thinks toucans can talk might be gunning for this one. Quite literally."

I explained about the bird's presence at Trinity during the murder, and last night's shooting at the church.

"So I'm not bringing him here just because you guys will be better at taking care of him — although that's certainly very important," I said in conclusion. "There's also the fact that you have much better security here than Michael and I could ever provide."

"You really think the toucan could be in danger?"

I nodded.

"Never fear!" Manoj drew himself up to his full height. "We will protect him!"

"No one gets through us to the bird," Axel commented over his shoulder.

"Excellent," I said. "I suppose I should confess to Grandfather that I'm bringing him a marked toucan."

"You will find him in the Small Mammal House," Manoj said. "Awaiting the birth."

He hurried to catch up with Axel and fuss

over the toucan before I could ask "what birth?"

Only one way to find out. I headed toward the Small Mammal House.

I made my way through the crowds of tourists — of course it was Saturday now, and apparently a reasonably large number of people had decided to weekend in Caerphilly. Randall would doubtless be pleased, since tourism was rapidly becoming a significant source of income for both the town and its businesses — although I suspected this morning he was probably worrying about the possibility that the dramatic police response to the shooting at Trinity would discourage vacationers. Was I more cynical to think it was just as likely to encourage them?

I strolled into the Small Mammal House. Nothing much seemed to be going on out in the public areas.

As usual, the meerkats had drawn the biggest crowd, partly because they'd cornered the market on cute and partly because unlike many of the other animals they didn't spent the majority of their days hiding in the farthest corner of their habitat.

A couple of cat lovers were cooing baby talk to the sand cat, who was lying on a branch gazing out through the glass with his ears laid back and the tip of his tail twitching, as if to express his disapproval of their undignified way of addressing him. I'd always gotten the impression that in spite of being the size of an ordinary house cat — and a fairly small house cat at that — the sand cat resented being relegated to the Small Mammal House and felt it would be much more suitable to his feline dignity if he were housed with his larger relatives in the Big Cat House.

A couple of teenagers were tapping on the glass of the lesser Madagascar hedgehog tenrec's habitat and wondering loudly why the stupid animal wouldn't come out and show himself. I thought of pointing out to them the large sign announcing that the habitat's occupant was not on display today — it was right beside the sign telling people not to tap on the glass. But I reminded myself how strong an advocate Grandfather was of learning by doing and left them to figure it out for themselves. If they were lucky, they'd grasp the importance of reading the signs before they got to the Big Cat House or the Bear Cave.

None of the animals on display looked pregnant, much less in the throes of labor, so I went over to the door marked STAFF ONLY! DO NOT ENTER! I punched the access code into the keypad, slipped in, and slammed the door behind me before any of the tourists noticed what I was up to and tried to enter on my heels.

Normally the staff-only sections of the zoo were fairly quiet except during the feeding-time frenzy. But I could see at least a dozen staff members racing up and down the corridor or gathered in a clump at its far end. As I proceeded down the corridor I could see they were all staring through what looked like a picture window, except that it gave a view not of the outside world but into a room with a sign over its door that read CLINIC AND NURSERY.

"Is this where the blessed event is taking place?" I asked a passing staff member.

"In the clinic," she said. "Nothing visible yet, but if all goes well, they'll bring the pups to the window for us to see."

She dashed off as if on some urgent obstetric mission. Annoying that she couldn't have just said what kind of new arrivals they were expecting. Still, pups did narrow the field a bit. If it was the ill-tempered sand cat's mate giving birth, she'd have said kittens. Pups could mean wolves — Grandfather was particularly fond of wolves. But wolf litters weren't that rare at the zoo, so no matter how pleased Grandfather was at the birth of more tiny predators, the rest of the staff wouldn't get this worked up. And besides, the wolves didn't live in the Small Mammal House. The meerkats did, and I seemed to recall that their offspring were also called pups — but like his wolves Grandfather's meerkats were remarkably good at producing litters. No one made this much fuss over them.

I had just decided to break down and ask someone what we were expecting when Grandfather burst out of the clinic/nursery door, dressed in pale blue surgical scrubs.

"Victory!" he shouted. "We now have two healthy Screaming Hairy Armadillo pups!"

"Seriously?" I muttered.

CHAPTER 24

"Ar-ma-dil-*lo*! Ar-ma-dil-*lo*!"

Some of the assembled staff members were merely cheering and thumping each other on the back while others had formed an impromptu conga line, shuffling up and down the corridors chanting "Ar-ma-dil-*lo*!" over and over again. And everyone seemed to be congratulating Grandfather as if he were the proud new father.

"Clarence is going to bring them to the window," Grandfather announced.

I almost got trampled in the rush to the window. Fortunately, most of the assembled staff were relatively short — did Grandfather have a hiring bias in favor of people he could loom over? — so I was easily able to peer over people's heads.

Clarence Rutledge, also in scrubs and gloves, was holding up a dollhouse-sized armadillo. It didn't look particularly hairy, but then a lot of mammals — including humans — tended to be born without their full complement of hair or fur. I couldn't hear any screaming, but maybe the glass was soundproofed.

"Isn't he cute?" one staffer cooed.

Well, yes, he was. Baby animals usually were. I made a mental note to check on the way out to see what the newborns would grow up to look like. I had a feeling cute was a transient phase for Screaming Hairy Armadillo pups.

"He's adorable!" a staffer exclaimed.

"He or she," another staffer said.

"Has Dr. Blake said which?"

"He says it could be a few weeks before we can tell."

I left them to coo over the tiny, wriggling pup and strolled over to where Grandfather was basking in the armadillo's reflected glory.

"I dropped the toucan off with Manoj," I said. "I know it's not as exciting as a brace of brand-new Screaming Hairy Armadillos, but the toucan can use your help." I explained the possibility that Mr. Hagley's killer might be after Nimitz.

"I need to schedule another series of wildlife lectures," Grandfather said.

Someone who didn't know the way his mind worked might have taken that for a non sequitur.

"That would be nice," I said. "But your lecture would mostly attract people who already know a fair amount about birds and animals. Including the fact that toucans can't talk. I doubt if Caerphilly's criminal population would have much interest. So if you're hoping the person who's gunning for the toucan would show up and learn that the bird can't squeal on him, I rather doubt it."

"Good point." He sighed. "Well, I need to make a few phone calls. I want to get in a little extra help on the security side of things."

"Calling in the Brigade?" I asked. Blake's Brigade, as we all called it, was a loosely organized but fanatically loyal group of volunteers who could always be counted on to drop everything and come when Grandfather called for their help.

"Not a bad idea," Grandfather said. "Although I think the first thing I'm going to do is call Randall to see if he can lend me a few of his more capable cousins."

"Good grief. Well, if you insist on bringing armed Shiffleys into the picture, make sure they know that not everyone who comes galumphing through the woods will be a bad guy. Last night's shooting brought

248

the out-of-town law enforcement swarming like mosquitoes to a picnic."

"I'm sure Randall will brief them." Grandfather waved one hand dismissively.

Yes, Randall would brief them, if I had anything to say about it.

I returned to the public area of the Small Mammal House. The surly teenagers had joined the crowd around the meerkats, although their faces showed that they clearly considered it beneath them to gaze at anything so ostentatiously cute.

I hunted down the Screaming Hairy Armadillo habitat. There were three of them there, trundling around like small tanks. They weren't really all that hairy, except by comparison to other armadillos — I could see only thin wisps of hair sticking out between the plates of their shells. I wondered if whoever had designed creatures for the Star Wars movies had been thinking about Screaming Hairy Armadillos the day they'd come up with Yoda.

I checked the time. Nine thirty. Which meant the chief was probably even now meeting with James Donovan, the law professor, P. Jefferson Blair's friend. By the time I went into town, found a parking space within hiking distance of the law school, and made my way to Donovan's office, the chief would probably be finished with him.

While I was driving into town, I could hear my phone, which I'd stowed inside my purse, pinging with messages — five of them in quick succession. Was some crisis going on? When I had to stop at a stop sign on the outskirts of town, I dug into my purse for the phone and scanned it.

No crises. Just everyone I knew texting me.

Mason's mother informed me that she was on her way to deliver the boys.

Mother texted that she was heading over to our house with Cordelia.

Michael reported the boys' safe return and reminded me that we needed to order more grain for the llamas.

Osgood Shiffley had replaced my window and would be dropping off the car by noon.

And Dad wanted to know when we were going to visit Ragnar.

I texted "OK" or "thanks!" to everyone but Dad. He got "later" instead.

Then I continued my journey to the end of the campus where the law school had its quarters.

Professor Donovan's office was in the main law school building, affectionately known as Nameless Hall. It had originally been called the Nathaniel J. Pruitt Building, after a local judge so conservative that he was rumored to have called Calvin Coolidge a "damned revolutionary." But after the downfall and disgrace of the Pruitt family the college had decided the building needed a new name. Since it also needed a major overhaul, the college had offered the renaming rights to the distinguished alumnus who provided the bulk of the money for the renovations. Unfortunately the donor had died before announcing his choice of names, and his highly litigious family had been squabbling over the issue ever since.

Nowadays, unofficially renaming the building had become a traditional prank among Caerphilly College students. As I climbed the impressive stone stairway to the front door, I wasn't surprised to see that, as usual, the blank space on the building's façade where the bronze name plaque had been removed was covered with a painted sign. Today, I noted with approval, it was the ATTICUS FINCH SCHOOL OF JUSTICE.

Over my years as a Caerphilly College faculty spouse I'd developed a certain ability to interpret all sorts of subtle clues to a faculty member's status. In addition to being in the main law school building, James Donovan's office was conveniently located, decently sized, and blessed with one of the limited number of windows. I deduced that while Donovan wasn't likely to be named dean of the law school anytime soon, he was probably tenured and well regarded.

His door was open about a foot, and I didn't see the chief inside, so I knocked.

"Come in," he called out. But he looked slightly surprised when I entered. Maybe he was expecting a student — although it was Saturday. I'd gotten the impression that any faculty member found in his or her office on a Saturday was seeking peace and quiet, not interaction with students.

Donovan looked to be in his forties or early fifties, with thinning sandy hair. He stood up when I entered, revealing that he was almost as tall as Michael's six four, though he was so lanky that he gave the impression of being even taller.

"Meg Langslow." I held out my hand. "Has Chief Burke already talked to you? He said it would be okay to for me to drop by after he did."

"He just left," Donovan said as he shook my hand. "You're with the police?" He didn't seem hostile or upset — just puzzled. He waved me to one of his guest chairs.

"With Trinity Episcopal," I explained. "Running errands for Reverend Robyn

Smith, who's out on maternity leave."

"How can I help you, then?"

I probably should have just come right out and asked what he wanted done with Blair's ashes, but what harm would it do to see if I could get him talking?

"We were told to contact you," I said. "I gather you were a good friend of Paul Blair's — or P. Jefferson Blair. Not sure what you knew him as."

"I knew him as Paul when we went to college together," Donovan said. "And retrained myself to call him Jeff when he showed up again to start a new life. Which would have been a lot easier in any town other than Caerphilly, but that was Jeff."

"Stubborn?"

"Impractical."

"I can see that," I said. "Apart from impractical, what was he like?"

Donovan leaned back and took a deep breath.

"He was a nice guy," he said. "And also he was an idiot. Book smart, of course, but no common sense. No street smarts. Archie van der Lynden and Fitz Marshall got their hooks into him freshman year. Dazzled him with their money and their social connections. Got him into their fraternity."

"What did they get out of it?" I asked.

"Passing grades." Donovan snorted. "Neither one of them would have lasted a semester without Jeff's help. He tutored them, wrote their papers. I kept hoping Jeff would see through them, but they hung on till junior year, with him still fetching and carrying for them. And then Archie recruited him for his mother's plot to cheat the insurance company. You heard about that, I gather."

I nodded.

"They told him it was a prank, of course. Just another part of the entertainment. And if you ask me, he believed them. The judge and the jury agreed, which was why he got such a light sentence. Of course, it helped that the gun he was carrying wasn't even loaded. They gave him the minimum — five years. Still, it almost killed his poor mother, and it certainly derailed his career."

"He still managed to become a professor," I pointed out.

"Adjunct professor," Donovan said. "The indentured servants of the academic world. And teaching English literature to freshmen wasn't ever what he had in mind. He was originally planning to go to law school, you know. That's how we met — both doing the pre-law track. He wanted to go into some kind of socially responsible legal work —

become a public defender, or take on big environmental cases. He had to give that up, of course. The Virginia Bar doesn't have a hard and fast rule against admitting convicted felons, but they certainly don't make it easy. And Caerphilly's law school wouldn't take him. Maybe they would have if Mrs. Van der Lynden was still around to pressure them — that's how he got back into the college, of course. But she died before he finished his bachelor's degree. So he studied his options, decided the English Department would be the path of least resistance, and got on with his life. At least for a little while."

"The police report said he had an accident while cleaning his gun," I said.

"Yeah, right." Donovan rolled his eyes. "No one really believed that. No one who knew him, anyway. He'd never seemed to have the slightest interest in guns — in fact, if anything, I'd have thought he was pretty much against them after the New Year's Eve gun battle he lived through out at the Van der Lynden castle. Everyone figured he'd lost heart and decided to end it all."

"Including you?"

He shrugged slightly and seemed lost in thought. I waited as patiently as I could manage.

"At the time I kind of wondered if maybe it was something from the jewel robbery coming back to haunt him," he said finally. "What if one of the real robbers thought he knew something and came back to try to get it out of him? Or just wanted to take revenge and shot him? I did a little research, but as far as I could figure out, both of the real robbers would still have been in prison at the time. So I figured I was just being paranoid. He decided to end it all, went out and bought a gun, and did it."

I nodded. I wondered if it had occurred to him that even if the robbers themselves were still in prison, they could have friends and allies on the outside. If Chief Burke had been in charge, he would definitely have checked to see if Blair had actually bought the gun — had the police in 2000 done that? And even if he had bought a gun, had he done so to end his life — or to defend it?

"Did he ever say anything about getting threats?" I asked.

"Not exactly." He frowned. "He had chronic insomnia, and sometimes when he looked particularly haggard, I'd ask what the trouble was, and he'd say it was his past coming back to haunt him. I always assumed he just meant his conscience was bothering him, or the old memories, but after his death I did sometimes wonder if it wasn't just a mental thing. If maybe someone from the past was bothering him. No way to find out now."

He stared gloomily into space for a few moments. Then he seemed to pull himself up.

"I already told pretty much all of this to Chief Burke," he said. "Is there some official reason why I'm telling you?"

"Just me being nosy," I said. "Officially, I'm supposed to be representing Trinity Episcopal. Extending our sincere apologies and asking what you want us to do with Jeff's ashes."

"What I want you to do with them?" Donovan looked startled. "Can't they just stay there?"

"Of course they can," I said. "If that's what you want. Well, technically they're not there right now — I think the police took them away for safekeeping. But as soon as we get the okay, from them, we can put him back in his niche."

"Good." He looked down at the papers on his desk but I suspected he wasn't thinking about the student paper that lay there, so copiously marked with red ink that it almost looked as if it were bleeding.

I picked up my tote to leave. And then I

set it down again. This might be my best chance to get information out of Donovan. Surely there was something else I could ask him to get him talking again.

"Tell me," I asked. "Was he well-off?"

CHAPTER 25

"Well-off? Jeff?" Donovan snorted, looked up, and frowned. "Why? Is there a cost to putting him back in his crevice? Some kind of restocking fee?"

"Of course not," I said. "And even if there were, under the circumstances, Trinity would take care of it. I should have preceded that question with 'on a completely different subject' or something."

"Then why the interest in his bank account?"

"You wondered yourself if someone who thought he knew where the loot was hidden had come back."

"Which would have been pretty stupid of them, because he didn't know a thing." Donovan was shaking his head firmly. "If he had, he probably could have made a deal with the prosecutor. Had the charges against him dropped in return for cooperating with their investigation."

"Makes sense," I said. "But if he was well-off, someone might assume it was from the robbery rather than from earnings or inheritance. That could explain them coming after him."

"Okay, that I get," Donovan said. "But he wasn't well-off. He didn't come from money, and you certainly don't get rich on an adjunct's salary. He was up to his ears in debt when he died. Fortunately, most of it was student loan debt, the kind that's wiped out if you die before you've paid it off, so his poor mother didn't get stuck with it. His department actually took up a collection to pay off most of the rest of it."

"Interesting." And it really was, since, as I'd been reminded several times lately, niches at Trinity didn't come cheap. I wondered if Donovan knew this.

"How'd he end up buried at Trinity?" I asked.

"That's the church he went to," Donovan said. "So the minister arranged it."

"Dr. Womble?"

"That's him." Donovan smiled — a fairly common reaction for anyone who'd met Trinity's former rector. "Funny old guy, but really nice. He took care of everything. I gather they have some kind of fund to take care of members of the congregation who die broke."

Quite possibly we did, but I didn't think it covered buying them a niche at Trinity. I decided Donovan didn't need to know that.

"On another completely different topic," I said. "I don't suppose you kept in touch at all with Archie van der Lynden."

"We didn't move in the same circles," Donovan said. "Not before the robbery and certainly not after. Why?"

"I need to find him," I said. "For much the same reason I came to see you. His mother's ashes were disturbed. I assume what he'd want is for Trinity to put her back in her niche, but so far I haven't been able to reach him. The only contact I've got is a law firm, and so far they're not being helpful. They haven't even gotten back to the chief."

"Well, give it time," Donovan said. "If I were a defense attorney representing scum like Archie, I'd make sure I knew exactly what he'd been up to before I got in touch with law enforcement. If I even talked to them at all. They're not under any obligation to do so, you know."

"Yeah, but from what I've gathered, this isn't a criminal defense firm," I said. "It's a fancy estate and trust outfit called Wellington Blodgett."

261

"Wellington Blodgett? They're representing Archie? Sounds . . . implausible. His mother, maybe, back in the day before she lost all her dough, but Archie?"

"Maybe he's part of their pro bono clientele."

"Also implausible. A firm like that tends to encourage their attorneys to take on a less unsavory sort of pro bono client. Hang on — I have an idea."

He picked up his phone and dialed a number. Only four digits, so I assumed it was a college extension.

"Jeannie? Can you work your magic on those files for me? . . . Long story, but I want to find out if we have any graduates working at a white-shoe firm in Richmond called Wellington Blodgett. . . . Yeah, preferably a reasonably senior one. . . . Sure thing."

He pressed the mute button and glanced up at me.

"Jeannie's the dean's admin. She keeps a detailed record of where all the law school grads end up. Invaluable for fund-raising purposes. If we have a graduate at Wellington Blodgett, we might get some inside scoop about how they ended up representing Archie."

I nodded. He waited, staring tensely at

the phone, for a few more moments. Then he jerked to attention, unmuted the phone, and picked up a pen.

"I'm ready. . . . uh-huh . . . uh-huh. . . . Great! Thanks! I owe you one."

He hung up the phone and, with a flourish, handed me a piece of paper on which he'd written *J. Elliott Vanderbilt, Coll. '89, Law '92.*

"I don't even have to look him up," he said. "Big man on campus back when we were undergrads. One of Archie's frat brothers. Quite possibly the stupidest human being ever admitted to Caerphilly's law school — certainly the stupidest in my class. And now a partner at Wellington Blodgett! Well, money can't buy everything, but apparently it can buy a partnership at a ritzy law firm. I doubt if Archie's a pro bono client. More likely Elliott's private charity case. Maybe he does Archie a favor now and then, for old times' sake. Rattles a saber. Talks his old buddy out of a jam. Of course, I'm not sure knowing this gets you one bit closer to talking to Archie."

"But you never know." I tucked the paper into my notebook. "Thank you."

"Say, is it true that the police found Mrs. Van der Lynden's jewels in the crypt?" Donovan asked. "That's the rumor that's been

263

going around."

"Jewels, plural, no," I said. "They found a ring with a red stone. No idea if it's valuable, much less if it belonged to Mrs. Van der Lynden. Why?"

"You'd think the police would have made that a priority." Donovan shook his head as if sadly disappointed.

"I'm sure finding out's a priority," I said. "Alas, bringing me up to speed on what they've learned isn't. I'm sure they'll make a public announcement when they're ready."

"I bet it is Mrs. Van der Lynden's," he said. "Wish Jeff were here to see this. We used to wonder sometimes if the jewels would ever turn up."

"What did you and he think had happened?"

"We never settled on one theory. Archie, his mother, one of the staff, one of the robbers. Who knows? All I know is that Jeff didn't have them."

I nodded.

"I'll let you know when we've got Jeff safely stowed in his niche again," I said as I stood up.

"Appreciate it."

He picked up his red pen and focused on the student paper in front of him with a visible effort. I slipped away and closed the door behind me.

On my way out of the building, I noticed that while I'd been inside the latest set of pranksters had renamed it the DENNY CRANE SCHOOL OF LAW.

Back at my car, I checked my phone before taking off. A text from Dad asked simply, "Ragnar?"

"Not now," I replied. "But soon."

Dad's burglary reenactment plans could wait. I was going to see Dr. Womble. Dad would be miffed when he heard I'd gone to visit the retired rector without him, but putting the two of them in the same room would torpedo any chance of steering the conversation into useful channels.

Before heading out, I took a few moments to rummage through the box of items for Dr. Womble. Apart from the letter from Archie, none of the other items seemed related to recent events or to the Van der Lynden robbery. But perhaps it would be a good idea to encourage Dr. Womble to root through the box while I was there, to see what random revelations its contents sparked. I closed up the box and set out for the Wombles' retirement cottage.

Although they referred to their retirement home as a cottage, it was actually a rambling old farmhouse tucked away in a wooded glade a few miles from town. They'd converted the former barn into a library, although that didn't mean there weren't plenty of books to fill shelves in every room in the house — including the tiny hall powder room.

Mrs. Womble answered the door, releasing the unmistakable odor of freshly baked chocolate cookies into the wild.

"Hello, Meg," she said. "Glad to see you're okay after last night's excitement. Here to see Rufus, I assume — he's back in the library. You can take him his tray."

She ushered me briskly down the hall and into a kitchen in which every horizontal surface was covered with racks of cooling cookies. She picked up a tray with a pitcher of lemonade, two glasses, and a plate of cookies.

"Second breakfast?" I asked. Dr. Womble's eating habits were modeled on those of the hobbits.

"Goodness, he had that an hour ago. Elevenses. I suppose if you're taking that box to Rufus I should bring the tray."

"The box isn't heavy," I said. "Just put the tray on top."

She did so, and let me out the back door before returning to her baking. Had she anticipated my arrival? Or had I fortuitously rung the doorbell just as she was about to deliver refreshments? Not for the first time I wondered how someone so efficient and down to earth had ended up married to Dr. Womble.

I found Dr. Womble sprawled in one of the half-dozen disreputable but comfortable easy chairs drawn into a rough circle in the center of the barn floor, with several large stacks of books on the floor around him. He looked up and smiled with delight when he saw me.

"Good afternoon, Meg!" he exclaimed. "Have you ever eaten breadfruit?"

"Not that I can recall." Not knowing whether this was a rhetorical question or an offer of hospitality, after setting my tray-laden box on the floor I glanced around. I saw no plates of anything that could possibly be breadfruit, though there was one containing a paring knife and some relatively fresh orange peels. There were a few empty plates, though. Perhaps Wyclif and Wilberforce, the household's enormous gray tabbies, had eaten the breadfruit? They were lying in two of the armchairs, looking remarkably sleek and contented.

"I wonder where one could find some," Dr. Womble went on. "I really am quite curious to try it."

"I could ask around if you like." I moved aside enough books to set the tray on the low table in front of Dr. Womble. In any other home I'd have thought of it as a coffee table, but here it was obviously more of a book, tea, and lemonade table. I poured us each a glass of the lemonade. Then I glanced around to see if I could figure out what had inspired Dr. Womble's sudden interest in breadfruit.

"That's what the *Bounty*'s mission was all about, you know," he was saying. "Bringing back several hundred little breadfruit trees from the South Pacific to the Caribbean.

"That's *Bounty* as in *Mutiny on the . . .?*" Light was beginning to dawn.

"Yes. Such a tragic tale. Poor Captain Bligh. He wasn't perfect, of course, but he wasn't the villain he's been painted. The real story was so much more nuanced."

As he talked, I studied the heaps of books around him. Books about Tahiti. Books about the West Indies. Books about Australia. Books about tropical plants, sailing ships, naval battles, Captain Cook's voyages of discovery, the American Revolution, and the Napoleonic Wars. I wasn't sure how the poetry of Wordsworth and the history of the Isle of Man fit into the *Bounty* saga, but I had no doubt I'd soon find out if I didn't figure out a way to steer the conversation in the direction I wanted.

Inspiration struck when I spotted a copy of a familiar book: *The Bounty: The True Story of the Mutiny on the Bounty,* by Caroline Alexander.

"Oh my goodness!" I exclaimed. "You're reading Alexander's book about the *Bounty*! You *must* talk to Dad about it. He's been urging me to read it for years, so he'd have someone to discuss it with."

"Why yes!" His face lit up. "Do you know what I find the most interesting aspect of the whole thing?"

"Not another word!" I held up my hands as if stopping traffic. "No spoilers! Not till I've read it. And I'm going to take this as a sign that I should have done so long ago. I can drop by this evening and borrow Dad's copy, and meanwhile I'll see if I can get him out here so the two of you can have a discussion."

Dad might refuse to be diverted from his crime reenactment project, but if I could manage to rekindle his passion for rehashing the history of the *Bounty,* even if only for an afternoon, life would be much more peaceful for so many people around us.

"In fact, I could go to get him now." I took a large gulp of my lemonade and stood up.

"No, no," Dr. Womble said. "Do stay — you haven't even had one of Emma's cookies."

"That's true." I sat down again. "And I did come by for a reason. May I pick your brain about something?"

He nodded. So I reached into the box, pulled out the letter from Archie, and handed it to him.

CHAPTER 26

He looked at the letter and sighed. A melancholy expression replaced his eager excitement.

"Poor man," he said.

"Archie van der Lynden?"

He nodded. He reached over to the plate containing the orange peels, snagged the paring knife, cleaned it off on his sweater, and used it to slice open the envelope.

He pulled out a sheet of ruled paper that had obviously been torn from a spiral-bound notebook, all the messy little paper tags falling off it. He read it slowly, and then handed it to me.

Archie's handwriting was large and sprawling, and the lines slanted downward, ignoring the thin blue rules. The letter read:

Dear Dr. Womble: Here at Inchness doing a little tune up, ha ha! The cigar thing fell thru, but I've got something better lined up for when I get out. If you want to make an investment, say the word, but if not, don't worry, the new plan's a sure thing and I hope to pay you back real soon. Yours, Archie.

"Cigar thing?" I asked.

"Some plan to take advantage of Cuba being open to tourism to import fine cigars more cheaply," Dr. Womble said. "I don't quite understand the details."

"I think that's what you'd call smuggling," I said. "I hope you didn't invest in it."

"Oh, I never invest in any of Archie's projects," he said, displaying more common sense than I'd have expected. "I lend him money from time to time — at least we call it lending. I'm sure he really does intend to pay it back."

He sipped his lemonade and seemed lost in sad contemplation. I considered several subtle ways of asking my next question and finally decided just to blurt it out.

"Do you have any idea where he is now?" I asked. "Because the chief wants to talk to him. As do I."

"Probably still at Inchness," Dr. Womble said. "It's a residential rehabilitation center for drug and alcohol dependency. He's been a patient there on and off for years now, and for the last ten years they've let him work there as a custodian. Which works out splendidly, because they can keep an eye on

272

him, and readmit him as soon as he starts to relapse. But still — very sad. He showed such promise as a young man. Was it about Archie you came to see me?"

"Partly," I said. "I had a few other questions, too. In all your years at Trinity, you've seen a lot of things that could have a bearing on Mr. Hagley's murder."

"Poor man." Dr. Womble shook his head. "I'll tell you anything I can. I can't share anything that would be covered by pastoral confidentiality, of course."

"Of course," I said. "Let's start with this: why did you arrange for the John Doe who was found at Trinity to be buried in our columbarium?"

I expected him be startled, but he only sighed. He took off his glasses and polished them on the bottom of his sweater, at approximately the same place where he'd cleaned off his paring knife. It didn't exactly feel like a delaying tactic — more like something he needed to do to gather himself for the effort of explaining — as if he needed to see as clearly as possible in order to explain clearly. But since the part of his sweater he'd used had evidently received contributions from more than one past meal, his earnest polishing didn't produce the results he expected.

"I only seem to have made things worse." He sighed, and gazed sadly at the glasses, as if deeply disappointed in them.

Was he talking only about the glasses, or was he sidling obliquely toward some deeper revelation?

"Let's see what I can do with those." I held out my hand for the glasses. "I fix up Dad's all the time."

He surrendered them willingly enough, though with a slightly surprised look. I snagged an ice cube from my lemonade, warmed it in my hand to produce a few drops of water, and used a paper napkin from the table to give the glasses a thorough cleaning, lenses, frames, and all.

"The John Doe," I prompted.

"Yes." He blinked owlishly at me. "It was in the winter sometime."

"January 12, 1995," I suggested. "At least that's the date inscribed on the John Doe's niche."

"January 12, 1995 it is, then," Dr. Womble said. "What a wonderful memory you have. Yes, and we were expecting rather a big snowstorm. I went to visit all my shut-ins, partly because I knew it might be a few days before I could get out to them again, and partly to make sure they had everything they needed to ride out the storm. And it took rather longer than I expected. Of course my shut-in visits usually do for some reason."

Actually, pretty much everything Dr. Womble did took longer than expected, even for those of us who were accustomed to his absentmindedness and distractibility. Books were usually the reason — books and conversations.

"It was very late — perhaps ten o'clock. I was coming back from Mrs. Petworth's house, and trying to decide whether to stop by Trinity to make sure everything was ready for the snow or just go straight home before the roads got worse, when I ran into Archie."

"Literally?" I asked.

"Very nearly. He was stumbling along the middle of the road a few blocks from Trinity and . . . well, he wasn't quite himself."

"Was he on drugs?" I asked.

"Only drink that day, as far as I could tell," he said. "Not that alcoholism is that much better than drug abuse, of course, except for the fact that you're not actually breaking the law when you buy spirits. And of course, the drug use followed all too soon. At that time he'd only been out of prison a few months, and a few of us were trying to help him make a new start. Not very successfully, as it turned out."

His face fell as if Archie's plummet from grace were entirely his fault. I thought of telling him it wasn't, but sensed that the question could very well spark a long, philosophical discussion on the nature of responsibility that, however fascinating, wouldn't bring me any closer to knowing what had happened either thirty years or two days ago. Fortunately I'd had some experience steering Dr. Womble back on track.

"So what did you do when you almost ran into Archie in the middle of the snowstorm?"

"I stopped, of course," Dr. Womble said. "And coaxed him into the car. I tried to find out where he was staying — his mother had died a year or two before he got out of prison, so he couldn't have been staying with her. He was rather vague about his plans, and after a bit, I came to the realization that perhaps he was embarrassed because he apparently hadn't made any arrangements about where to stay and had no money for either a room or a bus ticket out of town. He ended up in our guest room for a few weeks until I managed to get him into a residential substance abuse program."

A few weeks? Dr. Womble was a very good man, but Emma Womble had to be a saint for putting up with him all these years.

"At the Inchness Center?" I pointed to the return address on Archie's letter.

"It might have been," Dr. Womble said. "I'm afraid I don't remember. It was so long ago — and only the first of many such stays, unfortunately. Such a sad story — a young man you'd have thought would have a bright future ahead of him. And yet his whole life was blighted by one unfortunate mistake."

I was tempted to suggest that the fake jewel robbery probably wasn't Archie's first or only mistake, not by a long shot. Or that attempting to organize a complicated if unsuccessful plot to defraud an insurance company of several million dollars wasn't exactly the sort of mistake that a basically honest and well-intentioned young man would stumble into all that easily. And to point out that Archie's involvement with substance use appeared to have preceded the jewel robbery, since the person he originally tried to recruit to perform it was his drug dealer. But none of those comments would get me any closer to getting an answer to my question. And did all this have something to do with the John Doe, or had Dr. Womble forgotten my question and veered back onto Archie?

"Very sad," I said, "but I don't quite get what this has to do with John Doe being buried at Trinity."

"Oh, yes." Dr. Womble frowned and sat up straighter in his chair as if making a strenuous effort to get himself back on track. "Well, Archie was quite agitated. Kept calling me a good Samaritan and babbling about being attacked on the road to Jericho and killing fatted calves and — well quite a mishmash of vaguely Biblical-themed ravings. He did look as if he'd been in a bit of a scuffle, but unfortunately I made the understandable assumption that he was speaking metaphorically, and that in reality he'd gone a few rounds with the asphalt roadway." He smiled wryly.

"Why unfortunately?"

"Because he was, after a fashion, telling the truth. Apparently he'd gone out to Trinity to visit his mother's grave. This was before we started worrying about vandalism and locking up the columbarium. In fact, it was right after this that we did start locking it up — I thought that way people would have to come to the office in the daytime to get the key, and we'd have less chance of people tripping and hurting themselves in the churchyard."

"Or being mugged there," I suggested.

"That too." He nodded. "Anyway, Archie told me that while he was leaving the crypt after visiting his mother's grave, and somewhat distracted with grief, someone waylaid him in the graveyard; they'd fought, but Archie was able to escape. He was so . . . agitated and incoherent that at first I assumed he'd hallucinated the attack — he seemed rather confused about whether it was a man who had attacked him or a polar bear. And the next day he woke up so hysterical that for a while we thought he was having delirium tremens. He was quite obsessed with fear that the man who attacked him could have followed us home. So to calm him I went down to Trinity. I expected to find absolutely nothing — and instead, I found an unidentified man lying dead in the graveyard. A rather large man in a bulky white down jacket."

He stopped and stared into the distance, as if seeing it all over again.

"What did you do?"

"Called the police, of course. And then, God help me, I went inside, called Emma, and told her to reassure Archie that he could rest easy because his assailant was dead."

"And how much of this did you tell the police?"

"Almost none of it. I reported finding the body, of course. But for the rest — I thought I'd wait and see."

"Wait and see what?"

"Who the man was. And how he'd died. I was afraid that if they knew Archie was involved, they'd jump to all sorts of conclusions. Assume the worst. He was out on parole, you see, and they might have sent him back to finish his sentence. Even if they didn't, I was afraid the experience would derail him just as he was trying to make a new start. So I decided to wait, at least until the medical examiner had finished his autopsy and announced the results." His face was drawn and anxious, as if he was still waiting for the autopsy.

"And what did it reveal?"

"Accidental death." His face cleared slightly. "He'd been somewhat intoxicated, which probably caused him to stumble. He'd hit his head on a headstone, lapsed into unconsciousness, and frozen to death. So Archie wasn't to blame."

I wondered if he'd ever considered that the medical examiner might have reached an entirely different verdict if he'd known Archie had been there. Would John Doe's wounds still have looked like accidental death if the medical examiner knew the deceased had been fighting with someone? Tripping and hitting your head on a gravestone was one thing; getting shoved into it was another. And who had been medical examiner in Caerphilly back then — had it been someone like Dad, who was almost too ready to suspect homicide? Or someone who would be quick to close the book on what looked like the accidental death of a drunken vagrant? Yes, if Dr. Womble had revealed what he knew, Archie would probably have been questioned and might even have been charged with . . . what? Self-defense? Justifiable homicide? Involuntary manslaughter? Not being one of those many family lawyers, I had no idea. But he'd have been charged with something, and maybe the charges would have been valid.

I could understand why Dr. Womble had worried about derailing Archie's efforts to rebuild his life. But by the sound of it, Archie had managed to derail himself just fine without any help from the Caerphilly PD.

I suspected Dr. Womble had already thought of these points. Even if he hadn't, what good would it do to reproach him with them after more than twenty years?

"You don't think maybe Archie could have helped figure out who the John Doe was?" I asked instead.

"I showed him the picture," Dr. Womble said. "He didn't know the poor man. Even so, the shock of being attacked and then learning that his assailant had frozen to death had a profound impact on him. It shocked him into . . . well . . . ."

"Sobriety?" I suggested.

"Well, no. But into a recognition of the need to make serious changes in his life. So I did everything I could to get him into a decent treatment program. As I said, I can't remember if it was at Inchness or someplace else, but I made sure it was a very reliable place. That helped me get over the guilt."

"Guilt about what?"

"That I hadn't managed to save that poor unknown soul." Dr. Womble looked stricken. "If I'd been more diligent about my stewardship of Trinity — I should have gone there to check that everything was battened down before the storm. Or if I'd done a better job of getting information out of Archie. In either case, maybe I'd have found the poor man before he succumbed to the elements."

"Since Mrs. Womble was probably already worried sick about you being out in a snowstorm, I think you did the right thing by going straight home," I said. "And maybe if you had stopped by the church, some other less careful driver would have literally run over Archie. And don't expect me to give you a hard time about letting a poor drunk sleep it off unmolested. How were you supposed to know that someone's life depended on a bit of information hidden in an alcoholic's fuzzy brain?"

"You sound like the bishop." Dr. Womble chuckled softly. "And yes, I understand that it's a little morbid of me, dwelling on it like that. I don't usually — or I didn't until recent events brought it so forcefully back into my mind. But you did ask me why I arranged to have the poor dead man buried here at Trinity. It seemed the least I could do. And when I told Archie about it, he insisted on contributing what he could."

"I gather that wasn't much."

"Not really." Dr. Womble shook his head. "Sadly, his mother lost all her money before her death. Archie did have some income thanks to a trust fund from his grandfather Van der Lynden, but that was quite modest even thirty years ago."

"And I doubt if old Mr. Van der Lynden made provision for inflation," I said.

"Probably not," Dr. Womble agreed. "Though he did make provision for Archie's . . . feckless character. The trust was set up so Archie could never touch the principal. Not if he lived to be a hundred. So as the cost of living increased, he struggled until the maintenance job at Inchness came through."

I found myself wondering if Dr. Womble had had something to do with the maintenance job coming through.

"What about Paul Blair?" I asked. "Who returned to Caerphilly as P. Jefferson Blair. You arranged for his niche, too, didn't you?"

"Oh, yes." Dr. Womble nodded. "It was the least I could do. I wasn't able to save Jeff, you see. He was so unhappy — the estrangement from his family, the ruin of his intended career. The loneliness — he assumed no one would want a relationship with someone who had a prison record, and wouldn't give anyone a chance to change his mind."

"The police report said he was killed by accident while cleaning his gun."

"And even I know better than to take that at face value. No, it was suicide, and I failed to prevent it."

"So you paid for his niche."

"No, actually the college did. I suppose you could say I blackmailed them into it."

He looked curiously pleased with himself.

CHAPTER 27

"Blackmailed the college?" I liked his style. "How?"

"I found the syllabus of a class he was teaching that semester — I think it was called 'The Literature of Despair.' Every single writer on the reading list was someone who had committed suicide. Thomas Chatterton, Hart Crane, Ernest Hemingway, Sylvia Plath, Richard Brautigan, Carolyn Heilbrun, James Tiptree Jr., Virginia Woolf — I forget who else, but you get the idea."

"Sounds like a cry for help," I said.

"And one the college completely ignored. So I talked to the dean of the English Department and implied that I'd be talking to an attorney about the possibility of legal action. They managed to find the money to bury him properly and pay off his debts so his family wouldn't have to."

He smiled beatifically.

"How did you ever think of that?" I asked.

"I didn't, actually. A friend of Jeff's did."

"Let me guess — Professor James Donovan."

"How did you know?" Dr. Womble beamed. "Such a loyal friend. Of course we had to keep his part in it secret. He was working to get tenure, you see."

Yes, I could see. And even today Donovan might not be all that crazy about having his part in it revealed. Well, his secret would be safe with me.

"Look," I said. "You need to tell the chief about all this."

Dr. Womble looked stricken.

"Why?" he asked. "It's all ancient history. How can any of it have anything to do with poor Mr. Hagley's murder?"

"It may not," I said. "But what you've just told me could clear up a lot of the chief's unanswered questions. Questions that he's spending valuable time to answer when he could be spending that time on things that *are* related to the murder."

There was also the possibility that some of it might have everything to do with the murder. I couldn't see how, but then I wasn't the chief.

Dr. Womble still looked unhappy.

"How about if you let me tell him?" I suggested. "I could explain that it all came up in our discussion over what to do about everybody's ashes, and you had no idea any of it might be related to the murder."

"I suppose that would do," he said.

"And if Archie gets in touch with you, please see if you can get an address or a phone number for him," I said. "Or at least tell him we're trying to reach him. I need to confirm what he wants done about his mother's ashes, and the chief wants to talk to him so he can clear him of any suspicion in the murder."

Or see if he was implicated in the murder, but no sense worrying Dr. Womble about that.

"I'll try," he said. "Did I hear correctly that they found some of the missing jewelry in the crypt?"

"We found a ring," I said. "No idea if it's one of Mrs. Van der Lynden's jewels or a piece of costume jewelry someone dropped, but I suspect the chief's eager to talk to Archie about that, too."

Dr. Womble nodded.

"And I'll let Dad know you're eager to talk about the *Bounty*." Probably a good idea to distract him before he had second thoughts about sharing information.

So I endured twenty minutes or so of Dr. Womble's new enthusiasm. Under any other circumstances I'd have said *enjoyed* rather than *endured,* but I was impatient to share what I'd learned with the chief. So, fascinating as I found Dr. Womble's thoughts on the difference between jackfruit and breadfruit, the sinister connection between the *Bounty*'s mission and the slave economy in the West Indies, and his assertion that the mutineers who escaped hanging appeared to have done so less by proving their innocence than by hiring persuasive attorneys and using their aristocratic contacts — I was relieved when Emma Womble appeared to announce that Father Shakespeare had arrived to see him.

"I'll dash right out to welcome him." Dr. Womble suited the action to the words, and would have overturned the lemonade pitcher if both Mrs. Womble and I hadn't reached out to steady it.

"Father Shakespeare?" I queried. "Is that a real name?"

"Seems to be," she said. "He's tomorrow's supply priest — and an old friend of Rufus's. He's going to stay the night with us. They'll be up all night, talking over their exciting days in Selma and Montgomery."

"Wow," I said. "I remember hearing that Dr. Womble was active in the Civil Rights movement. I didn't know how active. He didn't tell me a thing about it when I tried to interview him for the parish newsletter a few months ago. Maybe I could get enough out of Father Shakespeare for another article."

"Catch him after services tomorrow," she said. "Right now he's taking Rufus fishing. And I'd better get a casserole ready, in case they spend so much time talking that they forget to bait their hooks."

I thanked her for the lemonade, and made only a token protest when she gave me a tin containing several dozen cookies for the boys.

Then I hurried back to my car. I picked up my phone to call the chief — but no. This merited an in-person visit. I called Michael to warn him I'd be a little later than planned.

"No problem," he said. "Ferreting out the town's most sensational secrets is bound to take a little time."

"Yes, and maybe not even possible, considering that most of the people who might know anything are dead."

"True — what was it Ben Franklin said? 'Two can keep a secret only if one of them is dead.' "

"Actually, what he said was, 'Three may keep a secret, if two of them are dead.' Trust me; I once won a family trivia competition with that, and it's stuck with me."

" 'Two can keep a secret' is catchier. Although not all that apropos, I suppose — you've run into way more than two people keeping secrets, and most of them are dead now. Besides — no Josh, we're not talking about the toucan. We're talking about Benjamin Franklin. . . . No, that's Ulysses S. Grant. Franklin is on the hundred-dollar bill . . . Okay, I'll show you, the next time I have both a fifty- and a hundred-dollar bill in my wallet."

"You might warn him not to hold his breath," I said with a chuckle. "I should go — I want to catch the chief. See you soon."

I drove back to town and dropped by the police station. I found Vern Shiffley sitting behind the front desk.

"Is the chief in?" I asked. "I wanted to share what I learned from Dr. Womble."

"He's in," Vern said. "And in a pretty cheerful mood for a change. Guess who our John Doe is probably going to turn out to be?"

I shook my head.

"Aaron Hempel," he said. "Younger brother of Bart Hempel, who in case you don't recognize the name was the ringleader of the jewel thieves."

"The one who's still in prison for the murder of Fitz Marshall?"

"He got out about six weeks ago," Vern said. "There's a statewide BOLO out on him. In fact, weirdly enough, we'd already put out a BOLO on Bart before we knew the John Doe was his brother."

"Because he got out of prison just before Mr. Hagley was murdered?" I asked.

"No, although we were kind of interested in talking to him for that reason. But we got really interested after Horace entered one of the bullets he recovered from your van into IBIS. The Integrated Ballistic Identification System," he added, remembering that I was a civilian.

"He got a match?"

"To a bullet recovered from a 1977 drug case down in Richmond," Vern said. "A case in which Bart Hempel was one of the major suspects."

He beamed as if he'd shared some fabulous news. Yeah, right. Was it supposed to cheer me, knowing that the person who'd taken a potshot at me was a convicted murderer, a known drug dealer, and a hardened ex-con?

"Fascinating," I managed to say aloud.

"I'll let the chief know you're here," Vern said.

The chief was indeed in a good mood, and my account of my conversation with Dr. Womble only seemed to improve it.

"It's coming together," he said. "In no small part thanks to the information you've shared. I've already been in contact with the Lee County Sheriff's Department. This Inchness place may be prohibited by HIPAA from talking about their patients, but if Archie's an employee, the door's wide open. I wish Dr. Womble had been more forthcoming at the time about Archie's encounter with his assailant in the graveyard, but I can understand his reluctance. Because yes, from what I know of how the department functioned in 1994, Archie might not have gotten a very fair hearing."

"Then again, if they'd known Archie was involved, they might have thought to show the John Doe's picture to Bart Hempel."

"Actually, according to the case file, they made a special trip up to Culpeper to do just that, because the part of the churchyard where they found the body was right outside the columbarium that contained Mrs. Van der Lynden's ashes, and they were still gung ho to solve the jewel robbery," the chief said. "And the picture they'd have shown him looked almost identical to his brother's mug shot picture from a DUI arrest a few months earlier, so I'll be interested in hearing why Mr. Hempel failed to recognize it."

"Maybe Bart Hempel was behind the attack on Archie," I suggested. "And was afraid if he identified his brother they'd realize he was involved."

"Although he was in no particular danger, as it turns out, since neither Archie nor Dr. Womble ever reported the attack."

"Well, keep me posted if it looks as if I'll have a chance to talk to Archie or Bart Hempel about their relatives' ashes," I said. "Meanwhile I'm going to see if I can keep Dad's latest project from interfering in your investigation."

"His latest project?" The chief's face had taken on a wary look.

"He wants to do a reenactment of the 1987 robbery," I said. "He thinks it will provide valuable clues to what really happened to the jewelry."

"Is he serious? After thirty years, the possibility of substantial renovations by one or both of the two owners who followed Mrs. Van der Lynden, and Heaven knows how many freelance treasure hunters combing the grounds? Because Lacey wasn't the only one, just the most obsessive. And do you really want to get involved?"

"I don't want to get involved, but I figure

he's going to do it whether I help him or not, so I want to keep an eye on the whole thing. And try to prevent it from interfering in your murder investigation. If I can get him and Ragnar so involved in planning the reenactment that they don't get around to having it for however many days it takes for you to wrap up your case, I figure that would be useful."

"Very."

"Also, I'm going to try to convince them that if you heard about their plan you would take a dim view of it."

"I do take a dim view of it," the chief said. "That doesn't mean there's anything I can do to stop them."

"Yes, but if I imply that there is, it will be much easier to keep them out of your hair. Do you really want them to show up asking to see the case file?"

"Good point," he said. "Although if it came to that, I'd refer them to Fred Singer, who should still have the complete copy of the case file we gave him when he wrote that article in December."

"Duly noted." I stood up and slung my tote over my shoulder. "And since Dad's already in touch with Fred, he may already have it. So if you need me for anything, I'll probably be out at Ragnar's farm, trying to inject some small note of sanity into the reenactment plans."

"Better you than me," the chief said.

I paused at the door and turned around.

"Look, I gather you're thinking it was probably Bart Hempel who took a shot at me last night," I said. "Any chance you could let me know when you've got him in custody? I think I'll feel more secure."

"Absolutely," the chief said. "In fact, check with Vern on the way out — we're expecting news momentarily."

When I reached the front desk, Vern was on the phone — with a police officer in another jurisdiction, I deduced. I tried to look as if I was merely waiting rather than actively eavesdropping.

"We appreciate it, Fred," he was saying. "And if there's ever anything we can do for you, just say the word. Well, no, we don't get *that* many fugitives up here, but the ones we do get stick out like a sore thumb, so it's pretty easy to catch 'em. You bet. Bye."

"On the trail of Hempel?" I asked.

"Yup." Vern beamed. "We asked the police down in Hampton and Newport News and nearby jurisdictions to check out his old haunts and known associates. We weren't optimistic — after all, if you get yourself sent to prison for twenty-five or thirty years, when you come out you're gonna find that your favorite haunts have fallen to the wrecking ball, and most of your known associates have either died or gone to prison themselves. But we lucked out — Virginia Beach just confirmed that they've picked him up."

"Good news, then."

"Yup." Vern leaned back in his chair and let a broad grin cross his face. "Let's hope it's all over but the interrogating."

"Congratulations."

I went back to my car. And when I got there, I texted Dad.

"So when would you like to go to Ragnar's?"

I slipped the phone into the compartment in the center console, hoping Dad was off doing something so absorbing that he wouldn't even look at his phone for a few hours. Or that he'd lost interest in the idea of holding his reenactment. Or —

My phone buzzed.

"Can you pick me up now?"

CHAPTER 28

The fact that Dad had texted back almost immediately wasn't a good sign. He'd probably been hunched over his phone waiting to hear from me. Which meant his obsession with the idea of reenacting the jewel robbery was pretty intense.

I sighed, texted back, "OK," and started the car.

"I'm at Trinity," he added.

When I got to the church I found Mother and several other ladies from the Altar Guild getting the sanctuary ready for the next morning's services. They seemed delighted to see me arrive to collect Dad, which probably meant he'd been trying too hard to make himself useful.

"I only wish we knew for sure the supply priest will actually show up," Mother fretted, as she frowned at a vase of lilies that seemed determined to droop more than she considered suitable.

"Why wouldn't he?" I asked. Was Dr. Womble apt to lead Father Shakespeare astray, taking him fishing on Sunday morning?

"Mr. Hagley was the one arranging the supply priests this quarter," she said. "And we can't exactly ask him if he booked one before getting himself knocked off, can we? I think the diocese frowns on séances."

She sounded positively testy.

"If it will make you feel any better, a Father Shakespeare arrived at the Wombles while I was there," I said. "And Mrs. Womble said he was tomorrow's supply priest."

"Thank you, dear," Mother said. "That puts my mind at ease."

"It doesn't entirely put mine at ease," one of the other ladies said. "That name sounds familiar — haven't we had him before?"

"I think you're right," Mother said. "I wonder if he's the cheerful one with the lovely Australian accent."

"If Junius Hagley booked him, it's probably the one who always sounds as if he has a bad head cold," the other lady said. "The officious one."

"He's a friend of Dr. Womble's," I said. "So my money's on the cheerful Aussie. Come on, Dad. Let's go see Ragnar."

Ragnar's farm — an estate, really, though Ragnar always referred to it as "the farm" — was a few miles out of town. I started off the journey telling Dad about Dr. Womble's newfound fascination with the *Bounty*, in hopes of distracting him from the reenactment project, but it didn't work. He sat on the edge of his seat, peering ahead, until Ragnar's front gates came in sight.

"Here we are," Dad exclaimed. "Start visualizing. It's New Year's Eve, and we're going to a masked ball."

He sat up straight and half closed his eyes, the better to superimpose 1987 over the present day.

I kept my eyes wide open, which tended to improve my driving.

Two large brick pillars flanked the asphalt driveway leading into what was now Ragnar's house. I had no idea if the pillars had even existed in 1987, but in Mrs. Winkleson's day, they'd been painted white. One of Ragnar's first improvements — to his mind, at least — had been to paint them an inky matte black. He'd also replaced the round white concrete balls that had previously topped the pillars with large, menacing gray gargoyles. The black wrought-iron gate was a holdover from Mrs. Winkleson's reign, allowed to stay because it was, after all, black and made of wrought iron, one of Ragnar's favorite things in the universe. But unbeknownst to the gate, its days were numbered. Ragnar wanted it replaced with a larger and much more elaborate gate. With dragons. So far I'd done forty-seven trial designs for the dragon gates, and Ragnar had pronounced my latest effort almost perfect. I was guardedly optimistic about achieving perfection with sketch forty-eight or forty-nine, but lately helping Robyn had taken up most the time I'd have usually spent either at my anvil or with my sketch pad.

The gates stood wide open — another change from Mrs. Winkleson's day. She'd have made us wait at the gate until one of her overworked staff finally noticed the buzzer. According to the newspaper reports, Mrs. Van der Lynden had stationed James Washington here for security on the night of the New Year's ball. So did that mean the wrought-iron gates had been here at the time of the robbery? Even if they had, they wouldn't have been much of a barrier. A moderately active jewel thief could have climbed them easily. And that was assuming it was dark and he failed to notice that to the right and left of the pillars only an ordinary barbed wire fence barred the way.

I suspected Dad probably had a romantic vision of our local jewel robbers scuttling over the red tile roofs of a Mediterranean villa, like Cary Grant in *To Catch a Thief.* So far I couldn't see that the crime would have challenged the physical abilities of the most sedentary crook.

I paused in the gateway and contemplated the gates for a moment.

"What's wrong?" Dad asked.

"Nothing's wrong," I said. "I'm just studying the gates."

"We can get out if you like, so you can get a closer look."

"I don't need a closer look," I said. "I've repaired them several times. For what it's worth, I think they're old enough to have been here in Mrs. Van der Lynden's time."

"Progress!" Dad beamed at the gates as if they'd done something useful and important.

I hoped he wasn't going to attempt anything truly annoying, like trying to talk Ragnar into painting the brick columns white and restoring the concrete balls.

"We should find out what Mrs. Van der Lynden called the place." I pointed to the black-and-gray plaque that proclaimed RAGNARSHEIM. Mrs. Winkleson had had a small black-and-white sign calling it RAVEN HILL.

"I'm not sure she called it anything." Dad frowned down at the pile of clippings in his lap. "All the newspapers just call it the stately mansion of the Van der Lynden family."

"Doesn't make for a very catchy sign. And the letters would be so small you'd have trouble reading them," I added, remembering the tiny type they'd had to use to fit Beatrice Helen Falkenhausen van der Lynden on the plaque that had covered her niche.

"Archie van der Lynden would know," Dad said. "You could ask him when you talk to him about his mother's ashes."

"If the chief is ever able to put us in touch, I will."

We were following the asphalt driveway now as it curved gently to the left through lines of flowering cherry trees on either side. White cherry blossoms drifted down onto the windshield and eventually fell off as we made our slow way along the lane. Beyond the cherry trees I could see fields of white daffodils, white daisies, white flowers whose names escaped me — Mrs. Winkleson had imposed a rigid black-and-white color scheme on the whole estate, so all the flowers were white. Ragnar had largely left this aspect of the landscaping alone, initially because Mother Nature didn't make many flowers in black and gray, his favorite colors. Nearer the house he'd added in a few blood-red roses and poppies, and he'd set aside one part of the formal gardens for experimentation with black flowers. But he'd become reconciled to the white flowers after noticing how eerie they looked by moonlight.

"All this would have been dark when the guests were arriving," Dad announced. He was frowning, apparently at the landscape's rebellious inability to conform to the picture in his mind's eye. "Look! There's Ragnar's gardener. One of his gardeners, anyway. He must need several." He pointed to a man standing on a ladder, pruning one of the cherry trees. "I don't suppose there's any real reason to interrogate Ragnar's staff." He looked wistful, as if he thought interrogating the gardener might be rather fun.

I took my eyes off the road long enough to glance over at the pruner.

"That's not a gardener," I said. "That's Fred something-or-other. Former bandmate of Ragnar's — I forget which band. Bass player. Ragnar takes in strays, as he puts it. Human strays."

"He has a lot of needy friends, then?"

"Friends, friends of friends, random acquaintances he picks up at concerts or in the bookstore or the coffeehouse. I'm not even sure he knows where some of them came from. I've never been out here when Ragnar didn't have at least a dozen people staying with him for however long it takes them to get back on their feet."

"Back on their feet?" Dad twisted in his seat to keep his eyes on the pruner we'd just passed. "Not physically, I hope."

"Sometimes. I remember one guest who'd broken his leg, and since he lived in a fifth-floor walkup in Brooklyn he stayed here until he was back in action. Quite a lot of them are down-on-their-luck musicians or actors between gigs. Artists who can't afford studio space. Guys whose wives or girlfriends have thrown them out. The occasional drunk or addict trying to clean up his act — if Ragnar ever needed work, he'd make an awesome sober companion. And of course he usually does have employees, although their numbers vary greatly for no apparent reason, but it's hard to tell them from the guests, which can be disconcerting."

"Why?" Dad frowned. "It all sounds wonderful."

"It is," I said. "But all the same, if I'm asking someone to hold the ladder while I install a wrought-iron chandelier, I want to know if he's on salary or in withdrawal."

"Oh, dear," Dad murmured. "I can understand."

"Still, they're mostly harmless. He doesn't get many bad apples — just people who, as he puts it, need a little more time to find themselves." Of course, some of his guests had been looking — not all that diligently, from what I could see — for years. But since Ragnar required them to perform at least a small amount of useful work, the complete deadbeats tended to depart rather quickly. And Ragnar, who was a sociable creature, could always be assured of finding someone — usually at least half-a-dozen someones — to keep him company whenever he wanted it, and help out with whatever new project had caught his fancy.

"He's a good egg," I said aloud.

Dad nodded, and returned to squinting at the scenery.

I wondered if I could manage to leave Dad here to plot his reenactment with Ragnar's help. And immediately felt guilty. Dad got such a lot of pleasure out of things like this, and if I hadn't been busy, I'd have really enjoyed helping him. But I was busy. And —

"Oh, look!"

CHAPTER 29

"Look at what?" I had slammed on the brakes in case Dad was pointing out something in the road ahead of us.

"Oh, dear — I didn't mean to startle you," Dad said. "It's just that the swans and the gazebo look so beautiful in the sunlight."

"Yes, they do." I set the car in motion again.

Dad was craning his neck to get a better view to our left where, beyond the cherry trees, was a lake presided over by a small flock of beautiful and evil-tempered black swans. Some of them were swimming serenely over the surface of the lake, while the rest perched on the black wrought-iron railings of the glossy black gazebo. I nodded at the nice effect I'd achieved with the railings. I'd have felt guilty replacing all the intricate white wooden fretwork that used to grace the gazebo with wrought iron if not for the fact that the swans liked to sit on the

307

wooden railings while using the gazebo as their privy — which meant the only time the fretwork had looked nice was for a couple of hours after one of Mrs. Winkleson's long-suffering maids had scrubbed it. From what I could remember, there seemed to have been a staff member whose full-time job was cleaning up after the swans. Ragnar took a more laissez-faire approach to the gazebo, which meant we all mostly enjoyed it from afar.

In the fields I could see a few of the black-and-white belted Galloway cows that had presumably come with the farm, but Ragnar also added quite a number of black Angus cows. And there were several new additions to the herd — yet another breed of black cows, of course. The newcomers bore enormous sweeping semi-circular horns that made them look like cartoon Vikings in exaggerated helmets.

"Slow down a bit," Dad ordered, pointing to the Viking cows. "Could those be Camargue cattle?" Dad had become quite fascinated with heritage animal breeds.

"You'll have to ask Ragnar," I said.

We also saw humans dotting the landscape. A gray-haired woman sitting on a stool in front of an easel — probably a guest. A tall, rangy man in blue jeans and a straw cowboy hat mending the barbed wire that kept the cows off the road — could be employee or guest. A pudgy figure trudging toward the swan-bespattered gazebo with a bucket in one hand and a scrub brush in the other — an employee, I fervently hoped.

Dad might be regretting the landscape's refusal to re-create a late December evening, but I decided that if Mrs. Winkleson were around to see her former home, no doubt she'd be reasonably pleased with how little Ragnar had done to change the black-and-white color scheme of the grounds. A much greater proportion of black than before, but she'd probably have found that acceptable.

The house, though, would have given her fits. I paused in the drive for a moment right at the foot of the sweeping marble stairs that led up to the front portico. In Mrs. Winkleson's time, the steps had been bare, unadorned, and a little intimidating. Nothing had interrupted the impressive sweep of the marble until you reached the portico above, where two stately marble urns flanked the top of the steps, each holding a boxwood shrub that looked just a little too small for its setting, as if cowed by all the marble.

Now the steps were lined on either side

by elaborate statues of dragons and castles and armored warriors.

"Oh, dear," Dad said. "That's going to make an authentic re-creation of the start of the party rather difficult."

I stifled the urge to ask who cared about the start of the party — wasn't it the actual jewel robbery we were interested in?

"You mean the statues?" I asked.

"Yes." Dad brooded. "I assume they're fixed in place somehow."

"Actually, they're not," I said. "They're chess pieces. The back terrace has a giant chessboard made of black and white marble tiles, and when he wants to have an outdoor game, he just gets everybody to help him haul all the statues around to the back terrace."

"I see." Dad nodded and narrowed his eyes again. Hard to tell if he was still trying to visualize the arrival of Mrs. Van der Lynden's guests or if he'd detoured into visualizing Ragnar and his motley crew of guests hauling the life-sized statues up the marble steps.

While he was pondering, I set the car in motion again. We pulled into the parking lot, which was screened from the front door by a tall brick wall, painted black and topped with an intricate menacing sort of iron fretwork I'd devised, kind of a cross between spikes and oversized barbed wire. Ragnar had loved it, calling it exactly what Sauron would have wanted for the walls of Mordor. I was just glad that so far he'd only had me install it on a few highly visible walls that no one would ever have needed to climb to get anyplace they wanted to go.

"Let's take the elevator," I suggested as we got out of the car.

"He's installed an elevator?" Dad did not seem pleased.

"It was there when he came," I said. "No idea if Mrs. Winkleson installed it or if it was already there when she moved in."

I parked the car as close as I could to the row of vine-covered trellises that spanned the whole parking lot on the side closest to the house. Underneath the vines, you could make out that the trellises were still painted white, probably because Ragnar didn't have the heart to disturb the vines enough to paint them black. Then I led the way through a break in the trellises to the little covered porch they sheltered. At one end of the porch was a door that had been painted to look like a well-weathered castle postern. A small grotesque gargoyle head was mounted to the right of the door. I flipped the gargoyle up to reveal a modern key pad, typed in the proper code, and nodded with satisfaction when an audible click confirmed that the door was unlocked.

Dad had opened the door to the back seat and was reaching inside for something. His black medical bag, I assumed, though I had no idea why he couldn't just leave it in my car. It wasn't as if Ragnar didn't have first aid kits. But before I could speak up, he emerged holding something other than the medical bag. A brown leather briefcase. No doubt I'd find out its purpose in due time.

"This way." I held the door open and gestured for him to enter.

Before us lay a long corridor that looked like the ancient stone passageway of some medieval dungeon, broken at intervals by well-weathered cell doors. Iron torch holders flanked each door and studded the walls at intervals. If you looked closely, you could tell that the stone floor and walls were painted and the torch flames were fake, but still, it was a great illusion.

"Where does this go?" Dad asked.

"Where doesn't it go?" I headed down the corridor at a slow pace, to allow for the fact that Dad was doing more gawking than walking. "That branch to the right goes to the loading dock. Farther down is a side corridor to the mechanical room — boilers, water heaters, and such. In addition to the passenger elevator on this end, there's also a dumbwaiter farther down to haul supplies to the kitchen. There's a side passage that leads to the garage. And eventually you come out into the back garden."

"Was this all here back in 1987?"

"No idea." I shrugged as I hit the elevator button. "It was all here when Ragnar came. He just repainted it to his taste."

"This place is like a sieve," Dad muttered. "How can we possibly trace the movement of the robbers with all these possible escape routes down here?"

"And wait till you see all the doors and French windows upstairs."

The elevator doors opened and I stepped inside.

Dad hesitated, clutching his briefcase to his chest.

"Do we just barge in?" he asked. "Shouldn't we let Ragnar know we're about to pop out in the middle of his living room?"

"His front hall, actually." I planted my thumb on the elevator door's open button. "The security code I typed in is the guest code — it sends a message to Ragnar's phone, and if he likes he can see who's entering through the cameras hidden in those torch sconces. Get inside before the

313

buzzer goes off."

"This is impossible." Dad stepped inside. His shoulders drooped and his face wore a despondent look.

I took pity on him.

"Chin up," I said. "It's not as if we were trying to re-create the robbery for the boringly literal minds of a television audience. We only need to re-create it in our minds, the better to assist our little gray cells."

I narrowed my eyes as I said this, and tapped my forehead solemnly. Dad nodded and narrowed his eyes to match mine, but he didn't look very encouraged.

The elevator door opened to reveal Ragnar, resplendent in faded jeans, heavy boots, and a black t-shirt from the 2003 European tour of Sinister Vegetation, one of the many now-defunct heavy metal bands in which he'd played. He flung his arms out in exuberant welcome.

"Meg! Dr. Langslow! You're — Is something wrong? Is the septic field acting up again?"

"Nothing wrong as far as I know." Ragnar and I exchanged hugs. "Has your septic field been acting up lately?"

"No, but you both had really funny expressions on your faces. As if you smelled something bad."

"We were visualizing." Dad narrowed his eyes to demonstrate. "We want to reenact the jewel robbery. So we're trying to see our surroundings as they would have been in 1987."

"Ah." Ragnar narrowed his own eyes and peered around for a few moments. Then he sighed, shook his head, and opened his eyes wide again.

"It only looks blurry to me," he said. "Evidently I am not very skilled at this visualization."

"That's okay." I patted his shoulder. "Neither are we."

"I brought along something to help with that." Dad lifted up the briefcase as if the mere sight of it would inspire us. Ragnar and I just blinked. "Is there someplace where we can spread out my papers?"

"The library." Ragnar turned to lead the way down the right-hand hallway. "So this reenactment — you mean to recreate the events of 1987? Like a play?"

"Exactly," Dad said. "And we will see what we can learn from them. Perhaps we will solve the mystery of the missing jewels."

"May I have a part?" Ragnar asked. "I would greatly like to portray a dangerous criminal. Ah, here we are."

He flung open the library door.

"Wow," Dad said as we entered the room. "Now that's a library."

What I'd taken for a pile of books in one corner shook slightly, and a slender young man in a faded gray sweatshirt and heavy glasses scuttled out, rather the way a silverfish would when you opened an old book.

"So sorry," he almost whispered as he slipped out of the room. "Didn't mean to intrude."

"It's okay, Hosmer," Ragnar called. "You can stay."

But Hosmer was long gone.

"One of your guests?" I asked.

"Hosmer alphabetizes the books," Ragnar explained. "His idea, not mine, but I have to admit, it's starting to be useful. I'd gotten to the point where I couldn't find anything."

"How long's he been here?"

"A few weeks, I guess." Ragnar shrugged. I suspected it was more like a few months.

I glanced over to see, not to my surprise, that Dad was happily planted in front of a shelf.

I'd been in Ragnar's library before, but this was Dad's first time, so discussion of the jewel robbery came to a halt for the time being while he explored the shelves. Understandable, since Ragnar's library was the real thing. Back in Mrs. Winkleson's day, the shelves had been largely filled with expensive knickknacks. A few hundred books had graced the shelves here and there, in clumps, but they'd clearly been bought by the yard for the effect — most of them were leather-bound with titles stamped in gold. Impressive from a distance, but close up you realized you were looking at the bound proceedings of early-twentieth-century medical symposia, five-volume novels by long-forgotten lady authors with three names, bowdlerized editions of Shakespeare, and obsolete legal texts.

Ragnar had filled the room with books. Real books, that looked as if they'd actually been read. Hosmer's scheme appeared to be to arrange everything alphabetically by author rather than trying to divide them up into subjects — not a bad system. It was easy to find things, and meant serendipity could lead to you a book you hadn't realized you wanted to read before you found it. And I enjoyed the incongruous juxtapositions — H. P. Lovecraft lurked just below Laura Lippman. John Donne leaned against John Gregory Dunne. Dashiell Hammett was flanked by Barbara Hambly and Charlaine Harris. Proust — in French — nestled next to Terry Pratchett.

It occurred to me that if Ragnar and I just tiptoed quietly out, Dad probably wouldn't notice we'd gone for hours. He might even find some book so fascinating that he'd sit down and start reading it from cover to cover — allowing me to get back to the growing crop of chores ripening in my notebook. But before I got a chance to suggest this to Ragnar, he spoke up.

"So, what's in the briefcase?"

Dad started in an almost guilty manner and replaced the book in which he'd been browsing — a copy of Oliver Sacks's autobiography, I noticed. He picked up the briefcase and trotted over to a wide Mission-style table that sat in the middle of the library. Ragnar and I hurried to move the books that were piled here and there on the table — carefully, so as not to upset any organization Hosmer had been working on. Dad set the briefcase down on the table and opened it with a flourish.

"A floor plan of the crime scene!" he exclaimed as he pulled out a large sheet of paper. Ragnar and I examined it briefly in silence. From the floor plan's grainy texture I suspected it was an enlargement of a diagram that had appeared in the *Clarion*. Actually two diagrams — one of the upper floor of the mansion, with Mrs. Van der

Lynden's bedroom located near the top of the stairs, and one of the front hall and ballroom — now the oversized living room. Dad was probably delighted that the diagrams included not only the location of all the doors, windows, and furniture, but also an arrow pointing to the wall safe in Mrs. Van der Lynden's bedroom, dotted lines to show the path the burglars had taken on their way out of the house, and in the front hall, little outlines of human figures to show where the bodies of the slain burglars had fallen.

"These look the same," Ragnar exclaimed with great enthusiasm. "Of course I have totally redecorated, but the floor plans are still the same. At least in the main part of the house. We can ignore the wings that Mrs. Winkleson added."

I wasn't sure how he planned to ignore them, since they'd at least doubled the size of the house. Not my problem.

"And the big bedroom at the top of the stairs — that is my bedroom, and the safe is still there."

He and Dad actually exchanged a fist bump — where had Dad learned to do that? From the boys? I couldn't quite share their enthusiasm.

"That's nice," I said. "But how does it

help us find the loot? Much less solve Mr. Hagley's murder?"

"Meg, don't you see?" Ragnar said. "The reenactment will be perfect! The house is exactly the same!"

I looked around at the black velvet window coverings. The wrought-iron sconces and chandeliers. The gargoyle bookends scattered here and there among the volumes. The painting over the library's fireplace, a huge oil depiction of a brooding dragon — according to Ragnar, an original by Frank Frazetta, a fantasy artist even I had heard of. I knew that unless Ragnar had recently redecorated, the living room contained a black-and-red sofa shaped like a coffin. And in a rare break from his usual medieval taste, his bedroom contained not only the one-of-a-kind king-sized wrought-iron canopy bed that I'd made for him, but also a sofa made from the rear seat and back end of a black-and-red 1965 Ford Mustang. Mrs. Van der Lynden and the Dames of Caerphilly would probably faint at the sight of any of it.

"Oh, exactly the same," I echoed, while doing my best to keep a straight face.

"Let's go check out the safe," Ragnar said.

He and Dad raced off.

CHAPTER 30

I started to rise to follow them and changed my mind. I didn't share Dad's fascination with the reenactment. But I was curious about the robbery. I decided to stay behind and see what other information Dad had brought in his briefcase.

A diagram of the estate's grounds, with all the various buildings marked, from the house itself down to the minor outbuildings, like the gazebo and the gatehouse, which had both existed at the time of the robbery. The house was considerably smaller without those imposing wings, but making allowances for the difference in color schemes, the main part of the house looked the same. Only one barn rather than the current three. A separate garage that had either been replaced by or incorporated into the left wing.

The briefcase also contained a batch of photocopies of newspaper articles, along with several dozen photos. Most of the photos were black-and-white shots, probably taken by the *Clarion*'s photographer for the society page. Mrs. Van der Lynden in her glittering ball gown. I paused to study that one. Her pursed lips were dark in the photo, which probably meant she was wearing bright red lipstick — had that been back in style then? Her dress had the exaggerated shoulder pads that were popular back in the '80s, but she didn't quite have enough neck to carry off the look. I suspected she was trying to channel Bette Davis, but it came out more like Miss Piggy. She was wearing glittering earrings and a necklace, but nothing that impressive. I leafed through more photos of Dames and their escorts. Everyone was in sequins and shoulder pads, but most of them had much more impressive jewelry. I wondered if they'd all found that suspicious — that the woman who had the means to outshine them all had suddenly given up conspicuous consumption for what probably passed in their circles for understated elegance.

And then I ran across a photo of Archie van der Lynden. I studied that one intently. Not that I had any hope of tracking him down — I might not even recognize him if I ran into him. Thirty years changes anyone, and if Archie had been battling substance abuse for most of his adult life, he could be more changed than most. But maybe I could get a clue to his character. He was wearing a white tuxedo with a dark rose in the buttonhole — red, presumably, though the picture was black and white. He slouched slightly, his right hand in his pocket. A lock of his blond hair fell casually over his forehead. His face, though technically handsome, was curiously unpleasant. It was the expression, half self-satisfied smirk, half sneer. A thought came to my mind unbidden — the portrait of Dorian Gray, just at the point where he decides he needs to hide it. Not someone I'd have looked forward to meeting, I decided.

Of course, thirty years could change a person inside as well as out. I hoped they had done good things to Archie. But I wasn't optimistic.

I moved on to other pictures. Mug shots of the three bank robbers. Two looked rather furtive and unprepossessing, while the third — Bart Hempel, the ringleader — was striking, almost handsome in a thuggish way.

The two so-called gentleman burglars. William Fitzgerald "Fitz" Marshall, the one who'd been killed. His face wasn't unpleasant like Archie's, though it wasn't handsome, either. Regular features — I'd give him that. His face had a vague apologetic air — and an ever-so-slightly bloated look that reminded me of a few of my college classmates who'd majored in grain alcohol with a minor in weed. I felt the impulse to shake Fitz and tell him to shape up. That I'd seen where that path led, and it wouldn't end well. And then I reminded myself that it had already ended rather badly for him, three decades ago. Dad had added in his obituary from the Caerphilly student newspaper. Considering that obituaries were usually written to show the deceased in the most favorable light, the student rag was remarkably restrained in its praise of Fitz. Son of a successful alumnus of Caerphilly law school — the article actually had almost as much information about Judge Marshall as about his son. Fitz had been a business major with a love for football and lacrosse, who took an active part in campus social life. I suspected this was obit-speak for a party animal who'd been admitted thanks to his father's influence and would have been lucky if he managed to pass enough courses to graduate.

And Paul Jefferson Blair. His picture surprised me. He didn't seem to fit in with Archie and Fitz. He looked . . . well, normal.

Clean cut. Good looking in an unassuming way. I flipped through the articles to see what they said about him. Not much. A political science major with a 3.5 average and plans to attend law school after he graduated. What had possessed him to go along with Archie's crazy scheme? I had a feeling James Donovan might have been able to shed some light on that if he wanted to. But I felt a curious disinclination to pry.

"He's suffered enough," I murmured, putting Blair's photo back in the folder.

Dad and Ragnar dashed back into the room, full of excitement. Three or four of Ragnar's flock trailed in behind them.

"The safe's just as it was," Dad exclaimed.

"Go start rounding everyone up," Ragnar said to one of his guests. "This is going to be awesome."

"Meg?" Dad was looking at me. "Are you all right?"

"My head's aching a little."

"I have aspirin," Ragnar said. "And acetaminophen."

"I also have more interesting stuff," one of the guests said.

Ragnar gave him a withering stare.

"Herbal stuff," the guest added hastily.

"I just need some fresh air and a little exercise." And some time by myself, but it would be rude to say so. "I'm going to stroll down to the lake. Carry on without me."

I fled out the oversized double front doors and stood at the top of the stairs, surveying the landscape. The swans appeared to be savagely demolishing a stand of some kind of aquatic grass at the far end of the lake, so I decided it would be safe to head for the gazebo. Not that I necessarily wanted to hang out in the gazebo, but it gave me a destination.

I hadn't been lying about the headache — just exaggerating a little. But I felt the slight throbbing ease as I ambled along the gravel path toward the lake.

I approached the gazebo itself with caution, remembering how foul it could get and how possessive the swans could be of it. Grandfather had once arranged for a rather melodramatic sign at his zoo, listing the top ten birds most likely to kill you. Mute swans had made the list at number five, following cassowaries, ostriches, Australian magpies, and the European herring gull. Toucans probably wouldn't even have made the top hundred. I couldn't remember off-hand what magpies and herring gulls did that was particularly lethal, but in addition to having long powerful necks with sharp beaks, the swans would beat their victims with their wings. Ragnar's black swans had a slightly smaller wingspan than mute swans — six feet rather than seven — but I wasn't sure that would make much difference if they ganged up on you, and they had the same hair-trigger tempers.

But the swans were absent, and as I got closer, I could tell the gazebo's condition wasn't that bad at the moment. Obviously the swans had been there, but either they didn't spend as much time hanging out on the wrought-iron railings as they had on the wooden ones or whoever Ragnar had assigned to gazebo-cleaning duty was doing a good job.

As I was about to step into the gazebo, a sudden flurry of motion at its far side startled me, and I stopped where I was, in case I'd stirred up a territorial swan. But it was a human figure, scuttling away through the rushes in much the same way Hosmer had fled the library. In fact, for a moment, I wondered if it was Hosmer, but Hosmer had been slight and with wispy pale blond hair. This was a stocky, bearded man with a disheveled mane of light brown hair.

"Sorry to disturb you," I called after the fleeing figure. But I wasn't sure he heard.

"Why are so many of Ragnar's guests so . . . . eccentric?" I muttered to myself.

"And why does Dad fit in so perfectly?" I felt guilty almost immediately. Ragnar had a good heart. Some of the strays he took in would never survive on their own in the outside world, but here they had a home, and could usually find ways to make themselves useful. I had probably flushed out the guest who was responsible for the gazebo's much-improved condition. Perhaps I should make a point of telling Ragnar how much I appreciated the change. And he could pass it along to the guest.

And as for Dad — most of the time I enjoyed his energy and enthusiasm. Clearly I was a little overtired today.

I strolled across to the far side of the gazebo and stood looking out over the lake. The view in that direction was very calm and peaceful, not only because the lake was so beautiful but also because I couldn't see even a corner of the house in which all the chaos was happening. And from a practical standpoint, gazing over the lake was the prudent thing to do, in case the swans tired of their grass demolition activities and tried to sneak up on me.

I saw motion to my right. I pretended to be totally focused on the distant swans while using my peripheral vision to check out what was happening closer at hand. A wizened, bearded face was peering out of the reeds by the water's edge.

So much for finding peace and quiet in the gazebo. I was about to give up and head back to the house when I heard a crunch of gravel behind me.

the reeds by the water's edge.

So much for finding peace and quiet in
back to the house when I heard a crunch of

CHAPTER 31

I whirled around to see who was coming.
Clearly I was still a little more easily startled
than usual — probably an after-effect of the
shooting. But it was only Ragnar lumbering
toward the gazebo.

"You are psychic!" he said, beaming. "Just
the other day, I said to myself that I must
tell Meg that the gazebo needs repair. And
here you are!"

He was pointing toward one of the metal
railings. Yes, it needed repair. It looked as if
something heavy had landed on the railing
and even done a little damage to the stone
floor.

"I don't have my tools with me at the moment," I said. "But I'll put it on my list. By
the way, someone's been keeping the gazebo
in very good condition."

"Buddy." He nodded and peered around.
"He puts a great deal of work into it. He
hangs out here a lot — I'm surprised he's

not here."

"I suspect I scared him away."

"Yes — he's very shy. Almost antisocial — he never joins in any of the group activities." Ragnar, who hated to do anything alone, shook his head in bewilderment. "I suppose he still has much healing to do. He is one of the walking wounded, I think."

I found myself wondering if Buddy was another former bandmate, one of the many who hadn't kept his feet on the ground as well as Ragnar during the heady and probably drug-and-alcohol-filled days of their success. I knew better than to ask, though. Ragnar respected his guest's privacy. And from what I'd seen of Buddy's face, he looked a little too old to be Ragnar's contemporary. Perhaps a mentor? Some ancient drumming guru? He looked vaguely familiar, so maybe I'd seen him in some of the many onstage and backstage pictures Ragnar had used to decorate the music room.

Not that it mattered. He was one of Ragnar's flock now. So I changed the subject.

"Look," I said. "I have an idea. What if I added some fretwork to the top of the railing to make it less appealing for the swans to sit there? A miniature version of the Mordor–style wall topping."

"Awesome!" Ragnar said.

Then he narrowed his eyes and stared at the railings.

"Yes, I can almost see it," he announced. "This visualization thing goes much better with wrought iron."

For Ragnar, almost anything went better with wrought iron.

Just then my phone buzzed. I pulled it out and looked at the screen.

"Mother just texted me," I said. "I'm pretty sure she needs me to do something — look, can you hold down the fort here? Help Dad figure out what he needs to do for his reenactment? And if I don't get back by the time he's ready to go home, just call me."

"I can definitely hold down the fort! Give my greetings to your mother."

Ragnar strode back to the house as if he expected to repel boarders from the ramparts. I pulled out my phone and called Mother.

"Please tell me that you have an urgent errand for me to do, so I didn't just tell a whopper of a lie," I said.

"Well, it's not that urgent," she said. "And I'd do it myself, but Viola and I are helping Robyn with more organizing, and I hate to interrupt the momentum. So if you have the time today — Lettice Forsythe found a ginger jar that would be perfect for Mrs. Van der Lynden. Could you drop by her shop? And then take the jar to Maudie?"

"Can do." I started walking toward my car.

"And if you happen to be anywhere near Trinity . . ."

"Which you know to be highly likely, since Morton's is only three blocks away."

". . . I left my umbrella and rain hat there."

"Not that you'll need them before tomorrow's service."

"It's a very nice hat and the umbrella your brother brought me from Paris," she said. "I'd hate to see them go missing overnight."

"One umbrella and rain hat rescue coming up."

As I passed by the front of the house, I heard cheering coming from inside. I was almost tempted to trot up the marble steps to find out what was going on.

Almost.

On my way back to the front gate, I noticed that the various guests and employees were no longer at work on the grounds — though I did see Hosmer, sitting under a cherry tree, reading a book. Clearly, with the exception of a few shy souls like Hosmer and Buddy, the entire population of Ragnarsheim was getting sucked into the reenactment.

But not me! Not for the moment, anyway. And then I contemplated, briefly, the curious experience of being delighted to have Mother delegate her errands to me. Over the years, I'd gotten much better at weaseling out of doing chores for Mother when I wanted to. But right now, I was perfectly content to fetch and carry umbrellas and ginger jars.

I might even find a chance to drop by the police station or Randall Shiffley's office to find out how the chief's investigation was going.

Lettice Forsythe's shop was in a well-preserved white gingerbread Victorian on a side street, about a block and a half from the town square. A sign hanging from a white wooden post by the sidewalk spelled out the name of the shop, which I think was *Forsythe's* — but the letters were so small and flowery that I'd never been able to confirm this theory. Locals called it "Lettice's shop" and tourists tended to enthuse about "that wonderful little shop with the sheep on the porch." Not a real sheep, of course, but a life-sized wooden sheep covered with woolen curls, sporting a wry ceramic face. One of these days I'd ask Lettice if there was a story behind the sheep.

But not today, unfortunately. The shop was closed.

Odd. Most of the shops in town had already gone on their summer schedules, staying open seven days a week from ten A.M. until ten P.M. It was only two in the afternoon.

I went up to the door and peered inside, in case Lettice had accidentally forgotten to flip her sign from closed to open this morning. No. No one inside, and the lights were off. Although the posted hours on the door did, indeed, promise that they'd be open today.

Well, I could pick up the ginger jar tomorrow. Maybe Lettice would bring it to Trinity for tomorrow's service and save me the trip. Then —

"Meg?"

Lettice's voice. I looked around but saw no one.

"You can't see me," she said. "I spotted you on my security system. Just a minute; I'll come down and let you in."

So I waited on the porch until Lettice appeared behind the door, unlocked it, and let me in, to the tinkling accompaniment of the door chime. Clearly she'd already retired to the second floor apartment where she lived, as her diminutive frame was clad in jeans and a *Caerphilly Days* t-shirt. Since I thought of her as one of Mother's cronies — they shared a passion for Wedgwood and Chinese porcelain — I was surprised to realize that she was probably only forty-five or fifty. The sedate and conservative clothes she wore in the shop made her seem much older. Probably deliberate.

"Your mother mentioned you'd be dropping by for the jar," she said. "After what happened to you last night, I decided to close down early. What if the shooter is still lurking in town?"

I considered suggesting that she stop worrying, since I seemed to have been his target, but I decided it would only make her more nervous, now that she'd brought the target into her shop.

"There it is!" She pointed to a blue-and-white porcelain jar standing on the counter at the back of the room, next to her antique brass cash register.

"Very nice," I said. "Almost a pity to see such a beautiful antique disappear forever into the crypt."

"I'd agree with you if it was an antique, but this one's only a reproduction," she said. "Let me find a box for it." She darted through a door behind the sales desk, into the back of the shop.

336

"Was the broken one — ?"

"A very valuable antique." Lettice emerged with a box and a handful of old newspapers in which she began wrapping the jar. "If Mrs. Van der Lynden had donated it to a museum, that lovely thing would still be intact. We don't want any more nonsense like *that* in town. So your mother and I decided we'd rebury her in a reproduction. Perfectly nice, but of no interest whatsoever to any sinister grave robbers."

"Sensible," I said.

"By the way," she asked. "Do you know if the ring they found in the crypt was Mrs. Van der Lynden's?"

"I haven't heard."

She finished wrapping the jar. But instead of starting to wrap the top, she set it down and went into the back of the shop again. She returned and handed me a file folder.

I opened the folder and found myself staring at a larger-than-life photo of the ruby ring.

"Either that's the ring I saw in the crypt or an exact duplicate," I said. "Not that I could tell one ruby from another — assuming it's a ruby — but the setting's pretty unusual."

"Precisely." She nodded and began wrapping the ginger jar's top in more newspaper. "Art deco style. Made by Van Cleef and Arpels in the 1920s. Evidently the Van der Lyndens had some real money in the family back then."

"The necklace isn't too shabby, either." I was leafing through the rest of the photos in the folder. Right behind the photo of the ring was one of a necklace with dozens of glittering diamonds. "How do you happen to have these photos?"

"Right after the robbery, the police sent around photos to all the jewelry stores, antique stores, and pawn shops within miles. My dad owned the shop back then, and when I took over and cleaned out the files, I found this. Maybe I should have thrown it out with the rest of the paper clutter, but I thought it was interesting."

"And besides, the case is still unsolved," I pointed out. "So it's turned out to be useful."

"Very true." She smiled as she tucked the newspaper-wrapped lid in with the jar and stood up. "The idea was to make sure we'd recognize the jewelry so we could notify the police if anyone tried to sell us any of it. Of course they'd have had to be pretty stupid to try to sell any of it here in town."

"But criminals aren't rocket scientists."

"Quite right." She nodded, and reached out to take the photo of the ring. "I think it's interesting that you found the ring. That and the necklace were probably the most valuable of the collection. But the necklace would be relatively easy to dispose of — a lot of carats there, but none of the individual stones are that recognizable in and of themselves. A savvy thief could easily break it up to sell the stones, individually or in matched pairs, without sacrificing much if any of the value. The ring, though — only so many rubies that size and quality around, and the setting's not only distinctive but quite valuable in its own right."

Curious how much Lettice knew about how criminals fence stolen jewels. Was this something antique dealers picked up if they dealt in estate jewelry? Or was she, like Dad, a mystery buff?

"So the ring would be hard to sell discreetly?" I asked aloud.

"Impossible, unless you had the kind of contacts that would let you offer it privately to the sort of customer who wouldn't care about its provenance. In fact, except for the necklace, that would be the same for most of the more valuable pieces. Too distinctive to sell that easily."

"So you're suggesting if someone did get

their hands on Mrs. Van der Lynden's jewelry, they wouldn't suddenly find themselves rolling in dough."

"Yes." She nodded absently, still looking at the photo. "Unless they were experienced jewel thieves with the right kind of contacts. The criminals Archie tried to hire were not professional jewel thieves. They wouldn't have had the slightest idea how to liquidate a haul like this. Neither would Archie van der Lynden and his frat house gang."

"So what do you think happened to them?" I wasn't sure why I was asking. I had yet to talk to anyone who wasn't positive that either Archie or Mrs. Van der Lynden had had the jewels. Still, it would be interesting to see if Lettice was on Team Archie or Team Mommie Dearest.

"Well, I don't think Mrs. Van der Lynden buried them in her backyard." She smiled. "No matter what Lacey Shiffley thought, rest her soul. I'd bet they were never stolen to begin with. Mrs. Van der Lynden hid them. Of course, she wouldn't have ever been able to wear them in public again, but for some people, just owning them would be enough. She always struck me that way."

"You knew her?"

"I saw her in the shop plenty of times. I used to help out Dad here after school and over the summer. She was one of the ones he warned me to keep an eye on. A time or two she'd been about to leave still wearing rings or earrings she'd been trying on. And claimed it was just absentmindedness, of course. Getting back to the robbery — I can well imagine her sitting in her pink satin bedroom, wearing all the jewels that were supposed to have been stolen, and gloating about the big check the insurance company was going to send her."

"Like Gollum brooding over his precious," I suggested. "You don't think having her only child go to prison dampened her enthusiasm a little?"

"From what I hear, she expected him to get off with a slap on the wrist. In fact, considering that two people died as a result of his silly plan, I think his getting out after five years or so pretty much was a slap on the wrist. And yeah, his going to prison upset her, but if you ask me she minded the insurance company's balking more."

"You're not the only one who thinks Mrs. Van der Lynden was behind it all," I said. "But what if her plan backfired on her?"

"Backfired how?"

"What if she hid the jewelry only to have someone come along and steal it from her hiding place," I said. "Which wouldn't have mattered so much if she'd at least got the insurance money."

"Oh, God, she'd go ballistic." Lettice clapped her hand over her mouth as if to smother a surprisingly girlish giggle.

"And she'd be stuck with her original story," I went on. "No way she could say, 'excuse me, I was lying before, but now someone's stolen my jewelry for real.' Can you imagine?"

Lettice's face sudden grew serious.

"You know," she said. "I can. Before the robbery she'd come in occasionally — to our shop and any others in town that sold jewelry or antiques. Mostly window-shopping from what I remember — which made sense when I heard later on that she'd lost all her money. But after the robbery she was in here all the time. Never asked about her jewelry, but she'd study everything in the case. Since Dad and I both thought she was behind the robbery, we used to laugh about it — here she was again, pretending to be looking for her jewels. But what if she really was looking?"

"Maybe she ended up losing her money, her jewelry, and her son," I said. "She died while he was in prison."

Lettice nodded.

"I went to her estate sale," she said.

342

"Didn't find a thing worth putting in the shop — anything of value she'd already sold off. So yes, she did come to a sad end."

We stood for a few moments, gazing at the box containing the reproduction ginger jar that would soon become Mrs. Van der Lynden's last resting place.

"Well, you'd better take that over to Maudie," Lettice said. "Be careful out there."

"I will."

I hauled the box out and stowed it carefully in the back of the Twinmobile. Lettice peered out as if keeping watch until I was safely on my way. I wasn't sure why she was so nervous — it was broad daylight, for heavens' sake — but I hoped her jumpy mood wouldn't rub off on me. Not the right mood for visiting a funeral home.

CHAPTER 32

As I pulled into Morton's parking lot, I reminded myself that there was nothing intrinsically creepy about the place. The thought didn't improve my mood.

Once again the parking lot was nearly empty. Was it unneighborly of me to be glad their business was slow this week?

Maudie very much approved of the ginger jar — both its obvious beauty and the fact that it wasn't a priceless antique.

"The things people want to bury with their loved ones sometimes . . ." She shook her head. "What part of 'you can't take it with you' do they not get? It's worse, I think, the times when the family wants to make a sentimental gesture and you just know their loved one would rather they had the money to take care of themselves. Which reminds me — have you had a chance to talk to young Mr. Hagley again?"

"Haven't seen him all day," I said. "Is he

back in town?"

"If he is, he hasn't come by here. I was just wondering whether to offer him the employee discount on his father's arrangements."

"That would be nice," I said. "And — wait. *Employee* discount? I didn't know Mr. Hagley worked here. I thought he'd been in banking."

"This was after he retired," Maudie said. "He's been one of our gentlemen for quite a few years now."

"Gentlemen?" Somehow this called to mind the professional mourners who occasionally appeared in the pages of Dickens' novels, dressed entirely in black, marching gravely ahead of the horse-drawn hearses. Mr. Hagley, with his gloomy air and perpetual scowl would actually have been rather good at this. But I had yet to see professional mourners as a feature of any local funerals — so what in the world did the gentlemen do?

"We pride ourselves on our strong customer service." Apparently Maudie guessed my question. "Only way a family-owned business can compete against the chains these days. So we let everyone know that you can call us any time, day or night, to start making whatever arrangements you need."

"I can see that would be a good customer service feature," I said. "But where do these gentlemen fit in?"

"People used to know they could just call the house if there was no one here," Maudie said. "But after Daddy got so sick, we didn't want him awakened all the time — he'd be like an old fire horse, charging down here in the middle of the night. So we decided there should always be someone here to answer the calls. Or the doorbell, occasionally. We have a little bedroom in the back where the gentleman on duty can sleep. We used to have one of our . . . less skilled employees on night duty, but after a few unfortunate incidents we realized we need someone with more social graces."

"I'm trying to imagine someone with fewer social graces than Mr. Hagley," I said.

"Well, he could be brusque at times, but at least he maintained a certain level of dignity," Maudie said. "Unlike our former watchman, who once told a grieving relative not to get her panties in a twist because someone would come out to pick up the stiff in the morning."

"Okay, I see what you mean." I hoped Maudie wasn't upset that I chuckled. "Even

Mr. Hagley wouldn't say that. So you replaced the uncouth night watchman with Mr. Hagley and all was well."

"Actually, we replaced the night watchman with Jim Washington," Maudie said. "Alternating with Reggie Thistlethwaite. And then after Jim died, his widow recommended her brother-in-law for the job."

"Brother-in-law? Junius Hagley was Jim Washington's brother-in-law?"

"Yes — they married sisters," Maudie said. "Dolores and Mary Margaret Kelly. Though I never got the impression the two sisters were all that close. Of course, that could be because they led such very different lives — the Hagleys moved in rather affluent circles, at least while he was an officer at the bank, and even before Mrs. Van der Lynden fired him, Mr. Washington was never that successful in a worldly, financial sense. The Hagleys were definitely there to support Mrs. Washington when her husband died, no doubt about that, but their manner was always a little . . ." She looked slightly uncomfortable, as if suddenly realizing she was overstepping the bounds of her usual discretion.

"A little condescending, maybe?" I asked.

"Possibly." Her expression said "exactly!" — though just for a moment. "I have to admit, that given the circumstances, I was rather surprised that Mrs. Washington recommended Mr. Hagley to me."

"Maybe it pleased her to see her brother-in-law taking her husband's hand-me-down job," I said. "Because, no offense to your business, which is probably a wonderful place for a retired gentleman to work — but you'd think a successful banker could afford not to work anywhere."

"Yes," Maudie said. "Of course, he always insisted that he only did it because he liked to keep busy. Still. At any rate, he did work for us, albeit part time, for nearly a decade, so we really should give him the employee discount. But do you think his son will be insulted if we offer it? You talked to him more than I did."

"I have no idea," I said. "But don't offer it. Just tell him that since his father was a valued employee for so many years, you will of course be charging the discounted employee rates for all of your services. And if he protests, just say you insist."

"I like that," she said. "Good thinking. I'm going to call him now to give him an update on what's going on in town, and I'll work it into the conversation."

She glided off. Was her swift, silent, yet graceful and unhurried gait natural, or something she'd picked up wherever funeral home staff learned their trade?

I drifted back out to the parking lot and over to the Twinmobile without paying much attention to my surroundings. My brain was racing, turning over what Maudie had told me.

I started the car and pulled out of the funeral home's parking lot almost on auto-pilot. Except that when I pulled out into the street, I turned left instead of right.

Right would take me to Trinity, where I still had to pick up Mother's stray belongings. Left?

Left would take me past the police station. I decided maybe the left turn was my subconscious telling me I needed to tell Chief Burke what I'd just found out. Or if he'd already gone home, I could leave a note for him at the station instead of calling and interrupting his dinner.

But his car was in the station parking lot. Along with several other cars. Aida Butler was sitting behind the desk in the reception area. From the way she came to attention when I pushed the door open, I deduced she was waiting for something or someone. Someone other than me.

"Please tell me you're not here to report another crime," she said. "Because that would be three days in a row."

"I only wanted to give the chief some information I just came across," I said. "If he's not busy."

Aida was already punching the intercom button.

"Chief? Meg Langslow wants to see you."

"Just for a moment," I said.

"Send her back."

The chief was keyed up, too. He did a better job of hiding it, but I noticed he had to stop himself from drumming his fingers on his desk.

"If I'm interrupting anything," I began.

"If you were, I'd tell you," he said. "At some point, you will be, but I'll let you know. What's up?"

"I'm not trying to horn in on your investigation," I said. "So feel free to tell me to go away and let you get on with it, but —"

"I gather you have some information for me?"

"Maybe. Did you know that Mrs. Washington and Mrs. Hagley were sisters?"

"Sisters?" He frowned and cocked his head slightly. "Are you sure?"

"According to Maudie Morton. Who has seen them in action as a family at two funerals, so I think she'd know."

"Interesting."

"You mean because now all six niches that were disturbed have some connection to the Van der Lynden robbery? Or because now Mr. Hagley has a connection?"

"Interesting on both counts," the chief said. "But I'm not sure what it has to do with the case." Although I noticed he'd taken out his notebook and was scribbling in it.

"Did you also know that both Mr. Hagley and Mr. Washington worked at the funeral home?"

I explained what Maudie had told me about her gentlemen.

"You're suggesting that one or both of them could have had access to the urns of people whose remains are destined to be interred at Trinity," the chief said when I finished. "And could have hidden the missing jewels in them."

"Yes. In the urns or in the niches."

"And where does that get us?"

"I don't know. But it's suspicious, isn't it? Or am I just being paranoid? It doesn't sound very logical when I say it out loud."

"It's worth considering," the chief said. "Jim Washington could have had access to four of the urns — Mrs. Van der Lynden, James Blair, Lacey Shiffley, and the John Doe. Mr. Hagley would have had access to his wife's urn, and possibly Washington's, if he started working at Morton's almost immediately upon Washington's death. Though I'd think it would take him a while to learn the ropes well enough to pull off a stunt like that."

"Or maybe once he learned the ropes he figured out what Washington could have done," I suggested. "Or maybe it was Mrs. Washington who hid the jewels — she'd have had access to her husband's urn and niche. And Hagley could have figured that out once he went to work at Morton's. Or maybe after his wife died."

"Why would either Mr. or Mrs. Washington hide the jewels in the first place?" The chief had on his skeptical face. "They struggled financially after Mrs. Van der Lynden fired him. You'd think they could have used the money."

"Maybe they had no idea how to fence stolen jewelry and didn't want to get caught," I suggested. "Or maybe they were overcome with guilt and wanted to make sure the loot was never found. And maybe Mr. Hagley had always suspected them but only recently figured out their hiding place."

"I like that theory a little better than the notion that Mr. Hagley buried the jewels in his wife's niche with the idea of reclaiming them a year or two later. But it doesn't get us any closer to figuring out who killed Mr. Hagley."

"Whoever he recruited to help him pry open the niches. He was on the frail side — I'm not sure he could have done it himself."

"So unless you have some idea who he would have asked to help him, your new information doesn't get me any closer to my killer."

I shook my head.

"I'll have to contact Maudie to see who would have had access to the various urns and niches." The chief was scribbling in his notebook. "There were no family present for most of them — Lacey had Judge Jane, Blair had James Donovan. Not sure there was anyone other than Dr. Womble for the John Doe. Or for Mrs. Van der Lynden — Archie was still in prison at the time, and either didn't get or didn't ask for compassionate leave to attend the funeral."

"Speaking of Archie — has he turned up?"

The chief shook his head.

"Weird," I said. "You'd think by now that even if his lawyers haven't been able to reach him, he'd have seen something about the case on the news."

"Possibly." The chief sounded pensive. "Frankly, I'm preparing myself for the possibility that we may never be able to talk to Mr. Archie van der Lynden. From what Dr. Womble said, it sounds as if he was already in very bad shape when he got out of prison. If even an unworldly man like Dr. Womble could tell that he was deep in the throes of addiction . . . and that was twenty-five years ago."

"You think he could be dead?"

"Well, I did until you showed me that note to Dr. Womble. Though that was six months old — no proof that he's still alive today. And the note doesn't rule out the possibility that he's institutionalized. Long-term drug abuse takes a toll."

We fell silent. I realized with a pang of guilt that I'd probably find it a relief if it turned out that Archie had died. I wasn't sure I wanted to see what thirty years had done to that handsome yet strangely repellent face. And I wasn't sure it would be any better to find out he was institutionalized somewhere, hallucinating cigar smuggling scams and asking for handouts almost as a reflex.

"But let's hope I'm wrong," the chief said. "Maybe Archie's out there doing some good in the world."

He didn't sound as if he thought it very likely.

"Getting back to the idea of someone stowing the jewels in an urn . . . ," I said. "Okay, maybe it's not very likely. But I thought of it. What if whoever killed Mr. Hagley thought of it, too? What if someone was aware that both Mr. Washington and Mr. Hagley worked at Morton's, and suspected them of complicity in the jewel robbery? And killed Mr. Hagley while trying to prove his suspicions."

"In other words, Mr. Hagley was merely trying to reclaim his wife's ashes, but whoever helped him had deeper suspicions," the chief said. "And I'll keep it in mind. At the moment —"

Just then the intercom buzzed.

"Chief? They're arriving."

CHAPTER 33

"Roger." He turned back to me. "Sorry to cut this short, but something has come up."

Something both he and Aida had been expecting.

"I'll get out of your way," I said. "Thanks for listening."

"Thank you for keeping me informed," he said as he held the door for me.

Out in the reception area, Horace had joined Aida, and they were both watching the front door with fierce, predatory expressions, like cats who'd seen a mouse disappear into a crevice. I paused.

"Is it okay to go outside now?" I asked.

"Why wouldn't it be?" Horace asked.

"Because both of you are staring through the door as if you expected Billy the Kid to come bursting in any second now."

They both laughed at that, and relaxed a little.

"You're not far off," Aida said. "They

picked up Bart Hempel early this morning down in Virginia Beach. The ringleader of the real jewel robbers," she added, in case I'd forgotten who Hempel was. "The chief sent Vern down to pick him up, and he just let us know he's a few blocks away."

"If Vern was a few blocks away when you buzzed the chief, he and his prisoner are probably about to walk through the door now," I said. "Maybe I should keep clear of the doorway until you've got Hempel safely stowed in the interrogation room."

"Interview room," Horace corrected absently, his eyes still on the doorway. Aida raised her eyebrows and rolled her eyes, as if to say she knew perfectly well that I was only staying put so I could catch a glimpse of Hempel. But they didn't order me out, so I made sure I was well clear of the path Vern and his prisoner would take through the reception room and settled in to watch the door with them.

Hempel was a mess. From the way he shuffled as he entered the station, I thought at first Vern must have put leg irons as well as handcuffs on him. No, his legs were unfettered. Was the shuffle some holdover from his prison time? Or did he have some kind of neurological condition that affected his gait? He was tall and broad, but his whole body had a bulky, bloated look, like a football player or wrestler gone to seed. The mane of thick, curly hair I'd seen in his mug shot had thinned, grayed, and begun receding from the top of his head. His face was slack and wrinkled. I remembered that one of the newspaper articles had identified him as Bart Hempel, 25. If that was so, he was only in his fifties, but he looked as old as Grandfather — and a lot less vigorous.

Although his hands were cuffed behind his back, Vern was keeping a watchful eye on him — and probably would keep doing so until Hempel was safely stowed in the interview room. I'd have just come right out and called it an interrogation room, especially when someone like Hempel was occupying it. As he passed me, he threw a quick, frowning glance my way and I had to make a conscious effort not to shudder. Life had not been kind to Hempel, but even in his current somewhat-diminished state, he wasn't someone I would ever want to meet in a dark alley. He wasn't even someone I'd want to meet in a well-lit street unless I had at least a brace of burly cousins with me.

"Room Two," Aida told Vern.

Vern nodded as if this was information he needed to know. Anyone who'd spent any appreciable amount of time in the Caerphilly Police Station knew that it only had two interview rooms. Room Two was the one in which the chair intended for the prisoner was bolted to the floor, the better to keep its occupant from coming over the table at you. Not something they had to use all that often, but I was glad they had it today.

Aida, Horace, and I watched Vern disappear. When the interview room door closed behind him and his prisoner, the two of them exchanged a look of — triumph? Not quite. But definitely satisfaction mixed with impatient anticipation. You didn't have to be law enforcement to see what they were thinking. They'd brought in the guy. Now it was up to the chief.

I wished them good night and headed out to my car with a curious sense of anticlimax. However interesting my news about the Hagleys and the Washingtons might be, it was probably irrelevant and useless. And I hadn't even had time to tell him about Mrs. Van der Lynden haunting the local antique and jewelry stores after the robbery. Probably also irrelevant. The police had a genuine bad guy in custody. Hempel would probably turn out to be Mr. Hagley's killer.

Of course, it was always possible that Hempel would have an alibi. If it turned out that on Thursday evening he had been leading a prayer meeting or teaching an embroidery class or — more likely — locked up in some other county's drunk tank — the chief might suddenly take a lot more interest in my information.

Meanwhile, it was time I relaxed with my family. One more errand, and then I could head for home. I pulled into the Trinity parking lot, which was empty except for the now-repaired van. I nodded with satisfaction at seeing that. I parked my car and strolled up the front walk to the familiar bright red double doors.

Before fumbling in my purse for my key to the doors, I reached out and pulled the right handle, almost out of habit.

The door swung open.

If it had been after dark, I'd have gone right back to my car and called 911. But this early in the day, finding the church unlocked wasn't really that weird. There could be people here. Okay, empty parking lot. But still . . . people who lived within walking distance, or who would be picked up by friends or family when they finished whatever they were doing here.

Although I didn't know of any planned activities for Saturday afternoon — we tried to keep Saturday free from church meetings so people could spend time with their families. Apart from the Altar Guild doing their prep for tomorrow's service, which had probably finished hours ago, no one was scheduled to be here. Not that I knew of, anyway.

I kept my eyes and ears peeled as I walked as quietly as possible through the vestibule into the office corridor.

Mother's umbrella and rain hat were sitting neatly on the bench just outside Robyn's office. Not an unreasonable place to set something down, but a rather hard place to overlook them.

It occurred to me to wonder if Mother had actually forgotten them, or if she had deliberately left them behind.

"And why would she do that?" I asked myself.

To get me over to Trinity. I pulled out my phone and opened a document I kept saved in it — the roster of Key Holders, showing who was responsible for each day. And then I nodded. Sally Penworthy was Key Holder of the day. Mother considered Sally flighty — and I didn't disagree with her. That was probably why Sally had been given Key Holder duty on Saturday, which tended to be the lightest duty of the week.

But Sally wasn't here. She tended not to

stay on site like the other Key Holders —
she'd just show up when she thought all the
meetings would be over and lock the front
door. Either she'd already come and gone
way too early, or she was planning to drop
by later to do her usual half-baked job of
checking things out and securing the
church.

I could go back home and leave her to it.

But when we'd already had two crimes on
the grounds, did I really want to do that?

Not really.

Obviously Mother knew that if I found
the church unlocked, or anything else amiss,
I'd do my usual thorough job of securing
the building. So she hadn't forgotten her
umbrella and rain hat. She'd —

"Deliberately left behind," I murmured.
And not just the umbrella and rain hat. An
idea was forming in my mind.

I still had my key ring in my hand, although I hadn't needed it to unlock the
front door. I unlocked Robyn's office and
sat down on the love seat to think for a moment.

Then I called the police station. The non-
emergency number.

"I knew you'd call when you heard the
news," Aida Butler said, instead of hello.

"Hello to you, too, and what news?"

"Bart Hempel is alibied for the time of the murder."

CHAPTER 34

If Bart Hempel was alibied for the murder,
then I definitely needed to tell the chief
what I'd just realized.

"He must have blurted out his alibi as
soon as he walked into the interrogation —
sorry, interview room," I said aloud.

"Yeah. Dude could have given it up to the
Virginia Beach police and saved Vern the
trip."

"Maybe he wanted free transportation to
Caerphilly for some reason," I suggested.
"Are they sure his alibi will hold up?"

"The chief made a couple of phone calls
and so far it's good," she said. "He was playing the organ for a choir practice of the
Methodist church he's been attending since
he got out of prison. His alibi includes five
sopranos, three altos, and I forget how many
tenors, baritones, and basses. Plus the
minister, who doubles as the choir director.
So yeah, I think it will hold up."

"Damn." I had liked Bart Hempel as the killer. Someone from out of town. Someone I didn't know and never would. Ah, well.

"Keep it under your hat," she said. "The chief wants to lull the real killer into a sense of complacency. But I figure you should know."

"In case the real killer isn't lulled and decides to take another potshot at me? Charming. Could I speak to the chief?"

"I'll ask." She put the phone on hold. After a short pause, the chief came on.

"Before you ask," he said. "Yes, now that Bart Hempel is no longer a suspect, I will be looking more closely at the interesting connection between the Hagleys and the Washingtons."

"That's good," I said. "Meanwhile I had another idea. Possibly a crazy one."

"It's a crazy case," the chief said.

"What if the ring wasn't left behind by mistake," I said. "What if it was left behind on purpose? In fact, not even left behind on purpose — deliberately brought to the crypt and planted there."

"Why? And by whom?"

"The why would depend on the whom, I think," I said. "For example, if you had someone who felt guilty about taking the jewels, they could have left behind the ring where it would be found and returned to whoever owns it now."

"Presumably Archie van der Lynden would be the owner," the chief said. "Or possibly his creditors. But I'm not sure I buy the idea of a guilty thief."

"No, it seems unlikely," I said. "I could see Paul Blair doing it, from what I've heard about him. But he's long dead. Bad example, I guess. Not a guilt offering, then, but maybe a message."

"Saying what?"

"Here's the ring. I've got the rest of it. What's your offer?"

"Interesting message," he said. "But from whom and to whom?"

"From whoever has the jewels to someone they think would want them. Want them and be able to pay for them, which probably leaves out Archie van der Lynden."

"Maybe." He sounded dubious. "But why not just sell the jewels to a fence?"

"Maybe it's someone who doesn't know how to do that," I said. "If you suddenly came into possession of some jewels that didn't belong to you, would you know where to find a fence? Well, yeah, you probably would because I'm sure you've arrested a few over the years. But I wouldn't. A lot of people wouldn't. So they leave the ring, and someone interested in buying the rest of the jewels finds out they're available."

"That'd be taking rather a chance," he said. "What if whoever found the ring had just pocketed it?"

"By killing Mr. Hagley, they made it pretty darn certain that the police would be the ones to find the ring."

"The police or the person they knew would be locking up the church that night." He chuckled slightly. "I think anyone who knew you would consider you a reasonably trustworthy ring finder."

"That would mean the killer is someone I know. Probably someone who belonged at Trinity." I didn't much like the idea.

"Or someone who'd done their research. So your theory is that someone dropped the ring in the crypt, knowing that word of its reappearance would get out and someone they know to be interested in the jewels would know that they were on the market."

"And then they contact that someone to start the negotiations."

"Where does Hagley fit into your theory?"

"Maybe he was the person who had the jewels," I suggested. "And someone suspected as much and ambushed him in the crypt. Or maybe like me, he saw a light on in the crypt, went out to investigate, and surprised someone who killed him to keep his identity a secret."

The chief pondered for a bit.

"Unfortunately," he said. "Your suggestion opens up a whole lot of new theories of the crime without disproving any of the ones I've already thought of."

"Sorry," I said. "I just think it's way too much of a coincidence. Mrs. Hagley and Mrs. Washington are sisters. Mr. Washington is canned — unfairly — when the jewels disappear. Mr. Hagley is killed when one of them reappears. What if one of them — or all of them — was in on it?"

"I suppose I should find grounds to search Mrs. Washington's bungalow," the chief said. "See if the jewels — or any other suspicious objects — turn up. And it might be worthwhile doing a much more thorough search of the Hagleys' house. Although obviously if any of them were connected with the theft, they've had thirty years to find the perfect hiding place."

"Maybe the perfect hiding place was our crypt," I said. "Although searching their houses is probably a good idea. And check out their finances, to see if any of them have been living above their means."

He didn't speak for a few moments.

"I'll be talking to Mrs. Washington," he

said. "Although at the moment I still need to have a few more discussions with Mr. Hempel, so he'll be remaining as our guest tonight. He's alibied for Thursday night, but not for last night, when someone fired two shots at you from a gun he claims not to have seen for thirty years. And I'm not yet satisfied with his account of why he didn't identify his brother when my predecessor showed him the photograph of our John Doe."

"If you're worried that I'm going to go over and browbeat Mrs. Washington into confessing that she's the killer and that she'd been hiding the Van der Lynden jewels in her basement all these years, relax," I said. "I'm going home. I might have to drop by Ragnar's tonight to pick up Dad later, but apart from that, I plan to spend some quality time with the family."

"Good," he said. "And in case you're worried, I've stepped up patrols near Trinity and your house. And I've assigned Vern to keep watch out at your grandfather's zoo to make sure his cousins don't shoot too many random trespassers tonight."

"Thanks," I said. "Talk to you soon."

"Yes," he said. "But not, I hope, too soon. I'd like a quiet night for a change."

I ended the call and sighed.

"Me, too," I muttered. "Me, too"

I closed my eyes and took a deep breath. I was planning to take several of them while mentally pushing Mrs. Washington and Bart Hempel and everything connected to the Van der Lynden jewel robbery and Mr. Hagley's death out of my mind so I could go home to my family with a calm, uncluttered mind.

But as I was exhaling that first deep breath I heard a slight noise. I opened my eyes to see Mrs. Washington.

She stood just outside the doorway to Robyn's office. She was neatly dressed in a navy blue dress that made her diminutive figure look almost doll-like, and a matching navy blue hat. Normally I'd have found her a welcome sight compared to, say, the hulking Bart Hempel. But something about her set off all my mental alarms. The rigid, tense body posture. The death grip on her navy leather purse. The look of pure hatred in her eyes.

"How dare you?" she began. "I've never done anything to you. I lead a quiet, respectable life, and you're accusing me and my family of all sorts of horrible things. How dare you?"

Her voice shook, but I suspected it was anger, not fear. And I noticed that she was only gripping the purse with one white-knuckled hand. Her right hand was inserted in the purse.

I had a bad feeling about this.

"Mrs. Washington," I began.

"Don't talk to me," she said. "Don't try to make excuses. You're trying to frame me. And insult the memory of my dead husband. I'll see that you pay for this."

"Let's talk this over." I stood up. Possibly a tactical mistake. She clearly didn't like being loomed over. She took a step back.

"I'm sure if we —"

Her right arm tensed and I realized she was about to pull out whatever she had in her purse. Probably the gun. I lunged forward to grab her hand to keep her from aiming it at me.

She screamed and tried to throw herself backward away from me.

Thanks to our combined efforts, both of us got a healthy dose of pepper spray from the aerosol can she'd been trying to aim at me.

"My eyes! My eyes! What have you done to me?" Mrs. Washington had fallen down. I could just barely make out her writhing form on the hallway floor before the swelling completely shut my eyes. She was coughing and moaning. I could understand.

It wasn't just my eyes. My face, my nose, my whole respiratory tract felt as if they were on fire.

"Wretched woman," I tried to mutter, but trying to talk made my own coughs worse. And my nose was running so badly that I had to breathe through my mouth, which would set the cough off again.

Mrs. Washington wasn't talking anymore, either. Coughing, moaning, and — was that a choking sound?

I realized I should call 911. I reached into my pocket for my phone, but discarded that idea immediately. Since my cell phone didn't have physical buttons and I couldn't see the screen, using it would be difficult if not impossible. I groped my way back into Robyn's office and over to her desk. I felt around until I found the phone. Thank goodness our last round of cost-cutting hadn't eliminated the land line.

I managed to dial 911 by feel, and felt a surge of relief when Debbie Ann answered and asked me what my emergency was. If only I could cough out enough words.

"Help!" I croaked. "Trinity!"

"I know you're at Trinity," Debbie Ann said. "Help is on the way. Who is this? What's wrong?"

I tried to cough out "pepper spray," or my

name, but my throat wasn't cooperating. So I just hung on to the phone with one hand as I groped around the desk with the other, hoping to encounter the box of tissues Robyn usually kept there. And I kept coughing into the phone. It somehow seemed important to keep open what small connection I had to the outside world.

I heard someone run in. Surely not the police so soon?

"What's going on here? What's the meaning of this?"

Ah. Mr. Sedlak, the remaining misogynist. I would have given a lot to see the look on his face. I held up the phone and felt him take it. I relaxed back into the chair, listening as Mr. Sedlak proceeded to give Debbie Ann a highly colorful if not entirely accurate description of what he was seeing.

Why did it have to be Mr. Sedlak? Quite apart from the fact that I disliked feeling even slightly beholden to him, I knew he'd probably inflate his role in this afternoon's events out of all proportion. By this time tomorrow I'd be hearing how brave Mr. Sedlak saved me from certain death at the hands of a large gang of armed desperadoes.

"This could be some kind of terrorist attack!" Mr. Sedlak said at one point. "Anthrax! Or some kind of fast-acting poison.

Should I evacuate?"

"Let me have the phone, sir." Aida Butler had arrived on the scene. I felt relief wash over me. Could an ambulance be far behind?

After a few annoying protests, Mr. Sedlak surrendered the phone.

"Meg's here, and she can't talk yet, but if I had to make a guess, I'd say someone hit her with Mace or pepper spray. There's an older lady in the hallway who seems to have been affected as well."

"That would be Mrs. Washington." The chief had arrived. "And once she recovers from the effects of what I suspect is her own pepper spray —"

I nodded vigorously to indicate that he'd got it right.

"— I am looking forward to having a very interesting conversation with her."

CHAPTER 35

Happy as I'd been to see — well, hear — Aida and the chief arrive, I was delighted when Horace and eventually Dad showed up to offer what relief they could for my pepper spray pain. And Mrs. Washington's pain, too, but I was perhaps understandably less sympathetic to her sufferings. The skin of her face and one hand were mottled with red splotches, presumably from the pepper spray. I hoped mine didn't look quite as bad. Or if it did, that it was a short-term side effect.

Once I could talk again, it didn't take long to explain to the chief what had happened, and within a few minutes I was on my way home. Under my own steam. Dad offered to drive me, but didn't object too strenuously when I suggested that he should stay to keep an eye on Mrs. Washington. Either she had gotten a bigger dose of the pepper spray than I had or she was more sensitive to it, and she wasn't recovering as quickly.

"Or maybe she's pretending to be more affected by it," I suggested. "To delay talking to the chief."

Dad nodded solemnly. I could tell he was perfectly happy to stay on at the police station, and delighted at the prospect of using the need to monitor Mrs. Washington's recovery to eavesdrop on the chief's interrogation of her.

"And after we finish down here, I'm going back to Ragnar's to work on the reenactment," he added. "We're hoping to have our first run-through this evening. If you want to come along . . ."

"I think I should rest." I exaggerated my hoarseness slightly, to make sure he didn't try to talk me into it.

On the way home, I turned on the college radio station, which was having its usual Saturday all-day classic rock marathon, and tried to chill a bit by tapping my feet — well, the foot that wasn't on the gas pedal — to Bon Jovi and The Rolling Stones. Singing along would have been a more effective pick-me-up, but my throat wasn't yet recovered enough from the pepper spray.

I'd expected to find Michael and the four boys at our house — which wouldn't have been all that restful, but it would have made a nice change from shackled thugs and pepper spray. Instead, I found my grandmother Cordelia sitting on one of the overstuffed blue couches in our living room, sipping a margarita and using Tinkerbell as a footstool. Also a nice change, but not one I'd anticipated.

"What happened to your face?" Cordelia held up a green glass pitcher. "And shall I pour you a margarita? You look as if you could use one."

I accepted a margarita and sipped it as I explained about Mrs. Washington and the pepper spray. And then all the rest of my day. Cordelia made a good audience.

"I know I should just enjoy the peace and quiet," I said when I'd finished my tale. "But where are Michael and the boys?"

"They've gone out to Ragnar's house," Cordelia said. "Your father has decided that his reenactment of the jewel robbery needs a more seasoned hand at the helm."

"Michael's going to direct the reenactment?"

"Yes." She appeared to be trying not to laugh. "And all four boys were quite mutinous that your father had left them out."

I nodded. Yes, they would be. Both Josh and Jamie had already played children's roles in several local or college productions

377

and considered themselves stars in training. I wasn't sure either Mason or Adam had any theatrical ambitions, but if the twins were doing something, the other two Horsemen wouldn't want to be left out.

"Michael and I tried to explain that it was a grown-up party, so there really weren't any children's roles, to which Josh replied that they could play short grown-ups. So Michael took them along."

And there was also the fact that Dad's reenactment was just the sort of lunacy Michael liked to aid and abet.

"Oh, and Spike went with them," Cordelia added.

"Spike? Does he get a part, too?"

"Apparently he will be representing Mrs. Van der Lynden's Pekingese." Cordelia sipped the last of her margarita and studied the pitcher for a moment before shaking her head slightly. "Though I have no idea if her dog played an active part in the events of the robbery or if his is merely a cameo role. Anyway, you'll have some peace and quiet for a while. And I should head out. If your father is going to spend the whole evening out at Ragnar's, I think I should go over to distract your mother. Assuming you'll be okay here."

"I'll be fine," I said. "With any luck all the

weird red splotches from the pepper spray will have faded by the time the boys get home."

"I'll let myself out then." Cordelia gave me a quick kiss on the cheek and left. Her firm, brisk footsteps moved from the porch to the walkway. Then her car started, and its sound gradually disappeared into the distance.

I kept my eyes closed and took another sip of the margarita. Michael and the boys would be fine out at Ragnar's. They'd probably have a blast. They wouldn't starve — Ragnar had an excellent cook and was a firm believer that people — especially small but growing boys — should be fed with great regularity. Maybe I should just sit back, finish my margarita, and relax for a while.

That, of course, was the moment my phone rang. I picked it up and saw that Grandfather was calling, so I answered it.

"I might need you to come and take your toucan back," he said without any preamble.

"He's not my toucan, and why can't he just stay there?" I tried to keep my tone light.

"We had a security incident this afternoon. Someone tried to cut a hole in the fence. Might have gotten in if not for the hyenas."

"The hyenas?" I could feel my margarita glow vanishing. "What did they have to do with it? Isn't the toucan in the aviary?"

"We have a part of the fence where the security cameras keep going down — not sure yet if it's human vandalism or rodents chewing the wires. So I moved the hyenas and the wolves into habitats at that end of the zoo. If they start raising a racket, security goes to check the fence."

Grandfather sounded proud of his hyenas' success. I wondered briefly if he'd set it up so intruders actually ended up among the wolves or hyenas, rather than merely near them. Surely even Grandfather would have more sense. Then again, maybe not. I decided I didn't want to know right now.

"So with a little improvisation, the security system worked," I said aloud. "I still don't see why you want to throw the toucan out."

"It's for his own good," Grandfather said. "What if the intruder tries again? Say at feeding time, when the wolves and hyenas might be a little distracted?"

"Why don't you take the toucans off display and hide them someplace else in the zoo," I suggested. "The Big Cat House or the Bear Cave. People tend to avoid poking around and opening random doors in those buildings."

"I don't need to hide all the toucans," he said. "Just the one they're after."

"Oh, and you think someone so clueless he doesn't even know that toucans don't talk can tell one toucan from another? Do you really want any of your regular resident toucans to take the fall for Nimitz?"

A short silence.

"I suppose you could have a point," Grandfather said.

It took an effort, but I repressed the urge to utter some variation on "duh!" or "I told you so."

"Well," he went on. "Since you refuse to take responsibility for the danger in which you've placed our entire toucan population, I suppose I'll have to take protective action." With that he hung up — and a good thing, too, since it removed the temptation to actually utter one of the snarky replies that sprang into my head.

"Chill," I told myself. "He's only doing this because he's worried about the toucan."

Still, he'd broken my mellow mood. The fact that someone was prowling around the zoo, presumably looking for the toucan, could mean that whoever had taken a shot at me was targeting the zoo now, right?

Of course if that was the case, it would also mean that whoever had taken a shot at me was not locked up.

But the chief had both Bart Hempel and Mrs. Washington in custody. And seemed confident that one or the other of them would turn out to be responsible for all our recent unfortunate events. The attempted break-in at the zoo would probably turn out to be another contingent of rogue Goths bent on kidnapping some of the bats.

Yeah, but for the time being, I didn't feel like being all alone in the house. I wanted company. Preferably that of Michael and the boys.

I picked up the margarita pitcher, carried it out to the kitchen, and put it in the refrigerator for later. Then I grabbed my purse and headed for my car.

Before I took off, I detoured to the barn to grab my traveling blacksmith's kit — a sturdy canvas bag containing the tools I might need to do minor repairs to Ragnar's ironwork, including the damaged railings in the gazebo. Not that I expected to repair the gazebo tonight. But odds were it would take several days for Ragnar and Dad to work out their plans for the reenactment. Which meant I might be dashing out there on short notice more than once. If I had my tools with me, at least I had the chance of getting some useful work done in the process.

In fact, if Dad tried to suck me into taking a major role in his reenactment planning, it might be a good thing to come prepared to work. So I added a portable LED work light to the tools in the back of the Twinmobile.

I deliberately took a route toward Ragnar's that would not take me past Trinity. If more exciting events were unfolding at the church, I'd let other people discover them. I also detoured around the police station. Unfortunately, that detour led me close enough to Mrs. Washington's street to see flashing lights and several police vehicles outside her bungalow. No doubt the chief was searching it. I hoped I'd hear all the details later tonight. Or maybe in the morning. Not only the hows and whys of Mr. Hagley's murder, but also what had happened to the jewels. I found myself wondering how many people would greet the news of Mrs. Washington's arrest with some variation on either "But she seemed like such a nice lady" or "It's always the quiet ones you have to watch, isn't it?"

Still, the search seemed to suggest that perhaps the chief was close to wrapping up the case. Perhaps I shouldn't mention that to Dad, in case it spoiled his plans for the reenactment.

It was a beautiful clear night, with a nearly full moon. I found myself thinking that I could almost repair the gazebo by moonlight alone.

But I'd rather be at home. Maybe I could convince Dad to knock off early so his reenactors could get their beauty sleep. Michael and I could put the Four Horsemen to bed, then stay up and watch an old movie. Something black-and-white and sophisticated. We were still working our way through the latest Film Noir Classics DVD collection.

As I approached Ragnar's house, I could see that nearly every window was ablaze with light. I drove past the steps and into the parking lot, which was almost completely full. From the number of vehicles that were far from new and in bad repair, I suspected Michael had recruited some of his drama students to the cause.

Normally I'd have rung the doorbell and taken the elevator up, but I could see activity on the front terrace, and loud music was blaring out into the night — Glenn Miller's "In the Mood." Should I break the news to the reenactors that their soundtrack was a few decades off? First I had to get in, and if things were this lively in the house, I wasn't at all sure Ragnar would notice the doorbell. So I walked around to the marble stairs and began climbing.

All the giant chess pieces were gone, and the steps were back to the impressively stark, bare look I remembered from Mrs. Winkleson's day.

When I reached the terrace at the top of the stairs, I found the drama department out in full force. Several women students wearing maid costumes were at one end of the terrace practicing balancing trays of hors d'oeuvres or champagne flutes. Quite a few men in tuxedos and women in ball gowns were clustered near the entrance. Several of the ones I knew — or who knew I was their professor's wife — waved.

Near the top of the stairs a young man dressed all in black was leaning against one of the enormous planters, smoking a cigarette. I recognized him as Roddy, one of Michael's star pupils.

"Hey, Meg," he said. "Michael's inside."

"Are you one of the real robbers or the gentlemen robbers?" I asked.

"Real, of course." He put down his cigarette, reached up, and tugged on what I'd taken for a black knit cap, revealing it as a ski mask with which he covered his face.

"Pretty awesome, isn't it?"

Nearby another black-clad man was striding up and down, his ski mask already deployed, talking softly to himself. Presumably another of the real jewel thieves.

"Evan's working on his motivation," Roddy said.

"Isn't he always?" I murmured. Roddy nodded and chuckled. He was the sort of performer who could go from laughing over a card game in the dressing room one minute to tearing at your heartstrings on stage as Macbeth without turning a hair. Evan, by contrast, couldn't get through a one-line walk-on part as a footman without knowing his character's complete psychiatric diagnosis. He auditioned well, but directors rarely cast him twice. Giving him a leading role in the reenactment was probably a kindness on Michael's part.

As we watched, Evan stalked furtively up and down the terrace, now pausing dramatically to look around as if searching for the source of a noise, now drawing himself up to his full height, now assuming a menacing crouch and scowling as if an enemy stood before him. Then he reached into his pocket. I was expecting him to pull out a prop gun. Instead, he drew out a modest-sized salami and shook it at his invisible opponent.

"Clearly I have not studied the Van der Lynden jewel robbery closely enough," I said. "I was unaware that the robbers were armed with cold cuts. I shall need to rethink my whole theory of the crime."

"Ragnar disapproves of waving guns, even fake ones, in front of so many impressionable children," Roddy said. "So we're making do."

He drew out his own weapon — a large and very green banana — and sighted along it at the spot where Evan appeared to be holding a prisoner at sausage point.

"I do hope someone takes video," he said, turning back to me.

"Watch where you're pointing that thing," I said. "I'm going inside to see if Michael needs any help."

Roddy nodded, picked up his cigarette, and began blowing smoke rings in Evan's direction.

I braced myself for what strangeness I might find and headed into the house.

CHAPTER 36

My first thought was that I wished I'd brought some ear plugs. Since I hadn't, I'd make it a priority to find the source of the music and turn down the speakers. "In the Mood" had given way to Frankie Laine singing "All of Me," which might be pleasant if played at a normal volume instead of one that could drown out a jet engine.

In the hallway I found Michael, Dad, Ragnar, and several formally clad party guests kneeling on the floor around the plans of the house. Several other guests stood behind them, flipping through thick wads of paper.

"Transcripts from the 1988 trial," said a familiar voice. I glanced up to see Fred Singer of the *Clarion,* armed with his trusty digital camera. "When I first heard about your dad's reenactment notion, I thought it was ridiculous — but it is amazing how much information they're able to reconstruct from all the testimony."

It was still going to look ridiculous when it appeared in the *Clarion,* I thought, as I watched Fred snap several pictures of the solemn group clustered around the plans.

"They'd have been crazy to come in from the kitchen passage," Michael said.

"Yes." Dad nodded vigorously. "The guests wouldn't have seen them, but with at least twenty servants going back and forth constantly with trays of food and drink — not a good option."

"So I think they have to make their entrance from the loading dock." Michael pulled out his cell phone, tapped on it, and spoke into it. "Roddy? Can you grab Evan and Jared and go out to the loading dock?"

"I'm here." Evan appeared in the doorway. "Michael, we have a problem. I need to know my motivation for committing this robbery."

"Ten million dollars in loot doesn't motivate you?" Michael probably sounded calm enough to most people, but I could tell his patience was wearing thin. Probably not the first time they'd had this conversation.

"I just don't read Hempel as that mercenary."

I could have said that I'd seen Hempel and I had no trouble reading him that way. But if I did, Evan would want to stop the proceedings to question me, and it'd be a toss-up whether Michael or I finally broke down and strangled him.

"He's not mercenary," I said. "He needs the ten million to ransom his brother, Aaron, who's being held by a sinister international crime overlord. If he doesn't turn over the ten million by daybreak, the evil overlord will kill Aaron."

Most of the people there looked at me as if I'd suddenly lost my mind. Evan looked thoughtful.

"Yes. I think I can work with that," he said.

"Come on, then," Roddy said. "Let's get ready for our entrance."

Evan, still lost in contemplation, allowed Roddy to lead him over to the elevator. To my relief, everybody managed to hold in their giggles until the elevator doors had closed behind them.

"Thanks," Michael said.

"Meg! You can play a part! Maybe you could be Mrs. Van der Lynden." Dad beamed at me.

A young woman in a Marie Antoinette costume looked stricken.

"No, Meg is my assistant director," Michael said. "I need her eyes. And also her hands. For note taking." He handed me a pen and a yellow legal pad. "Places, everyone! Get ready for a run-through."

Everyone scurried about. Actors playing party guests swarmed into the living room — including Josh, Jamie, Adam, and Mason, who looked very serious and pretended not to notice me. "In the Mood" started up again. Actors with serving trays marshaled in the hallway. I spotted one of them filling her champagne flutes at the sink in the powder room off the foyer. The hors d'oeuvres trays each contained about a dozen neatly arranged individual Doritos. Michael and I and a few other uncostumed people — presumably representing the various tech services — clustered along one wall of the foyer.

"Action!" Michael shouted.

Laughter and chitchat rang out in the living room. The servants trooped in and began proffering Doritos and flutes of tap water to the guests.

Hollow laughter echoed through the foyer. I was the only one who started. Of course — Ragnar's doorbell. The rest of them had gotten used to it. An actor in a butler's outfit opened the door and admitted two more revelers.

"Cue Times Square," Michael called.

From the living room "In the Mood" vanished, replaced by the sound of televised cheering and the voice of Dick Clark.

Two men in black tuxedos slipped out of the living room into the foyer. They looked around furtively. Seeing no one, they reached into their pockets, took out black velvet eye masks, and donned them. Then they tiptoed up the broad main stairs to the second-floor hallway and disappeared.

For a minute or so we heard nothing except for Dick Clark and the Times Square crowd. Then we heard shouting coming from upstairs.

"Bang!" someone shouted.

"Bang *bang*!" another voice replied.

The various robbers appeared in the upstairs hallway — the two gentlemen robbers in tuxedos and black velvet masks, the three real robbers in black sweats and ski masks, and all waving bananas, salamis, or sub rolls in a menacing manner. The real robbers were holding black pillowcases stuffed full of something. The party guests crowded in to the archway between the living room and the foyer but wisely stayed out of the action.

A gentleman robber tussled with the real robber played by Evan. "Bang!" Evan shouted, and the gentleman robber slumped to the floor. But he managed to get off a parting shot with his sub roll, and Evan collapsed much more dramatically, allowing his salami to fall from his dying grasp right at the foot of the stairs. I wondered how he was going to react when Michael broke the news that he wasn't the one who got to do the death scene.

One of the remaining real robbers — Roddy, I think — picked up his fallen comrade's pillowcase. Then he and Jared raced out of the main door and could be heard thudding down the marble steps. The surviving gentleman robber had flattened himself against the wall at the top of the stairs and was looking down in horror at the casualties below. Probably not too far from what the real Paul Blair had done.

Several actors — representing doctors or guests with first-aid training — rushed to the side of the fallen gentleman robber. One of them, almost as an afterthought, made a cursory examination of the dead real robber. The rest of the guests reacted variously. Several men stood in the archway and ordered the others to stay in the living room. Several people ignored them and slipped out. A few women screamed.

The actor in the butler's uniform strode matter-of-factly across the foyer, opened the door to the closet that housed the telephone and security equipment, and mimed pushing 9-1-1 on the wall phone.

We heard a car start down in the parking lot.

"What happens when they get to the gate?" I asked Michael softly.

"They will wave their bananas at the actor playing James Washington, and he will open the gate for them," he replied, also softly. "I think we've gone far enough with this rendition." He stepped toward the center of the foyer and yelled "Cut! Everyone to the living room for notes."

The actors swarmed back into the living room, chattering animatedly. Evan picked himself up from the parquet floor and retrieved his salami.

"I think I was a little flat in my scene," he said. "Can we take it again?"

Michael either didn't hear him or pretended not to.

I joined the crowd in the living room, curious to see what kind of notes Michael would be giving. But I quickly realized that the session was less about critiquing the performance than about brainstorming, under Dad's direction, about what could have happened to Mrs. Van der Lynden's jewels.

"Okay," Dad said, to kick things off. "First let's consider the theory that the robbers actually made off with the jewels. So where are they?"

As various cast members proposed increasingly more convoluted and improbable theories, everyone seemed to be enjoying the session — Dad, in particular.

But I'd already spent way too much time thinking about the jewel robbery over the last couple of days. Had already tested and rejected those few theories that seemed even halfway plausible. I felt like standing up and saying, "Wake me when you start discussing how either Archie or his mother managed to hide the jewels."

Maybe that wasn't such a bad idea. My eyelids were drooping.

"Is there someplace I could catch forty winks?" I asked Ragnar. "I've had a really long day. And I want to be fresh for the next run-through."

"Of course!"

He showed me upstairs and down the long hall to one of the guest rooms. He lingered long enough to fuss over me, offering tea or aspirin, and pointing out that the attached bathroom had an excellent soaking tub. Then, reassured that all I wanted was a horizontal surface to become unconscious on, he hurried back to the living room.

I locked the door, nodded with satisfaction at the lock's no-nonsense click, and fell into bed.

I woke with a start, and it took a few moments to remember where I was.

I glanced at the clock. Ten o'clock. A pity I had no idea when I'd gone to sleep, so I could know how long a nap I'd taken.

Time to take the boys home and put them to bed. I stumbled into the bathroom and splashed some water on my face. Then I left the guest room and paused for a moment to remember which way led back to the foyer.

I heard voices in distance, so I headed down the corridor toward them.

As I approached the upstairs hallway, the one that looked down over the foyer, I saw a figure just inside my corridor. It was a man, standing there with his eyes closed, doing what looked like some kind of anxiety-relieving breathing exercise.

I didn't want to startle him, so I shuffled my feet a little as I got closer to him. He didn't seem to notice, even when I could almost touch him.

"Good evening," I said, keeping my tone calm and soothing.

It didn't help. His eyes flew open and an expression of horror crossed his face.

"Oh, my God!" he exclaimed. Then he ran inside shouting, "Ragnar! Meg's awake!

Meg's awake!"

He didn't sound the least bit happy to see me. He sounded scared. And guilty.

Usually the only people who fled like that upon my arrival were the boys, and only when they'd been up to something they knew was going to get them into big trouble.

CHAPTER 37

I followed the man downstairs. But I didn't have to ask what the problem was. Hosmer, the book alphabetizer, was standing in the middle of the foyer, holding the tattered remnants of what I deduced was a bejeweled dog collar. Ragnar had been patting him on the shoulder, but both of them were now staring at me with wide, anxious eyes. Behind them in the living room, people were looking under and behind furniture, all the while calling "Here, Spike! Good boy!" From the farther reaches of the house I could hear footsteps, accompanied by other voices also calling for Spike.

"Meg! Good to see you!" Ragnar said. "Except that we seem to have a little problem."

"Spike is usually more of a medium-to-large problem," I said. "Especially when he's allowed to run loose. I gather you tried to put that flimsy little collar on him."

"We did get it on him," Ragnar said. "Believe me, it wasn't easy. He has the soul of a Viking warrior, that one."

"And the teeth of a small demon." I noticed that both Hosmer and Ragnar had acquired a collection of bandages since last I'd seen them.

"Then I turned my back for a few minutes, and he did this." Hosmer held up the collar.

"There's a reason we put that heavy leather collar on him," I said. "Slows down his escapes."

"Don't worry," Ragnar said. "We will find him."

"Good," I said.

"I'm glad to see you're taking this so calmly," said a burly bearded guest.

"I'm very calm," I said. "I have every confidence that after he gets tired of giving you all the runaround, Spike will graciously allow himself to be captured. Of course, my boys would be inconsolable if anything happened to Spike. So if anything does, I will have to kill the person responsible. But I'll do it very calmly."

A pause.

"I think she's kidding," the bearded man said.

"You go on thinking that," I said.

"He can't have gone far," Ragnar said.

"Don't underestimate Spike," I said. "And besides, finding him's not the real problem. Getting a leash on him — that will be the challenge."

"Don't worry," Ragnar said. "I'm good with animals."

He ran off to join the search.

"He responds well to bacon," I called after him.

"Who doesn't?" the bearded man said, as he followed in Ragnar's wake.

"Where are Michael and the boys?" I asked Hosmer, the only one who hadn't already fled. "Are they running around looking for Spike?"

"Oh, no," Hosmer said. "Michael took them home before they realized Spike was missing. He told us to wake you when we found him. He told the boys Spike was probably napping with you, and you'd bring him home when you woke up."

"Good thinking."

"I'll just go check the kitchen," Hosmer said, sidling ever so casually away from me.

"At least Dad is here to patch everyone up when it's all over," I said — aloud, but to myself, since everyone else had run away.

I wasn't really all that worried about the Small Evil One. He was good at taking care of himself. But I couldn't go off and leave him. If I arrived home without him, the boys would insist on coming back to help find him. And the ruckus going on in the house right now was just the thing to inspire Spike to find a really good hiding place and stay put. He was probably listening to everyone call his name and thinking the kind of thoughts that were the canine equivalent of sardonic, mocking laughter. Did these idiots not understand that?

Evidently not. Or much else about dogs in general or Spike in particular. I went around the living room, shutting French doors that had been standing open, wondering if Spike might have escaped to explore the outdoors. I glanced outside as I did so. No sign of anyone searching the grounds. So I strolled back onto the front terrace and did my own deep breathing — but quietly, so I could listen for sounds that would suggest that Spike had been loosed upon the world. Because if he had, there would be sounds, sooner or later. He'd find something to bark obsessively at. He'd chase some creature that would protest as loudly as it could manage. Or he'd try to attack something that fought back, forcing him to retreat with noisy howls of mingled terror and rage.

And I wouldn't hear any of it here in the

house, with at least a dozen people stomping around and constantly calling Spike's name. I decided to head down to the gazebo again. It would be a good observation post — far enough from the house that I could hear what was going on around me, and with a sweeping view of that side of the grounds. I doubted anyone would even notice I was gone. And if anyone actually did and came out to look for me, I could suggest arming themselves with bacon and patrolling the grounds.

I was a little surprised Dad hadn't suggested an outdoor search. I'd have expected him to remember Spike's long-standing hatred of the swans. More than once we'd had to rescue Spike from militant groups of swans after he'd tried to attack one of their number. Bevies of swans, Dad would insist on calling them. I thought "mobs," would be a more accurate term when they were angry.

Fortunately, the swans would have gone to bed in their nesting grounds at the far end of the lake. Far away from the gazebo. Even farther from the house, though that wouldn't stop Spike from heading there.

And as long as I was going down to the gazebo, I could check the damage to the railings a little more closely. See if my traveling bag contained everything I'd need to repair them or if I needed to throw something else into the Twinmobile before my next visit.

I stopped by the Twinmobile, where I kept a bag of bacon treats for occasions when I needed to bribe Spike into good behavior. I stuck a couple of them in my pocket. Then I grabbed a flashlight, locked my tote in the car, and set out for the gazebo.

It was peaceful outside. I could still hear everyone calling Spike's name, but in the distance. I'd hear the raucous celebration when they found him. Or his imperious barking if they rousted him from whatever hiding place he'd found.

The gazebo was reasonably clean. The guest who took care of it — what had Ragnar called him? Buddy? Yes. Buddy appeared to have been doing a good job.

I pulled out my flashlight and shone it on the place where the iron had been damaged. I squatted down to get a better look.

Weird. One of the stone pavers was cracked, several iron bars were bent, and the tips of two bars were broken off completely. Earlier in the day I'd assumed the damage had occurred when something heavy had fallen on this corner of the gazebo. But the more I looked at it, the more it looked as if the damage to the iron had happened from below. Had one of the swans surged out of the water so forcefully that it broke the iron? It would take a remarkably violent surge. And while the swans did everything violently, I didn't quite think they could pull this off.

I realized that the paver beneath the damaged bars was not only cracked, it was also slightly askew — as if it had come loose from its mortar. If someone pried the stone up — say, with a crowbar — it might strike the iron hard enough and in just the right place to account for the damage.

I tugged at the stone. It felt a little loose. But it was a heavy stone. I'd need both hands to move it. I set the flashlight down on the stone next to it. Annoyingly, the round flashlight rolled off of the stone I'd set it on and onto the one I was about to lift.

Interesting. Was it my imagination or had the rolling flashlight sounded different on the two stones? I tapped them in turn. Not my imagination. The damaged stone sounded hollow.

I set the flashlight down again and looked around for something to wedge it in place with — a stick? A rock? Nothing came to hand, so I took my iPhone out of my pocket and used that. Probably safer not to have the phone in my pocket while I was trying to tug at the stone. I'd fallen into the lake once while replacing the railings. Immersion in the cold, slimy water hadn't been much fun for me, and my old phone had never recovered. I made sure the new one and the flashlight were a safe distance from the edge. Then I grabbed the damaged stone and lifted.

Something was still holding it down — the tip of one of the undamaged bits of railing — but it was definitely loose. I tried sliding it slightly toward me and then lifting. Bingo! The stone came up easily, revealing a neat stone-lined compartment underneath that was large enough to hold a couple of shoeboxes side by side.

"A secret compartment," I muttered. "Lacey Shiffley had the right idea after all."

Unfortunately, the compartment was now empty. But still, I was willing to bet I'd uncovered at least part of the secret of the missing jewels. The gazebo had been here at the time of the robbery — I remembered seeing it on Dad's copy of the diagram of the estate.

Of course, finding the compartment didn't answer the question of who might have used it to hide the jewels. Presumably Mrs. Van der Lynden had known about it, and possibly Archie. But unless one of them had possessed carpentry or masonry skills, someone else had to have made it. Someone who had still been working for the Van der Lyndens at the time of the robbery? Mr. Washington, perhaps? Randall Shiffley had said he was a handyman and gopher. Even if the secret compartment predated Mrs. Van der Lynden's purchase of the estate, whoever had built it could still be in town. Or someone cleaning up after the swans could have found it. It was only sheer luck that I hadn't stumbled across it while replacing the wooden railings with iron.

As I pondered this, I was running my flashlight along the edges of the secret compartment, studying how it was made. Something glinted in the beam. I reached down to pick it up.

A tiny little bit of gold-colored metal. I wasn't an expert on precious metals, but I could see nothing to suggest this wasn't gold. It seemed to be one side of the clasp that would hold an old-fashioned necklace closed.

"Whatever you just picked up, drop it," a hoarse, nasal voice said. "It's mine."

I glanced up to see the bearded, scowling face of Buddy, Ragnar's shy guest.

The moonlight washed the colors out of the scene, just as it had two nights ago when I'd found Mr. Hagley's body. It reminded me of those faded black-and-white photos of the Van der Lynden party I'd seen earlier that afternoon.

Buddy wasn't one of Ragnar's former bandmates. He was Archie van der Lynden.

And he was holding a gun.

Chapter 38

I was hoping I hadn't let any sign of recognition cross my face. If I could pretend I didn't know who he was . . . and that I didn't see the gun . . .

Well, it was worth a try.

"I have no idea what this is," I said, holding up the little bit of metal and narrowing my eyes as if the glare of the moonlight dazzled them. "I'm just trying to make sure the gazebo floor is structurally sound before repairing the railing. Now that I know the secret compartment is here, I can make sure the railing doesn't interfere with opening it, if that's what you're worried about."

It almost worked. He blinked a couple of times, and a puzzled look crossed his face. Then he frowned and tightened his grip on the gun.

"Nice try," he said. "But you know who I am."

"Buddy," I said. "Sorry, but I don't know

your last name, and I have no idea which band of Ragnar's you were in. I've never really been a big heavy metal fan."

"I bet you thought you'd found the treasure," he said. "But you're out of luck. I saw you messing around out here this afternoon, and I moved it."

"Treasure? That's nice." I tried to keep my voice nonchalant, and add in just a hint of disbelief that any treasure existed. "Why don't you let me get back to repairing the secret compartment?"

"I won't be needing the secret compartment anymore," he said. "I think it's time for the police to find the jewels and return them to their rightful owner. Me."

He smiled. Not a pleasant smile, and I found myself thinking, irrelevantly, that perhaps he could use some of the money he made from selling the jewels for some restorative dental work. Though even perfect teeth wouldn't make his smile anything but menacing.

I decided pretending not to know his identity wasn't getting me anywhere.

"So that's where the jewels were all these years?" I pointed to the secret compartment.

"Yeah," he said. "A lot more secure than most of the dumps I've been living in since

I got out. Whenever I really needed a cash infusion, I'd sneak back, grab a few things, and sell them. But I was getting down to the stuff that's impossible to sell on the black market for anything like what they're really worth. So I figured if I could arrange to have the stuff found, I could sell it out in the open. Except I didn't think it would work to just pretend to find the secret compartment."

"Someone might suspect you'd known about it all along."

"Yeah." He nodded. "Plus, what if finding it on Ragnar's land gave him some kind of claim on it? But I figured people would buy it if I could make it look as if Ma had had them buried with her."

"Tell me," I said. "Did you really call her 'Ma'?"

"Yeah." He cackled. "Drove her crazy. She wanted to be 'Ma *ma.*' Like zee French." He smiled and chuckled as if driving his mother crazy was one of his fondest childhood memories. Then he shook himself slightly and his face assumed a serious look.

"Just a few loose ends to wrap up," he said. "Get up."

I stood, moving as slowly as I could. Obviously I was one of the loose ends, and I didn't want to make myself easy to wrap up. In fact, I was puzzled why he hadn't knocked me off already. Not complaining about his failure to do so, mind you — just puzzled.

"I want the bird," he said.

"Bird?" I wasn't just pretending to be dense. It took me a moment to realize he probably meant the toucan. Okay, that explained why I was still alive.

"Don't play dumb. The parrot."

I couldn't help nodding. Just as I'd thought — he'd mistaken the toucan for a parrot. Though I was still puzzled about why he was so worried about it.

"Just out of curiosity," I said. "And since I assume I'm probably one of the loose ends you plan to wrap up, so you have no reason not to tell me — what did the parrot hear that you're so worried about him repeating?"

"Me arguing with that old fool in the church. He saw me go out to the crypt. Came out to see what was going on instead of calling the police like any sane person would. Of course, maybe that was because he was up to no good himself. He'd parked his car somewhere out of sight and was sneaking in to steal his wife's ashes. Turned out to be useful to me, though. Stupid church started locking the crypt door since

411

the last time I visited Ma's grave."

Which by my calculations meant he hadn't paid his respects in a quarter of a century. Well, everyone mourns in their own way.

"So I convinced the old goat I'd get his wife's ashes for him if he let me in, and he leads me into the church and gives me his crowbar and a key that's just sitting on a hook in the church office — pretty pitiful security if you ask me."

"And why lock up a graveyard, anyway?" I asked. "No one outside wants to be inside, and no one inside's likely to try to get out."

Archie frowned suspiciously.

"It's an old joke," I explained. "So you're worried the parrot would recognize you just from being in the office? They're not actually that smart."

"They repeat things," Archie said. "And the more they hear something, the more likely they'll repeat it. The old man recognized me. He kept calling me by name. 'Archie, Archie, Archie.' Over and over."

At any other time I might have admired his spot-on imitation of Mr. Hagley's hoarse, nasal, crowlike voice.

"And telling me, 'it's not a crypt, it's a calamari.' "

"Columbarium," I corrected absently.

"Whatever. I didn't worry about it at first

— I thought I'd convinced him to stay put in the office. Give me a few minutes privacy to commune with Ma, and then on the way out I'd pop open the front of his wife's niche and bring her jar back to him. He was going to be my witness. I'd come back and say 'Holy cow! Someone's already been prying open niches! And look what I found in the crypt!' And then I'd hold up that big, ugly ruby ring of Ma's and tell him to call the cops."

"What went wrong?" I asked.

"I guess the old goat didn't trust me. He followed me out there. I had to shut him up."

"You could have just told him you thought the jewelry was hidden in one of those niches and you had to see for yourself. I don't know what the penalty would be for prying open a niche, but I bet it's pretty minimal compared to the penalty for murder. And if they thought you were doing it to reclaim the stolen property you'd been trying to find for thirty years, they'd probably waive any penalty."

"Gee, too bad I didn't have you there to boss me around that night," Archie said. "Get moving. You're going to get me the bird."

"He's at the zoo," I said. "It'll be closed

by now."

"Yeah, I know," he said. "I figure you know the place well enough to help me get in. And show me where the bird is."

Oh, great. I was thrilled at the idea of trying to break into someplace guarded by an unknown number of armed Shiffleys. Though at least the chief had sent Vern there, which probably decreased the chances that we'd get shot in the dark.

Still, I'd rather manage my escape from Archie's clutches here at Ragnar's. I had the feeling the less time I spent in Archie's company, the better my chances for survival were.

What was up with those idiots in the house, anyway? Why didn't they come looking for me?

As if in answer to my mental question, a muddled blast of guitar, bass, and drum shattered the quiet night, startling both of us. If the music was this loud all the way down here at the lake, I couldn't imagine what it was like up in the house.

"Oh, God," Archie exclaimed. "Not that again."

"What in the world is it?"

"I think they're calling themselves Feral Slime this week," he said. "Couple of the other guests are trying to form a band."

"Someone should stop them." The only thing worse than dying here in Ragnar's gazebo would be dying here — or anywhere — with Feral Slime's ungodly racket filling my ears.

"Well, at least with that racket going on, they won't notice our departure."

Unfortunately he was right.

I tried to think of some reason to linger. Surely it wouldn't take long for Feral Slime to drive at least a few sane people out of the house.

"Close up the secret compartment before we go," Archie said. "No sense letting everyone find out about it. You never know. I might need to hide something again."

I stooped down and fumbled with the cover to the secret compartment. While I didn't want to annoy Archie too much, I figured I could delay our departure at least a few minutes if I pretended to have trouble lifting the heavy stone slab. And if I could manage to hurl the thing at him —

"Sometime this year," Archie said, tapping his foot.

"You know how heavy this thing is." My tone was probably a little surly, because I had just realized that hurling the heavy stone slab wasn't an option.

"Just — What the hell?"

Something ran into the gazebo and hurled itself at Archie's leg. At first I thought it was an exceptionally large and very wet rat. But after it bit Archie on the leg and scampered toward me I realized it wasn't a Rodent of Unusual Size. It was Spike.

"He bit me!" Archie howled. He pointed the gun at Spike instead of me — which would have been a relief if Spike had been the rat I'd originally mistaken him for. But annoying as Spike was, I took a dim view of anyone shooting him. Besides, he was running straight at me.

So I reached out, grabbed Spike as soon as he came close enough, and vaulted over the railing and into the lake.

The water was just as slimy as I remembered, and not a lot warmer than it had been in February. And jumping into the lake might not have saved me or Spike if Archie had been free to take potshots at us as I tried to scramble upright and wade to the shore.

But just then the swans arrived — several dozen of them. I deduced that Spike had found his way to their nesting grounds at the far end of the lake and done something to annoy them. Or maybe just woke them up — annoyed was the swans' default setting. Not finding Spike in the gazebo, they turned their wrath on Archie. By the time I made it to the shore they had knocked him down and were flailing at him with their powerful wings, with an occasional beak jab by way of variation.

Fortunately he'd attempted to flee from the gazebo when they'd attacked. He'd only gotten about six feet, but that meant he and the swans were far enough away that I thought I could risk wading back to the gazebo and fetching my phone.

As soon as I got close to the gazebo, Spike wriggled free of my arms and leaped onto its stone floor. Instead of acting grateful for being rescued, he drenched me by standing as close as possible while he shook the surplus water from his fur. Then he set off at a run to the house, howling in mingled fear and fury as he went. He'd probably bite the first person he met.

I put a little distance between me and the swans and called 911.

CHAPTER 39

"So glad to see you again, Dr. Shakespeare," Mother was saying to the genial supply priest. "And such a thoughtful sermon."

They exchanged a few more pleasantries, and then Mother sailed through the vestibule in the direction of the parish hall to make sure the potluck lunch was set up properly.

"Thoughtful," Lyndon Shakespeare repeated as he shook hands with me. "Is that a good thing or a bad thing? Robyn has already warned me that 'interesting' would mean there was nothing nice to say about it."

"Thoughtful is good," I said. "Thoughtful probably means Dad squirmed less than usual. Or possibly that you said something she can make use of at her next book club meeting."

"It's all good, then." He looked relieved. "How are you feeling after your ordeal?"

"Very glad it's over," I said. "You can't imagine what a treat it is to come here and find the biggest problem going on is that too many people brought potato salad instead of green bean casserole."

"I will feel free to indulge my unseemly passion for potato salad, then. My years in America have not made me a convert to the green bean casserole. Is it my imagination, or do we have a larger turnout than usual?"

"We don't usually manage standing-room-only outside of Christmas and Easter," I said. "And no offense to you, because it was a nice sermon, but I expect everyone turned up because they wanted to get the scoop on what happened last night."

"Me included." He laughed and shook his head. "Although I feel guilty keeping you from that lunch, and I notice that the line to shake hands with me is backing up so that people are beginning to sneak out the side doors — so just one question, if I may."

"Sure."

"Is it over now? I know it's been fretting Robyn, and I can't even imagine what you've gone through. Have they got the right bloke? Are things going to settle down finally?"

"They've definitely got the right bloke," I said. "For Hagley's murder, the attack on

419

me, and Aaron Hempel's murder, which they didn't even know was a murder until this week. Caerphilly is rapidly becoming a town devoid of mystery."

"I can't imagine that will last long," he said. "But let's enjoy the lull while we can. And let Robyn focus on Matt and the impending new arrival. See you later."

I was about to follow Mother to the parish hall, but in the vestibule I ran into Robyn. Matt had brought her to the service in a wheelchair and was standing guard to make sure she stayed in it. They were feeding some grapes to Nimitz — we'd had Grandfather bring him in so Robyn could see for herself that he was perfectly happy and healthy out at the zoo.

"Meg!" Robyn exclaimed. "So glad you're safe! Can you stay for the ceremony?"

"What ceremony?"

"The Restoration of Things Profaned. I thought it would help speed getting things back to normal around here, so we're going to do it after lunch — Dr. Womble, Father Shakespeare, and I. Don't worry; I'll stay in the chair and let them do any heavy lifting."

"I'd be delighted to," I said.

"Thanks for getting the household cleanup started," Matt said. "Especially for sending the Shiffleys over. I've learned my lesson —

next time I need something fixed, I'll ask Randall which one of his cousins would be interested."

"Good idea," I said. "In the long run it's cheaper than doing it yourself if you don't have time to finish."

"Yeah. And the Shiffleys are real interested in trading handyman work for paintings of their kids, so it should work out great."

He wheeled Robyn toward the parish hall.

I smiled as I watched them, wondering if perhaps I could safely delegate most of the future decluttering to Mother and Cordelia. And I glanced over at Nimitz, who, in spite the large tarp we'd laid down beneath his cage, was managing to create quite a mess for someone to clean up. Not me, luckily; I'd managed to weasel out of cleanup duty today.

"Meg?"

I turned to find Mrs. Washington standing in front of me. I must have looked alarmed, because she stepped back slightly and held up her hands as if in surrender.

"I'm here to apologize," she said.

"No need," I said.

"I think there is. I startled you yesterday."

"Startled?" Suddenly it seemed funny, and I burst out laughing. "You scared the Dickens out of me. I thought I was trapped alone in the church with a cold-blooded murderess who was also a diabolically clever jewel thief."

"When you come right down to it, I suppose I should be flattered." She laughed — in fact, you could almost call it a giggle. "Little old ladies like me spend too much of our lives feeling invisible. And here you were, suspecting me of being behind the biggest crime wave to hit Caerphilly in decades."

"I know better than to underestimate little old ladies," I said. "Have you met my grandmother Cordelia? A very formidable little old lady. And for that matter, my mother would kill me if I called her a little old lady, even a formidable one, so I'll just say that in a few decades she, too, will be quite possible the most formidable little old lady in the universe."

"You have quite a few formidable ladies here, of all ages," she said. "I hear good things about your woman priest, too. Junius has a lot to answer for."

"Like what?" Not that I disagreed, but I was curious which of Mr. Hagley's many sins was annoying her at the moment.

"You may notice that you haven't seen me here since James died, and not that often before. All these years I've assumed that

Trinity had to be as boring and narrow-minded as Junius."

"Oh, dear." Though true, I hadn't seen her here before.

"But I couldn't have been more wrong. I have no idea how he put up with this place all these years, or you with him. I feel as if I'm among kindred spirits for the first time in years. And if he wasn't dead already, I'd be sorely tempted to strangle Junius. It's as if for the past two decades he's robbed me of something that would have made my life so much richer."

"Don't let it make you bitter."

"I will do my best to let go of the bitterness," she said. "And I think showing up here again next Sunday will help. Tell me, what is St. Clotilda's Guild? Your mother — who I agree is very formidable — seems to think I should join it."

"It's the group that takes on good works and special projects," I said. "Joining would be a great way to get involved and meet all those formidable ladies."

"I'll think very seriously about it. For now, I should be going."

"Aren't you going to check out the potluck lunch?"

"I didn't bring anything."

"No problem," I said. "If everyone

brought something there wouldn't be room for it all. If you feel guilty, ask Mother what you can do to help."

"Well, if you're sure it's all right."

I made a shooing motion. She smiled, and stepped, still a little nervously, toward the parish hall — giving Nimitz's tarp a wide berth and ignoring his flirtatious head bobbing.

"Ms. Langslow?"

Professor James Donovan. Also someone I didn't remember seeing here at Trinity before.

"Just Meg." I shook his offered hand. "How are you?"

"And what am I doing here?" He smiled. "I came on account of Jeff. He never struck me as a deeply religious person, yet after he came back to Caerphilly, he became a regular here. I wanted to find out why."

"It grows on you," I said. "Though if you want to know why Jeff came here, you might want to talk to Dr. Womble."

"Is he the guy who gave the sermon? I have to admit, I would never have imagined that a sermon could range from Charles Darwin to Sojourner Truth to Charlie Brown and manage to make more than a little sense."

"That was Father Shakespeare, and he

and Dr. Womble are old friends," I said. "Go down to the parish hall, grab a plate of food, and talk to them."

"Are you trying to convert me?"

"No, just trying to feed you," I said.

"Okay then." He laughed and started to turn. Then his face grew serious again. "About Jeff," he began. Then he stopped and frowned as if not sure what to say. Or maybe not sure how I'd take whatever he was about to say.

"What about Jeff?" I prompted finally.

"When you put him back, is there some kind of . . . um . . . ceremony? Something brief, dignified."

"I'm sure between Dr. Womble, Father Shakespeare, and Robyn we can come up with something you'd approve of."

"Something Jeff would approve of. That's more important."

I nodded.

"And this time, can we put his full name on the plaque? Paul Jefferson Blair. I think he'd like it that way."

"Absolutely," I said. "Now go hit the chow line."

He smiled and turned toward the parish hall — though he stopped to stare for a few moments at Nimitz.

"Blessing of the animals?" he asked finally.

"That's not till October," I said. "He's just visiting."

Donovan shrugged and went into the parish hall.

"Nice that some people can relax and have a good time." Horace appeared beside me. "Some of us have to get back to work."

" 'A policeman's lot is not a happy one,' " I sang. "And here I thought the department would be pleased that I found the real killer."

"We are," he said. "But you have no idea how much we have to do to wrap it up. I was working all night, and still have hours of work ahead of me."

"So are you allowed to tell me if you found the rest of Mrs. Van der Lynden's jewels?" I asked.

"Not a big secret," he said. "We got the Shiffleys' dogs looking around, and found Archie's car hidden in a shed at the other end of Ragnar's farm."

"He has a car?" I said. "Somehow that surprises me."

"It sure surprised Ragnar, who's been driving him around whenever he needed to go anywhere for the last year or so."

"What a jerk!" I exclaimed.

"Even Ragnar seemed a little put out," Horace said. "And you know how mellow he is. Anyway, we found the guy at the rehab clinic who can testify that Archie was bribing him to get an alibi. And we found out from Bart Hempel that he'd given his gun to his brother Aaron, so we're pretty sure it will turn out that Archie got hold of it when he killed Aaron. And your dad's been studying the X-rays of Aaron's head wound, and he says the medical examiner in 1994 must have been blind or incompetent. No way the wound on his head could be from falling against a headstone. Blunt instrument all the way! So we might try to charge Archie with Aaron Hempel's murder, too."

"Awesome." I was delighted to be hearing that last bit of news from Horace, who merely gave me the highlights, rather than from Dad, who would have tried to share all the grisly medical details that had led him to this conclusion.

"Anyway, I should get back," he said. "Do you think your mother will kill me if I fill a paper plate and run?"

"She'll kill you if you don't take back a couple of platters for your colleagues down at the station," I said. "Just ask her."

He nodded and scurried toward the parish hall.

I managed to make it just inside the room — but nowhere near the food — when someone else hailed me.

"Ma'am?"

I turned to see Bart Hempel looming over me.

CHAPTER 40

"Sorry to bother you," Hempel said. "But I understand you're the lady I should talk to about what I want done with Aaron's ashes."

"Yes." I held out my hand. "Meg Langslow."

"Bart Hempel." His hand swallowed mine — and my hand was large for a woman — but his grip was gentle. In fact, his whole demeanor was mild and gentle. Strange how seeing someone led into a police station in handcuffs can influence your perceptions of him.

"Right now your brother's ashes are down at the police station for safekeeping," I said. "But I'm sure the chief would let you take them. Or we could send them wherever you'd like."

He frowned and looked down at his feet. Then he jerked his head up again as if he'd given himself an order to look me in the eye.

"Any way he can just stay here?"

"I don't see why not," I said. "I can't imagine anyone here would object." Actually, Mr. Hagley might have if he were still around, but Hempel didn't need to know that.

"Even though Aaron wasn't Episcopalian?" Hempel asked. "I don't rightly know what he was — if anything."

"We're pretty easygoing about that," I said. "And besides, after nearly a quarter of a century, we're kind of used to having him around. It will be nice to put a name to the face — or perhaps I should say the space."

Hempel nodded and looked down at the ground again. I waited.

"I was a stranger and ye took me in." His voice choked slightly. "Thank you."

He looked up again and I could see tears welling in his eyes.

"He's been here longer than he was anyplace else on this earth," he said. "And it's a good place." He looked around and nodded approvingly. "I can see that."

"When you get a chance, write down his full name for me, and his birth date." I had a feeling Hempel didn't want to break down in front of me, and having something practical to do might help. I tore a sheet out of my notebook and handed it to him, along with one of my pens. "We need to do a new plaque for his niche anyway. And remember, if you come to visit his grave, we usually keep the columbarium locked up to prevent vandalism — but just check in at the church office and they can let you in."

He nodded and took the offered pen and paper. He bent over to write on the closest flat surface — the wall beside the door — and printed his brother's name, birth date, and death dates in large, firm block capitals. Then he handed back the pen and paper.

"I'm working a twelve-step program," he said. "I need to put you and yours on the list of people I harmed."

"Not directly or deliberately," I said.

"Yeah, but if I hadn't sent Aaron to shake down Archie for a share of the loot I thought he had, Archie wouldn't have gotten hold of my gun and he couldn't have used it to try to kill you. Just because I didn't intend any of that doesn't mean I'm not responsible. I'm a different person now than I was then. Better, I hope. Anyway, if there's anything you can think of that would help me make amends, let me know."

"I can think of two things you could do that would please people around here, if you're game," I said. "See that man over there who's gesturing a little too wildly with that cup of punch?"

"The short, bald one?"

"That's him. My dad. He's a big mystery reader — and he's been trying to reconstruct exactly what happened at the Van der Lynden robbery. Will you talk to him?"

"Sure." Hempel shrugged. "Why not? As long as he'll be okay with exactly how unglamorous the whole thing was."

"I expect he has a lot of illusions that you'll need to shatter. But first — see the tall, white-haired man in the disreputable tweed suit? The one whose glasses are about to fall off his nose?"

He nodded.

"That's Dr. Rufus J. Womble. He was pastor here when your brother died. He's really the one who's responsible for Aaron being buried at Trinity. Go talk to him. Tell him a little about what your brother was like."

Hempel's face lit up.

"Thank you," he said. "I'll go do just that."

He shook my hand again and ambled off with a lighter step than before. I turned my attention to the buffet tables, but before I'd gone two feet I felt a hand on my arm.

"Ms. Langslow."

"Mr. Hagley." It felt odd to be calling someone else by the name I'd so long associated with Mother's bête noire. So I was relieved when he grimaced and held out his hand.

"Just Chuck, please. When you say Mr. Hagley, I look around for Dad."

"Me too, actually, and it's just Meg."

"I understand I have you to thank for finding Dad's killer."

"I helped," I said. "I think the police would have found him before too long."

"I assume this means we can arrange the funeral fairly soon," he said. "And in case you were wondering, yes, I would like to keep Mom and Dad here. So if you hear anything about who Dad was trying to sell the family slot to, tell them the deal's off. Why didn't Dad let me know if he needed money? I may be an ambulance chaser, but I'm a damned successful one. I gather he's been working part time at the funeral home for the last ten years — I always thought that was some kind of weird volunteer charity thing."

"Parents can be like that," I said. "They're so used to taking care of us that sometimes they can't handle it when they're the ones who need taking care of."

"Yeah." He shook his head as if still having a hard time believing it. "Anyway — the guy who preached today — it was pretty

433

good. Is he the one who'd be doing the sermon?"

"That could probably be arranged," I said. "Or you could ask Dr. Womble. I know your mother was very fond of him. And I think your dad found him only mildly exasperating."

"He must be a magician, then," Chuck said. "Either one of them will be fine. Once I hear from the chief when he's releasing Dad's body, I'll be in touch to arrange things."

He nodded and headed off for the buffet table. I was about to follow him when Dr. Womble appeared in front of me. He was holding two plates of food. He handed me one.

"Could we talk?" he asked. "Perhaps down the hall, where it's a bit quieter?"

We went out into the hall. I waited while Dr. Womble fed Nimitz a few bits of fruit, then followed him to one of the Sunday school classrooms. We set our plates down on the edge of a table on which one of the classes was building a Lego diorama of Palm Sunday and the Last Supper and pulled up two chairs.

"Did Bart Hempel find you?"

"Yes. Thank you for sending him to me. He's going to come over to the house this afternoon for a nice long talk about his brother."

"So what's up?"

"I rather think I need your help with something." He looked anxious, which was fairly unusual for him.

"You have it," I said. "What can I do?"

"I've been keeping a lot of secrets," he said. "Hazard of the profession, I suppose."

"Yes," I said. "Although I found out a few of them yesterday, I'm under no illusion that you've exhausted your supply."

"Heavens, no," he said. "And most of them I'll take to my grave — quite apart from pastoral confidentiality, why bring people's fears, failings, and foibles into the light? And it can be such a relief sometimes to unburden oneself without fear of embarrassment."

"Understandable." I wondered if I should remind him that he'd started off asking me for some kind of help.

"But I think this secret needs to come to light."

I waited.

"It's about Mrs. Van der Lynden's jewels."

"Don't tell me — you knew all this time where they were hidden?"

"Good heavens, no. If I had, I would have told the police. Too many people suffered from the loss of those wretched baubles."

"What about them, then?"

"They're worth a lot of money, aren't they?"

"Probably," I said. "Archie's been selling off what he could, so I have no idea how many pieces are left. Possibly not very many, but they'd be the most valuable pieces that he couldn't sell as easily. So yes, a lot of money."

"Thousands of dollars?"

"At least," I said. "Could be hundreds of thousands, depending on how much is left. A pity. Archie will probably spend it all on lawyers' fees, trying to keep himself out of the electric chair."

"Then we probably need to break the news to him as soon as possible."

"What news?"

"That the money's not his to spend. The jewels don't belong to him."

"Then who do they belong to?"

"Trinity."

"Trinity? Our Trinity?"

He nodded.

"How do you figure that?"

He sighed and took off his glasses to polish them on his sweater. Today's sweater looked as if he'd been sweeping chimneys in it, so I resigned myself to taking another

436

stab at cleaning them when he gave up.

"Mrs. Van der Lynden came to me a year or so before she died. She told me that she was going to disinherit Archie and leave everything to Trinity. I tried to talk her out of it — I wouldn't have discouraged her from leaving a substantial bequest to the church, but completely cutting out her only son? She was adamant. She'd already signed the documents. Left a copy with me in addition to the one on file with her attorney."

"Did she say why?"

"No." He shook his head. "She said he'd know. I asked if she'd told him, and she said she would when the time was right. Apparently she never did."

"How'd he react when he found out?" I asked. "But wait — he never did find out, did he? Because last night he acted as if he thought that if he could arrange for the jewelry to be found, they'd give it back to him as his mother's heir."

"We kept it from him — the attorney and I."

"How? I'm not a lawyer, but I'm related to an unreasonable number of them, and sometimes I overhear them talking. Isn't there some kind of law that you'd have to give him a copy of the will?"

"Yes, but she didn't do it with a will. Some

kind of trust. Apparently they're a lot more private. I consulted the bishop, of course, and he ran it by the chancellor, which is what they call the diocese's main lawyer. They both seemed to think it was all in order. I assumed Mrs. Van der Lynden would tell Archie — in fact, to tell the truth, I thought perhaps they'd had a temporary falling out, and that she'd redo the trust when they made up again."

"But they didn't."

"Apparently not. And apparently she didn't ever tell him. And while she'd been too ill to visit him for some months, the end came rather suddenly, so there was no time to arrange for compassionate leave so he could see her one last time."

I nodded, although from what I'd seen of Archie and heard of his mother, I wondered if either of them would have been that keen on a farewell visit.

"I was afraid of the effect it would have on him," Dr. Womble went on. "First losing his mother, then feeling abandoned, even rejected by her. I suppose it was almost a relief when Mrs. Van der Lynden's attorney explained that this was not going to be a windfall for Trinity — that we'd be lucky if her remaining assets were sufficient to cover her debts."

"And did they?"

"Not quite, but the bishop managed to convince a few of the creditors to write off their debts as a donation to the church. The rest were covered by the sale of her house — the smaller one she moved to after she sold the estate. We deposited about a thousand dollars in Archie's account — the one his trust fund went to — and convinced him that that was the extent of his inheritance. The bishop knew, of course, and Mrs. Van der Lynden's attorney, but we saw no reason for anyone else to know."

"Did Archie seem surprised at getting almost nothing?" I asked. "Disappointed?"

"Not at all." Dr. Womble began uselessly polishing his glasses again. "I rather think he knew how bad things were."

"And besides, he knew he had the jewelry waiting for him when he got out," I added. "So he wasn't worried. Wait — are you sure the trust covers the jewels?"

"Oh, yes." He smiled faintly. "I wondered about that at the time. I couldn't decide if it meant that she still had the jewels, or that she thought Archie did. Either way, she included them."

"I can understand why you kept it from Archie," I said.

"But if we'd been honest with him, perhaps it would have shaken him a bit. Inspired him to some kind of real reform."

"Or maybe it would just have made him more bitter and angry than he already was."

"You could be right. But still, on a more practical level, if he'd known he'd been disinherited, he wouldn't have come up with his crazy scheme for arranging to have the jewels found. And poor Mr. Hagley would still be alive."

"Archie would probably have come up with some other crazy scheme." I didn't quite know what to say about Mr. Hagley. Yes, Archie's scheme had cost him his life. I couldn't exactly say that I'd miss Mr. Hagley, but I certainly hadn't wished him dead. Just off the vestry and out of my hair — and Mother's. A thought hit me. "And just think how happy it would have made Mr. Hagley to know about the bequest to Trinity. He was always so concerned about our financial stability."

"I doubt if Trinity will get anything immediately," Dr. Womble said. "I expect there will be legal wranglings. Archie will try to fight it."

"You should tell Robyn right away," I said. "And then the two of you can tell the bishop. The legal wrangling will be his headache. Bishops are good at that sort of thing."

"Yes." Dr. Womble beamed beatifically. "Isn't it lucky they never made me a bishop?"

"Mommy?" Dr. Womble and I turned to see Josh and Jamie peering into the room. Then Michael appeared over their shoulders, carrying Nimitz on one arm. Nimitz was gurgling happily and rubbing his enormous beak against Michael's chin.

"The boys want to go along when we take Nimitz back to the zoo this afternoon."

"Not till we're finished with lunch," Jamie explained.

"And dessert," Josh added.

"Can't you just play with him here?" I wasn't keen on letting Nimitz into the Twin-mobile again.

"We need to see him alone," Josh said.

"We have to tell him something," Jamie said.

"Something important," Josh added.

"And private." Jamie looked very serious.

"Okay," I said. "I'll bite. What's so important that you need to tell the toucan?"

"We can't tell you," Jamie exclaimed.

Josh merely shook his head firmly.

"You'll tell a silly bird but not me. Why?"

They both grinned, Michael smothered a

chuckle, and I realized I'd been maneuvered into giving them the perfect straight line.

"Because!" they chanted in unison. "Toucan keep a secret!"

ABOUT THE AUTHOR

Donna Andrews was born in Yorktown, Virginia. She is the author of two amateur sleuth series: Turing Hopper Mystery series and A Meg Langslow Mystery series. Her first book, *Murder with Peacocks* (1999), which is part of A Meg Langslow Mystery series, won numerous awards for best first novel including the Lefty award for funniest mystery. *You've Got Murder* (2002), the first novel in the Turing Hopper Mystery series, won the Agatha Award for best mystery. She is a member of Sisters in Crime, Mystery Writers of America, and the Private Investigators and Security Association.